ENEMY IN THE Shadows

ENEMY IN THE Shadows

RUSSELL PELTON

outskirts press

Outskirts Press, Inc.
http://www.outskirtspress.com

ISBN: 978-1-4787-9983-2

Library of Congress Control Number: 2018910147

Pelton, Russell
Fiction/Suspense/Paperback
Title: Enemy in the Shadows: a fictional novel, Chicago 1991: Organized crime has moved into the ever expanding highly lucrative healthcare/dental industry including a front for money laundering.

PRINTED IN THE UNITED STATES OF AMERICA

Disclaimer

This is a work of fiction. Any resemblance of persons, places, or events depicted in this novel to actual persons, places, or events is entirely coincidental, except that Wrigley Field is a real Chicago ballpark, and the Billy Goat Tavern, Morton's Steakhouse, and Chef's Station are all, likewise, real.

Dedicated to all the individuals who stand up to bullying, whatever its source, and who finally say, "No! Not anymore! Not now and not here!" They are the true heroes of our streets and our cities.

The significant contributions and helpful guidance of my son, Michael Pelton in the creation of this book is recognized and deeply acknowledged.

Chapter 1

May 17, 1991

—

Darkness had settled over the far west side of Chicago. The businessmen had triple-locked their warehouses and shuttered their store fronts and fled to the suburbs, leaving only the rats and winos who slowly began moving from shadow to shadow. An occasional el rumbling westward stirred newspapers in the gutters. Otherwise all was still.

In a boarded-up garage off Pulaski Boulevard a meeting was taking place. A single hooded bulb hanging from the ceiling cast a circle of light around two men, standing and talking. Beyond the edge of the light were vague shapes of crates, cars and three other men.

Lenny Battaglia, in a powder-blue Italian silk suit and light-brown Gucci shoes, was thumbing through a wad of bills. His white-on-white shirt and paisley Ralph Lauren tie were accompanied by the white carnation in his lapel.

The large mole on his right cheek seemed to move back and forth as the overhead bulb slowly swung on its cord. After a moment, he looked up.

"Angie, you're three grand short! What the hell is going on here?"

"That can't be, Lenny!" the other man said, turning ashen. "This is what Sam gave me to give you. I'm sure it's right! Sam wouldn't short you guys."

"Angie, you know the deal. We're supposed to get ten grand a month from the clinic in Madison. There's only seven here. This is bullshit!"

At a nod from Battaglia, two men moved to Angie's side and grabbed his arms; one reached under Angie's jacket, pulled out his .38, and stuffed it under his belt. Terror swept across Angie's face. "Lenny, I swear. I don't know what's going on here. Jesus, I sure as hell wouldn't skim any of your dough. You gotta believe me!"

"Somehow, Angie, I *don't* believe you," Battaglia paused a moment. "Drop his pants."

The two men held Angie firmly while a third moved out of the shadows, unbuckled Angie's belt, unzipped his fly, and yanked the pants down.

"His jockeys, too." Battaglia walked to the wall, pulling a large pair of hedge trimmers down from a shelf.

" No, Lenny, don't do that! I don't know nothin!"

Battaglia opened the blades of the trimmers, walked up close to Angie, and thrust them strategically against his crotch. Angie flinched at the touch of the cold steel. "I'm going to ask you just one more time, Angie. Where's our fuckin' three grand? Believe me, it'll be better for you if you 'fess up."

Angie was heaving in uncontrollable sobs. He was unable to say a word.

"Last chance, Angie."

"All right," he gasped between sobs. "It's in my coat pocket…right side. I'm sorry, Lenny. I really am. I had to have it…my wife's medical bills…"

Battaglia looked into his eyes for a moment, then smiled as the giant blades slammed together. Angie's scream echoed off the concrete walls and ceiling.

"Fuckin' thieves don't deserve any mercy," Battaglia said as he turned, throwing the hedge trimmers into the shadows. Angie was dropped to the dusty floor in a heap. Both his hands clutched his groin as he convulsed in agony. Blood oozed between his fingers.

"Blow his brains out and dump him in the fuckin' river."

Battaglia went over to Angie's coat slung over a crate, he dug through the pockets and found the missing money. He added it to the wad Angie had given him earlier, peeled off a thousand for each of the other three men and pocketed the rest.

"All right. Here's the deal. Angie skimmed the whole ten grand. We got nothin'. Got it?"

The others nodded in agreement. They dragged Angie, still sobbing, over to a nearby car, threw him in the trunk, and slammed it shut. Lenny Battaglia waited for them to leave, adjusted his carnation, hit the buttons that turned out the lights and opened the warehouse's overhead door, got into his BMW and drove out into the night as the door slowly closed behind him. It had been a very profitable evening.

At nine o'clock the following Monday morning, Tony Jeffries took off his Panama hat and stepped out of the elevator into Wilson, Thompson & Gilchrist's reception room on the seventy-sixth floor of Chicago's Hancock Building. His weekend tan complimented his beige summer suit and wind-tossed brown hair. He slipped his aviator sunglasses into his jacket pocket and replaced them with his wire-rims.

"Good morning, Marion," he greeted the firm's receptionist as he walked through the room. "Beautiful day, isn't it?" He noticed the fresh pleasant fragrance of the multi-colored roses on Marion's desk.

"Good morning, Tony, yes, it certainly is," she replied, returning his smile. "Congratulations on your win last Friday." As an afterthought she added, "Oh yes, Mr. Gilchrist would like to see you first thing today."

Tony walked down the carpeted corridor to his office. He passed other attorneys in window offices to his right, with their secretaries in adjacent earth-tone carrels to his left. The boys from the mailroom were wheeling around their stainless-steel carts, distributing stacks of envelopes, boxes, and faxes that had come in that morning. The law firm was crackling back into life.

"Good morning, Mr. Jeffries."

"Good morning, Jack," Tony replied to a passing fresh-faced young attorney. "How'd you fellas do in your game this weekend?"

"Great," Jack answered excitedly. "We beat Cabot and Davis ten to one. We're in first place now."

"That's terrific, Jack. Keep it up." Tony turned and continued down the hall. *Columbia*, he thought. Tony, the chairman of the firm's hiring committee always associated the younger attorneys with the law schools they attended when they were first interviewed.

Wilson, Thompson & Gilchrist was an old law firm by Chicago standards. Founded in 1892, it had grown steadily over the years and now employed almost two hundred attorneys. It occupied five floors in the Hancock Building overlooking Chicago's Michigan Avenue. The firm's clientele included a wide variety of corporations, professional associations, and insurance companies. Its corporate litigation practice was fast-paced and lucrative, but was considered stodgy and sterile by firms handling personal-injury or criminal cases.

Tony had been a Chicagoan all his life. He grew up in Riverside, a western suburb, and attended law school at the University of Chicago. After three years in the Air Force, he joined Wilson, Jones & Thompson, as the firm was named at the time. In the intervening twenty years, he had built a reputation as an aggressive, successful civil litigator. Tony had seen the firm quintuple in size, and now headed one of its eight litigation groups.

"Morning, Judy," he said to his secretary as he walked into his office.

"Good morning," she replied with a smile. "Nice win on Friday. I heard all about it from Carol. I'll get you some coffee."

"Thanks. The toughest cases are always the sweetest ones to win," he quipped as he hung his Panama on the back of the door and dropped his briefcase onto his desk. Tony walked over to the window and looked down at Lake Michigan, Navy Pier, and Lake Shore Drive. The bright sunlight beaming through scattered clouds seemed to illuminate the deep blue-green of the lake. *God, this is magnificent*. As many times as he had looked out over the lake, he was still in awe on clear days like this. He could see across the lake the faint yellow line of the Michigan dunes, where his family had its summer home. He had just driven in from there that morning. To the right, in stark contrast to the clean beauty of the lakeshore, were the granite towers and dark canyons of the Loop.

Judy's cheerful voice brought him back to reality. "Here's your morning mail," she said, as she carried in a hefty stack of documents. "You might want to take a look at the letter from Bill Jackson at Trans American Airlines. I've put it on top. He's sent us a new case; here's the accompanying file. He'd like you to call him after you've had a chance to review the case. Also, here are your phone messages. Nothing unusual, everybody wants to talk to you first, before you get busy on other projects, including

Mr. Gilchrist." Judy placed the stack of documents and pink message slips on the right side of his desk.

She smiled as she left, returning a few moments later with a cup of black coffee. Judy, an attractive woman in her mid-twenties, had worked for Tony for about three years. Today she was wearing a light-blue dress that was both businesslike and feminine. Judy had come to know his clients and his files well, could recognize priority items when they arose, diverting less important matters until he was able to resolve the more critical problems at hand. She would also remind him when some temporarily forgotten project was nearing a deadline.

Tony skimmed through the stack of incoming mail and telephone messages. He made some mental priority evaluations. There were messages from last week, when he had been on trial, unable to return anything other than real emergency calls. He took a sip or two of coffee, pausing a moment to savor the aroma, French Vanilla, his favorite. He picked up his phone and called Cal Cizma, one of the close friends he usually met for a drink on Friday evenings at Ditka's bar to apologize for not being able to join them last week. Tony's team had been cleaning up on Friday, collecting the flotsam and jetsam from the trial they had just won. Henry Gilchrist, senior partner or not, could wait another five minutes.

"It's about time you got here, Anthony," Henry Gilchrist snorted as Tony walked into his office. Gilchrist was a short, rotund man of about seventy. Half-glasses were perched on the bridge of his nose and his gray mustache matched his thinning hair. The wall beside his desk was covered with plaques and citations that reflected decades of achievement in legal, political, and civic affairs; a fact that no one dealing with Henry Gilchrist was likely to miss. He had spent a lifetime building a solid practice and was considered an icon in the Chicago legal community.

"What's the problem, Henry?" Tony said as he eased himself into one of the two padded leather chairs in front of Gilchrist's desk.

"Our clients, the American Dental Society, its Commission on Dental Accreditation – CODA - and their directors have just been sued in an antitrust case. Dr. John Schofield, the ADS's executive director, is very upset. As I believe you know, CODA has been recognized by the U.S. Department of Education as the only body that can accredit dental programs in the states." Gilchrist leaned forward and handed Tony a half-inch-thick stapled document. "Here's the complaint with its exhibits. There are four antitrust counts for openers; then it wraps up with a defamation count that includes allegations of both slander and libel. Plaintiff's counsel is Jack Harrington. He thinks he has a winner here. He's asking for fifty million in damages, tripled because it's an antitrust violation."

"Harrington! These guys are serious."

"Yes. In fact, Harrington called me first thing this morning, advised me about the suit and told me that he has no intention of settling the case. This complaint was delivered to us ten minutes later. Harrington said he intends to take it to trial. He expects to get a massive judgment against the ADS and CODA, and make them beg for some settlement. Of course, the ADS's liability insurance certainly may not cover the cost of defending an antitrust case, much less any resulting judgment. Harrington plans to get a lot of publicity as well as a healthy legal fee out of this one."

"Well, nobody's ever accused Jack Harrington of being too cautious. He's always had balls," Tony replied, half to himself, as he took the complaint and began to thumb through it.

Gilchrist paused, nodded, then continued, "He's named all the officers of the ADS and members of CODA as co-defendants, asking that they be held jointly liable for any judgment. That's a bunch of nonsense, of course, but it's sure caught the attention of some folks at the ADS."

His voice trailed off; a stillness fell over the room. Tony continued skimming through the complaint. He grew uncomfortable as he realized that Gilchrist's initial reaction was probably correct; this could be a very difficult case to defend. One of the firm's major clients might be in serious trouble.

"What do we know about the plaintiffs" Tony asked, looking up at Gilchrist, who seemed more agitated than usual.

"The corporate plaintiff is a privately owned dental school that the ADS refuses to approve," Gilchrist explained. "It's named the Federal Dental Academy. Very patriotic, don't you think? Apparently, the school meets all the usual accreditation criteria, or so they claim. It's received State of Illinois approval as a post-graduate educational institution, but some of the people at the ADS don't like the man who owns the school. CODA just won't accredit it."

Tony resumed thumbing through the thick pleading as Gilchrist went on. "The school's leased a building on Lake Street just west of the Loop. They've apparently installed all the dental and lab equipment they need to get started, and they've got a faculty under contract. But they can't begin operating as an accredited dental school until they get CODA approval which CODA refuses to give."

"In other words," Tony replied, trying to get the facts straight in his mind, "the State of Illinois has to approve the institution and then the ADS, through CODA, has to approve it for dental accreditation, and there's the rub. CODA won't approve the dental program."

"Exactly."

"The ADS can't do that without an awfully good reason, Henry." Tony put the complaint aside momentarily. "It sounds like restraint of trade, unless we don't know all the facts. This might be a case that could be settled quickly if everything you've said is correct, maybe with CODA granting initial or provisional accreditation, or something along those lines."

"I wish it was that simple," said Gilchrist slowly as he turned in his chair and looked out over the lake. "But to make matters worse they've included the defamation count. It seems that various people at the ADS defamed the owner of this school in the process of denying its accreditation. That's count five."

"Terrific," replied Tony, flipping to that section of the complaint. "What's the defamation?"

"The complaint alleges that the program was turned down because the school's owned by an individual supposedly connected with organized crime, the Outfit. Some memos to that effect were circulated around the ADS."

"The mob? The so-called Outfit? Henry, this is 1991, not 1928, or even 1948. Those guys are all dead or in prison. Somebody's been watching too many *Godfather* films."

"That may very well be true, Anthony, but that's what they allege in their complaint."

"Is that the reason the school actually was turned down by CODA?"

"It may be," Gilchrist responded. "I understand that the ADS Trustee from Illinois, Bob Kaminsky, you've met him I believe, has been wandering around telling everyone that he knows all about these people and that they're definitely connected with the mob. His comments were supposedly off the record, but that kind of gossip spread fast. If that was the basis for the denial of accreditation, the ADS has both an antitrust and a defamation problem on its hands."

"Unbelievable! How the hell can Kaminsky go around saying things like that? Hasn't he ever heard of libel or slander?" Tony paused for a moment, then asked, "Who owns this Federal Dental Academy, anyway?"

Gilchrist lowered his chin, looking at Tony over his glasses. "All the stock in the company appears to be owned by one man; William O'Coogan, a prominent Lake Forest businessman. He primarily owns a large electrical contracting company. Harrington told me that he financed the school as a business investment. I understand that O'Coogan's outraged by this whole situation and intends to really punish the ADS. That's why he's the individual plaintiff under count five."

"I've heard of O'Coogan," Tony said. Bits of information swirled in the back of his mind. Finally, he was able to grab one of them. "Wasn't he president of the Chicago Athletic Association a couple of years ago?"

"That's right, probably how Jack Harrington got involved in this case. Harrington's not his regular lawyer, but they apparently became good friends when they served on the Board of the CAA together. It seems that when O'Coogan realized that he might have an antitrust case on his hands, he decided to get his friend Jack Harrington involved. Unfortunately for us, or rather for our client, he picked the best."

Tony continued thumbing through the complaint, a hundred thoughts flashing through his mind, then he looked up at Gilchrist. "Let me guess," he said with a tight-lipped smile. "You want me to handle this case and somehow save the ADS's ass; is that it?"

"That's it exactly, Anthony," Gilchrist replied, leaning forward and looking Tony hard in the eyes, "I don't know how you're going to handle it, but as far as our client is concerned it's a case that can't be lost. And as far as the plaintiffs are concerned, it's a case that won't be settled." He paused, leaning back in his leather chair. "Who do you have to work on it with you?"

Tony thought for a moment before replying. "I'll put Charlie Dickenson on it. He's my best associate. We've just settled the biggest case that he was working on, the O'Hare construction case, so he has some time available. We'll work on it together. I'll also get my new associate, Carol James, involved to do whatever basic research we need."

"Good, I'll tell the people at the ADS that this case is in good hands. We have one of our best litigation teams on it. You'll be responsible for this matter, just keep me advised from time to time."

Tony suddenly felt uncomfortable. "Now wait a minute, Henry. This is a tough case. It'll be very hard to defend, maybe impossible. I don't want anyone at the ADS to think that there isn't any exposure here..."

"Nonsense, Anthony," Gilchrist interrupted with a tight smile. "I have complete confidence in you. Get your man Dickenson involved and that James gal. Do whatever is necessary to win this thing, particularly that defamation count. See if you can get rid of it quickly; it really rankles people. If the press calls, you deal with them." He turned to his right and pushed a button. Looking back at Tony he added "Anthony, I'm really quite busy. I'm relieved that your group will be handling this matter. Give it your personal attention."

He was dismissed. Tony stood, picked up the bulky complaint, and walked to the door.

"Oh, Anthony."

"Yes?" Tony said, turning.

"Congratulations on your verdict in the Lawndale Hospital trial last Friday," Gilchrist added without looking up.

"Thank you," Tony answered as he turned back to the door and left.

As he walked down the circular staircase to his own office on 76, Tony had a sinking feeling that he had been handed a ticking time bomb. He was proud of being able to handle tough cases, but this one looked like it would be extremely difficult to win and impossible to settle. No matter what he did, there was a good chance he'd end up being hammered in a trial. *The old goat has set me up. If the case goes well, Gilchrist and his firm will have won it; if it goes badly, the fault will be entirely mine.*

Tony returned to his office. After mulling the case over, his view began to change. This was probably one of the biggest cases in the office. He'd handled tough ones before, some worse than this, and he'd won them all. *Alright, Jack Harrington, let's see how good you are against a real trial lawyer!* He asked Judy to take all his calls, closed the door, and began carefully reading through the complaint, this time taking notes. It was good. If the facts alleged were true (and Tony suspected that they were) the plaintiff dental school had a solid antitrust case against the ADS for restraint of trade for refusing to recommend its accreditation.

Tony gave Charlie Dickenson a call. Charlie was one of the senior associates in Tony's group with "street smarts" that made him a particularly effective litigator.

"Charlie, this is Tony. We've got a big new case in from the ADS. It's an antitrust suit with a defamation count tacked on. I know you've handled both types of cases, so I'd like you to work on this one with me. You free to talk about it now?"

"Absolutely. I'll be right up."

Within two minutes Charlie walked into Tony's office, pen and a yellow pad in hand, and took a chair. "All right Tony, what's this big new case all about?"

Tony briefly summarized it, adding, "The antitrust case is going to be tough to defend, it looks like our friends at the ADS may have been guilty of a little restraint of trade. But we're going to have to get a better handle on the facts to really judge that. My guess is that the libel and slander count is a red herring; it's designed to draw our attention away from the antitrust counts, where the real exposure is.

"Sounds like a big case, Tony. How do you want to staff it?"

"Let's get Carol James on board. She hasn't been involved in any big cases yet, and maybe it's time for her to get her feet wet. Initially, we'll have her handle any research that needs to be dealt with. Let her know about this assignment. We'll also need a paralegal we can call on as needed. That new fellow Larry Crowe hasn't been assigned any big project yet. Explain the case to him and have him put it on his list of responsibilities."

"Will do," Charlie responded, nodding and making another note.

"I'll have Judy make copies of the complaint and its exhibits delivered to you, Carol, and Larry by noon. The first thing you might want to do is check out our Mr. O'Coogan to see if there's anything unsavory about him."

Chapter 2

May 22

"This guy O'Coogan is as clean as Cardinal Bernardin," Charlie said as he dropped a hand-ful of papers on Tony's desk. "Maybe cleaner, Cardinal Bernardin has some friends in the Roman Curia that I wonder about."

It had been two days since they received the Federal Dental Academy's complaint. Tony and Charlie had spent nearly all their intervening time studying it and learning the underlying facts in an attempt to grasp some straws they could build into a defense. One fact had become painfully clear; a number of the staff at the American Dental Society had "understood" that William O'Coogan was in fact a member of organized crime. Some notes to that affect had been circulated. That was definitely a major reason why the ADS's Commission on Dental Accreditation had denied accreditation of the program.

Charlie Dickenson was a wiry young man in his early thirties. His thick black mustache, unkempt hair and unbuttoned shirt collar were more suggestive of a peace demonstrator in the sixties than an associate in a major law firm. But, in the six years since he'd graduated from Duke Law School he had established a reputation as a tough litigator. The firm had won more than one case because of the extra time and effort that Charlie had spent getting the job done right with the case nicely teed up for trial. Tony considered it a coup to have gotten him assigned to his group.

"I interviewed the chairman of the Chicago Crime Commission, Bill McNulty today and went through their files," Charlie continued as he sat down on Tony's beige leather couch. "That's a copy of their complete file on the guy," He pointed to the papers he had just dropped on Tony's desk. "They don't have one negative thing on O'Coogan. I also had our paralegal Larry run his name through all the electronic databases, and they only came up with one item that's even slightly derogatory. When O'Coogan was president of the Lake Forest United Way two years ago their fund raising fell 5 percent short of its goal. I'm not sure that's quite enough to convince a jury that our Mr. O'Coogan is in bed with a Mafia don. In the meantime, Carol's been doing some preliminary research into the antitrust issues raised; if half the plaintiffs' contentions are true, we're in trouble on that count too."

"Damn," Tony muttered. He had been afraid that was going to be Charlie's report. "Well, I've been trying all day to reach Dr. Kaminsky, the ADS Trustee who started the rumor but he's been out of his office. Hopefully, his rumors were based on something. Although with Kaminsky, you never can tell. He's a great gossip-monger, loves to pass on inside rumors about the darker side of the city. The problem is that I think he sometimes salts his rumors to make them more interesting."

"Well, that may be what happened here, Tony, but this guy O'Coogan looks clean. As clean as they come. And if that's true, I can understand why he's really pissed off."

"You're supposed to be helping with the defense of this case, not making things worse!" Tony quipped as he reached for a stack of papers on the credenza behind his desk. "These came in this afternoon from Harrington's office. They're the plaintiffs' first series of interrogatories to us, the plaintiffs' first request for the production of documents, and notices of the plaintiffs' first series of depositions." Tony handed Charlie the thick stack of xeroxed documents. "In a nut-shell, he wants to know who at CODA made the decision to not accredit the Academy and exactly what that decision was based on. He also wants copies of any internal memos or notes dealing with the Academy or O'Coogan."

"Isn't he jumping the gun a little?" Charlie asked. "We just filed our appearance yesterday; our response to the complaint isn't due for a couple of weeks."

"Oh, I know," Tony replied with a smile. "But this is Harrington's style. You'd better get used to it. He's going to be as aggressive as hell, you can count on that. To set your mind at ease, though, this case is assigned to Judge Katsoris. From my past experience with her, our time for answering all this won't begin to run until after we've responded to the complaint. It's a clever ploy, because some lawyers become preoccupied with responding or objecting to all this early discovery, and forget about looking closely at the complaint."

"Do you think there are any problems with the complaint?"

"I don't know, but I'd sure like to throw a motion to dismiss at them. That would be a good way to measure their fire; see how good their research is; find out how well they can write and function as a team under pressure. We wouldn't have to win the motions, in fact, I wouldn't expect us to, but it would tell us something about our opposition; about Harrington's back-up team. That would also buy us some time while we figured out what the hell kind of defense we can put together."

As the two lawyers analyzed possible defects in both the antitrust and the libel allegations, asking each other dozens of hypothetical questions, a thousand feet below them the late-May shadows extended over the lake. Rush hour traffic began streaming out of the Loop, turning north and south onto Lake Shore Drive.

"Pardon me, Tony," Judy said, sticking her head in the door. "I was just about to leave, but I know you wanted to know immediately if we were able to contact Dr. Kaminsky. Well, we have. He's in our reception room asking to speak to you."

Charlie and Tony exchanged surprised looks. “Well, show our guest in,” Tony responded after a pause.

A few moments later Dr. Robert Kaminsky was escorted into Tony’s office. He glanced at both attorneys, and gave Judy time to leave, shutting the door firmly behind her. Kaminsky was short and stocky, about five-six, with a thick cigar clenched in the corner of his mouth. White ashes were scattered down the front of his dark blue suit. He spoke out of the side of his mouth as though whispering a tip to an undercover cop. He was in his late fifties, with thick black hair speckled with gray. He was well dressed (except for the ashes) and wore a large diamond-studded ring. He appeared to be every inch the archetypical Chicago alderman and like an alderman, he had the reputation of knowing what was going on in the city’s darker crevices.

“Hello, Bob, how are you?” Tony said, rising as he offered the dentist his hand. “I think you’ve met my associate Charlie Dickenson before, haven’t you?”

“Right,” Kaminsky replied as he accepted the attorneys’ greetings, before dropping into the empty armchair facing Tony’s desk. Some ash fell off the end of his cigar into his lap and he brushed it away. “I heard that you fellas wanted to see me.” Kaminsky spoke with a faint accent that identified him as being from the Polish neighborhood on the northwest side. He paused, smiled and added, “And I know why.” You’ve got that suit filed against the ADS, and you want to know the inside story on that guy O’Coogan. Am I wrong?”

"No, Bob, you're absolutely right." Tony responded casually. "I hear that you know all about him. What can you tell us?" Charlie, seated off to the side, quietly picked up his yellow pad while lifting a pen out of his shirt pocket.

"The guy runs a couple of legit companies as a front but believe me he's a big money man for the Outfit. Took over this screwy new dental school this spring by force, literally threw out the guys who set it up. They were so scared they were afraid to gripe to anyone. In fact, one of the guys, the accountant, got out of town - flew to the West Coast - he was so scared of O'Coogan and his thugs. But one of the other fellas, a dentist, told me all about it. So, I know."

The two attorneys were listening intently with Charlie quietly taking notes. As Kaminsky paused to relight his cigar, Tony interjected, "Come on, Bob, why would the mob be interested in a dental school? That's small potatoes to them. That just doesn't make sense at all."

"You don't know anything, do you?" snorted the dentist. "Insurance! That's the name of the game. Dental insurance. They've got a deal with some of the biggest unions in the country. The union demands dental insurance for their members in all their contracts. The employees can only get that dental care at certain special clinics; 'closed panels' we call them. If the employee goes to some other dentist they pay through the nose, minimal reimbursement. No working stiff who needs serious dental work can afford that. Their clinics are manned by bottom-feeder dentists, usually from third-world countries, who are working for whatever they can get. A third of the dough that comes in goes to maintaining the office, including the docs' salaries; a third goes to the union local and the rest goes to the Outfit. When the dental school itself gets going, they'll staff the clinics completely with their graduates. In the meantime, they'll scrounge around for the cheapest stiffs they can find who can claim to be dentists and stick them in the clinics. That's the deal; or, that *was* the deal until I stopped 'em by letting the ADS know what the hell was going on." He paused to relight his cigar, exhaled a cloud of pungent smoke, leaned back in his chair and looked at Tony with a smug smile.

There was a long pause before Tony finally responded, "Bob, that's a fascinating story but what the hell makes you think that any of it is true?"

"I told you; I got it from the dentist who set up the school in the first place. He got his financing from these guys, but when the school was all ready to go, and they got their State of Illinois approval as an institution, they threw him out. Someone pulled a gun on him and said that he was out of there, just like that. So, he knows all about it, and he told me. There's other stuff going on with these guys, big stuff involving top mob bosses; but I don't know all the details. So, all I know is that it's being set up as an innocent little dental school, but it really is a well-disguised mob front."

"Bob, who have you told all this to?" Tony asked. He was afraid of the answer.

"Everyone at the ADS who would listen," replied Kaminsky proudly. "I made damn sure that those guys are never going to go anywhere in dentistry. Trustees and CODA members, I couldn't find personally, I gave them detailed notes. Hell, I'm an ADS trustee; and I met my responsibility!" He nodded emphatically.

"So much for the first two lines of defense on the libel and slander count," Charlie commented, leaning back in his chair with an air of resignation. He and Tony looked at each other and shook their heads.

"What the hell does that mean?" Kaminsky snapped.

"Bob, in every defamation or libel case," Tony answered, "there are three available defenses. The first two are that the libelous remarks weren't actually said, or, if they were, that they have some nice innocent meaning. Well, I guess we can't deny that you made those remarks in your capacity as an ADS trustee, and there's certainly nothing innocent in what you said about these guys. That leaves us with the third defense," Tony paused, then said, "*Truth*. We'll have to prove that what you said about O'Coogan and his cronies is absolutely true. We'll have to *prove* that."

Charlie leaned forward. "Dr. Kaminsky, do you have any personal knowledge of any of this, or is everything you know about this school and O'Coogan based on what you've learned from this other dentist?"

"You mean, can I swear under oath that every detail is absolutely true?"

"That's pretty much what I'm asking."

"Well, no, I couldn't do that. But you can take my word for it that everything I've told you is right. And the reason these mob guys are so mad is because it's all coming out now. I told the guys at the ADS, off the record of course, and now their plans are screwed up because the ADS and CODA won't approve their damn dental program."

"Bob, who is this dentist who told you all this? The fellow who set the school up in the first place?" asked Tony.

"Jack Roberts."

"Jack Roberts!" Tony shouted. He felt as though he'd just been kicked in the groin. "Are you talking about the guy who had his dental license yanked last year for drug dealing?"

"Yeah, that's the guy. But he's a very good dentist, I know."

"Didn't he also have his membership in the ADS revoked about five years ago because of ethics violations?" Tony shook his head in disbelief, then went on before Kaminsky could answer. "And isn't he the same guy who organized a medical center a few years back, lived like a baron off the investors' money for a couple of years, had his company file for bankruptcy, and left his investors high and dry?" Tony's voice was rising in intensity as he barked off his questions. "Is Jack Roberts the dentist who's the source of all your information?"

"Well, yeah; but that's why Roberts got involved with all this; he wanted to get a fresh start and do some teaching.

At least that's what he told me. When he couldn't get a job with any established dental school he decided to organize his own. He's always been an entrepreneur, you know; raises race horses on the side, I've been told. The trouble was that he couldn't get the financing he needed through regular sources, so he turned to, shall we say, *irregular* sources. That ended up being a mistake because they took over his place when he got it all set up."

"Where is Roberts now?" Tony demanded with a steely tone. "I think we'd like to talk to him ourselves.

"Damned if I know," shrugged Kaminsky. "I ran across him in Tosi's Restaurant over in Michigan a couple of months ago. I've known him since dental school. We had a few drinks at the bar and he filled me in on all this stuff. I think he said that he was moving out of the area."

"The problem we have, Bob, as I said a few minutes ago," Tony said, leaning back in his chair and lowering his voice, "is that we will have to prove that William O'Coogan is actually a member of the Outfit or clearly linked to it. He's sued the ADS for defamation because its staff and CODA members repeated these rumors and passed on your memos about him. You haven't given us too much to work with here."

"Well, that's your business, not mine," said Kaminsky, rising. "I'm just a wet-fingered dentist, not a lawyer. I've told you what I know. Frankly, I don't want to be involved in this case anymore. I did my job. I exposed those bastards for who they are! You can reach me through the ADS or my office on Milwaukee Avenue if you want to talk about it some more." He opened the door, nodded back to the two attorneys, and shut the door behind him. A few lingering cigar ashes settled onto the carpet.

"Well, that's just great," Tony said looking at Charlie. "Kaminsky admits that he libeled and slandered O'Coogan all over the place, and that his accusations were based 100 percent on the bar talk of the most disreputable dentist in the country." He shook his head. "Even if we could find Jack Roberts, I said if, and I'm not sure we can, we could never put him on the stand, Harrington would tear him apart." He paused, "frankly Charlie, I have this feeling that our case just got materially tougher."

"Tougher, hell!" Charlie replied, "Our case just got materially impossible."

Chapter 3

June 26

"Case number 91 C 5641," the clerk's voice boomed out. "*Federal Dental Academy and William O'Coogan versus the American Dental Society, et al.*" Tony rose and strode to the front of Judge Patricia Katsoris' courtroom. Behind him, Charlie stood up, following, yellow pad and pen in hand.

On the far side of the courtroom a tall, distinguished-looking attorney with flowing gray hair rose too. He paused to allow an associate to clear a path through the other attorneys who were hovering in the aisle awaiting their turn on Judge Katsoris's status call. He stepped forward with the silky ease of a man accustomed to dominating court-rooms. A number of the other attorneys whispered and nodded to each other.

Jack Harrington, the most prominent plaintiffs' antitrust attorney in Chicago, was making a personal appearance.

Judge Patricia Katsoris of the United States District Court for the Northern District of Illinois was holding her weekly call on the status of certain of her cases, particularly the new ones. A Harvard Law School graduate and a Reagan appointee, she enjoyed a reputation as a no-nonsense jurist who liked to keep her cases moving along. Initially viewed as a conservative, she had proven to be far less doctrinaire than most people had expected. She held the seat on the Northern District bench that since the Kennedy days had been traditionally reserved for a Greek-American.

Judge Katsoris' courtroom was located on the twenty-fifth floor of the Dirksen Federal Building. It was a large room with a twenty-foot ceiling and benches for well over a hundred attorneys and spectators. On days such as this, most of those seats were taken by attorneys. The polished paneled walls were adorned with portraits of distinguished jurists who had commanded those halls in the past. Behind the black-robed judge was the giant steel emblem of the United States of America. Tony remembered his awe the first time he had to argue a motion before one of the federal judges. He felt like Dorothy fearfully approaching the Great Wizard. It took him time to learn that judges, like wizards, are more mortal than they appear.

"Good morning, gentlemen," the judge said crisply when the four attorneys reached the lectern. Harrington's young associate stood one step behind his boss, taking notes.

Judge Patricia Katsoris was a thin woman in her late forties, one of the younger federal judges sitting in Chicago. She had medium-length brown hair and wore just enough make-up to overcome the severity of her requisite black robe.

"I have reviewed the defendants' motion to dismiss the complaint," she crisply said, "as well as the supporting and opposing memoranda, and I am prepared to issue my ruling at this time. I am denying the defendants' motion to dismiss. Although the defendants have raised some interesting points, on balance I am convinced that the plaintiffs have adequately stated their causes of action. The defendants' answer is due in twenty-eight days, with the plaintiffs' reply due fourteen days thereafter."

Tony had anticipated the judge's ruling. He had hoped that their motion to dismiss would at least slow the plaintiffs down. It did, if only a bit. But he had been able to measure his opponents' fire, which was his prime objective; they had filed their brief opposing his motion in a timely fashion; it reflected adequate but not incisive research; and raised no new cases that Tony's team wasn't already aware of. Harrington clearly had relied on one of his associates to prepare it. *This case will be decided,* Tony concluded, *in the courtroom, not because of the briefs filed.*

"I would like both sides to initiate whatever discovery they believe is appropriate immediately," Judge Katsoris continued. "I note that plaintiffs' counsel has already filed interrogatories and other discovery. Since the defendants' motion to dismiss has just been ruled on today, defendants shall have thirty days from today to respond to that discovery." The judge paused to look down at her calendar. "We'll have a report on the status of this case on September 11th. You gentlemen should advise me at that time when you think discovery will be completed. I'd like to be able to try this case in the late fall or early winter."

Damn, Tony thought. *She's already talking about closing discovery and setting a trial date. This is moving along faster than I had expected. I'm going to need all the time I can get to put a decent defense together.*

"Your Honor, the plaintiffs appreciate your well-reasoned ruling," Harrington stated, raising his voice. "I can assure the court that we will be most cooperative in bringing this case to a speedy trial. I feel compelled to say, Your Honor, that this is the most outrageous and egregious case of libel and slander that I have ever encountered in my years before the bar, not to mention the obvious and absolutely unjustifiable antitrust violations."

Taken aback by Harrington's outburst, Tony hesitated. He attempted to interrupt, but Harrington refused to give him the opportunity.

"When a prominent businessman like William O'Coogan, whose reputation I am sure the court is aware of, makes a good-faith investment in a fledgling dental school such as the Federal Dental Academy, he is entitled to be dealt with decently and fairly. Indeed, he should be welcomed by the community. Mr. O'Coogan made his investment with the hope that, as a result, the poor of this city and this state would have better access to proper dental care. Not to mention the jobs that the school will bring to this city. Instead, the pundits at the American Dental Society, who have an unholy obsession to control everything that touches on dentistry, decided to deny him that opportunity. They refuse to accredit his school, the responsibility for which has been delegated to them by the United States Department of Education. They did so even though the Federal Dental Academy had been approved as a proper post-graduate educational institution by the Department of Registration and Education of the State of Illinois. To make matters even more outrageous, the ADS staff was quick to explain to anyone who asked, that the denial was based, not on the merits of the school, but on their mistaken assertion that the school's owner, William O'Coogan, was a member of organized crime." By now Harrington was at a full roar, his voice dominating the courtroom. Neither Tony nor Judge Katsoris was able to interrupt. Two reporters sitting in the first bench were furiously scribbling notes. It was not a coincidence that they were there.

"Can you imagine that?" Harrington shouted, "A member of organized crime!" Without waiting for an answer, he pressed on. "We are speaking here of one of Chicago's most prominent and respected citizens; a man who is renowned for his civic contributions and philanthropic activities; a man who the mayor chose to personally escort Pope John Paul on his recent visit to our city. If the petty bureaucrats at the American Dental

Society can destroy the reputation of someone like Bill O'Coogan as capriciously as this, then I fear for our country and our way of life." Harrington lowered his voice and continued without pausing. "In addition, I should tell the court that I feel so strongly about the rightness of this cause, that I have volunteered to contribute a substantial portion of any fee that we may recover to the Chicago Symphony Orchestra. I don't want anyone to suspect for a moment that we are prosecuting this case for monetary gain." Harrington's voice rose again. "We are prosecuting this case, Your Honor, because it is the *right* thing to do; and to not do so would be a crime!" As Harrington finished, his young associate stepped up and handed him a handkerchief to wipe his brow.

The courtroom was silent.

"Well, be that as it may," the Judge added calmly after a moment, "we'll judge the merits of this case at the proper time, which I don't believe is now."

"Your Honor, if I might briefly respond for the record," Tony asserted himself, stepping forward. "Mr. Harrington's comments are not only inappropriate, but totally misstate the nature of this case. This is a garden-variety antitrust case. The defamation count is thrown in for window dressing and to distract the defense from the real issues at stake. I'm confident that, after some discovery, this entire case will be disposed of by summary judgment long before trial."

Turning to his distinguished opponent, Tony added with a slight smile, "However, if Mr. Harrington insists that the libel count is a significant part of this case, then I assume he has no objection to our conducting discovery into Mr. O'Coogan's finances and other business dealings, as well as those of the Federal Dental Academy. How else can we inquire into the truth of the matters alleged?" He gave Harrington a nod of mock deference as he finished.

The judge's raised eyebrows momentarily unnerved Tony. "If you intend to prove that William O'Coogan of this community is part of organized crime," she said, leaning back, "this should be a very interesting trial indeed!"

"My client has no objection whatsoever into that type of discovery," replied Harrington. "Mr. O'Coogan's civic and professional accomplishments are a matter of public record. I'm sure that counsel will be quite disappointed with what he finds. And to give counsel a head start on his review of Mr. O'Coogan's commitments, I will even tell him, now, in open court, where he can find the most comprehensive listing of my client's activities." He paused dramatically, concluding, "I am referring, of course, to the most recent publication of Who's Who in the World!"

"All right," interjected the judge, banging her gavel, "let the record reflect that defendants' oral motion to inquire into Plaintiff O'Coogan's personal finances and other business dealings, as well as that of the Federal Dental Academy, is granted without objection. Gentlemen, before you leave, let me ask you, would a settlement conference be productive in this case?"

"Absolutely not, Your Honor!" Harrington bellowed,

before Tony could respond. "The damages done to my client's reputation are so egregious that nothing short of a jury verdict in his favor, including substantial verdict, can adequately compensate Mr. O'Coogan for the injuries he's suffered at the hands of the defendants. We respectfully decline to participate in any settlement conference."

"Mr. Jeffries?" the judge asked as she turned to Tony.

"Well, that being the case," Tony confidently replied, "let's get on with our discovery. Put a jury in the box and let's have ourselves a trial."

"Gentlemen, get on with your discovery; I'll see you on September 11th. Mr. Clerk, call the next case."

The attorneys turned and walked toward the rear of the courtroom, brushing shoulders with counsel responding to the call of the next case. "That was a mixed bag, Tony," Charlie whispered. "I hated to lose the motion to dismiss, but I like where you ended up on the discovery question. Did you intend that to be a formal motion to inquire into O'Coogan's personal finances?"

"No, but let's not look a gift horse in the mouth. I don't think that Katsoris cares for Harrington's pomposity any more than we do. We have to decide what discovery to initiate immediately to take best advantage of this."

Out in the corridor, they paused to allow Jack Harrington and his entourage sweep by. Harrington was describing to the two trailing reporters the glowing details of William O'Coogan's contribution to the Chicago community. After they had turned the corner toward the elevators, Charlie added, "What about that bullshit about donating his fee to the Chicago Symphony? That's not enforceable!"

"I know, but Harrington's on the symphony board. So, if he gets a fee, and donates it, that will probably just satisfy a pledge that he's already made. And besides, what's a "substantial portion?" Five percent? Ten percent? Surely not one hundred percent?" Tony asked rhetorically with a smile. "Whatever it is, he'll claim it as a tax deduction. But he does put on a nice show, don't you think?"

"I guess so; but I think it would be very difficult to work for a guy like that on a regular basis."

"If that's meant as a compliment, I'll take it," Tony responded with a smile. "Let's get back to the shop and see where we can go with our discovery."

The two attorneys walked a few paces down the corridor and took the first elevator down. At ground level, they left the Dirksen Federal Building on the northwest side, and caught a cab going north on Dearborn Street. Tony felt lucky; it was often difficult to get a north-bound cab on Dearborn in that part of the loop. The taxi drove past the monumental Picasso in front of the Daley Center, and was slowed by some demonstrators overflowing the plaza. The Daley Center Plaza was almost always a focal point of some demonstration or another. Today's group was supporting one of the early contenders for the Democratic nomination for president, Senator Joshua Nightingale. After clearing the crowd, the cab turned right on Lake Street, then left on Michigan, delivering Tony and Charlie to the Hancock Building in a little over ten minutes.

"These came in while you were in court, Tony." Judy handed Tony a stack of pink telephone messages as the two attorneys returned to Tony's office. "The top one is from Bob Patsky. He told me to tell you that he really wants to settle the Atkinson case, for his client's sake, and he's willing to lower his settlement demand. I said that you'd try to get back to him today if you had time. The others are all self-explanatory. Oh, yes, Karen called from New Buffalo. She said that the weather was so nice that she's going to stay out there tonight reading some of her committee reports and will come in from Michigan tomorrow afternoon with the kids."

"Thanks, Judy. And could you bring us some coffee." Tony took the stack of messages and walked into his office, followed by Charlie. *Karen's probably the most conscientious member of the Illinois General Assembly*, Tony thought. *She's also probably the brightest, since she's figured out how to lie on the beach and get some work done at the same time*. Tony pictured her on the sand with her big floppy straw hat, reading drafts of proposed legislation. *She's probably wearing that very sexy blue number, too*. He smiled to himself.

"Anything exciting?" Charlie asked offhandedly.

"No. Nothing that can't wait until later in the day," Tony answered as they both shed their suit coats and dropped them on the couch.

As they were sitting down, Carol James walked in. An attractive brunette with medium length hair and subtle makeup, Carol stood about five foot four but looked taller in her light-gray business suit and low heels. "Hi Charlie, Tony. I'm glad I caught you," she said to Tony. "We received a call today from plaintiff's counsel in the Blessed Trinity Hospital case. He said they'd drop their appeal for a twenty-five-thousand-dollar settlement. What do you think?"

Judy reentered quietly, placed three cups of hot coffee on Tony's desk, then left.

"I think that means they're desperate for anything they can get. Remember, initially plaintiffs were demanding a million, but they got nothing from the jury; nada. They must know they can't have much of a chance on appeal. Tell you what, Carol, call Sister Mary Ann at the hospital and tell her what's happened. My recommendation to her is to only settle the case at this stage if we can do it for ten thousand or less. That's within our settlement authority from the insurer. It's also the low end of what an appeal will cost the hospital and is within their deductible. If she agrees, offer it. What do you think?"

"I agree entirely," Carol responded. "Okay, I'll take care of it."

After Carol left, Tony and Charlie began talking about what kind of discovery they should initially undertake.

"All right, Charlie," Tony began, pulling a copy of the Federal Rules of Civil Procedure from his bookcase. "We can file interrogatories about anything related to this case. We can also request the production of any relevant documents. Katsoris ruled today that data and documents relating to O'Coogan's personal finances and other business interests are relevant, so let's start making a list of the initial things we want produced and questions we want answered, including everything related to O'Coogan and the Academy."

Charlie already had a yellow pad and pen in hand. "I assume," he commented, as he began to write, "we'll want to know the names of all the current and past officers, directors and employees of the Dental Academy."

"Yes, including their last known addresses and the dates of their employment or relationship with the Academy as well as their annual compensation."

As Tony kept talking, his mind probing into the cracks and hidden holes that might be found around the edges of O'Coogan's vast world, Charlie continued taking notes. "We'll also want to know all the banks with which the Academy has ever done business, including all their account numbers." Tony paused before adding, "After we get that information, we'll subpoena the records of those accounts at all the banks named to see exactly who was giving and receiving money from the Academy. We should also demand the Academy's full tax returns since it was organized, as well as all their audits or financial statements prepared for anyone. We're certainly entitled to that."

"What about O'Coogan personally?" Charlie asked. "How do you want to go after him?"

"We'll do exactly the same thing with O'Coogan. Let's see what all his and his wife's bank records show. What the hell, get the kids returns and bank statements too. No telling what we might uncover. Also copies of his tax returns and any companies that he's controlled in the past five years, with all schedules and attachments."

"Do you want to define "controlled?"

"Good point. Yes, any entity in which he's owned 25 percent or more of the equity or serves as an officer or director."

"Got it," Charlie said, adding to his notes.

Tony paused for a moment, "There's something else I want you to check into. I want you to find out exactly how this school got approved by the Illinois Department of Registration and Education. The fact that they have state approval makes CODA's denial of their dental program's accreditation look suspect. It gives some credence to the plaintiffs' antitrust allegations. We should request copies of all documents exchanged between O'Coogan, the Academy, the state, and whoever it was at R&E who was involved with the Academy's approval, then set up a formal deposition of that person or those people. Perhaps we'll learn things we wouldn't learn otherwise." As Tony took a sip of his coffee, Charlie finished making his notes, then asked, "What about that renegade dentist, Roberts, who told Kaminsky that O'Coogan was a mobster? Should we try to find him?"

"Yes. We can't trust him, but if we can talk to Roberts maybe he'll tell us something that would be useful in defending the defamation count. Why don't you send a letter to him at his last known address, with copies to all the various attorneys who have represented him or sued him over the years? That'll be about half of the members of the Chicago Bar Association. Hopefully, someone has kept in touch with him and will forward our letter."

"Okay, this is a good start," Charlie commented as he finished writing. "I'll take care of that. I'll explain everything to the rest of the team and hand out their assignments."

The rest of Tony's day was filled with the usual routine of a practicing attorney. He had lunch with a client to discuss the best way to deal with a troublesome contract problem. After lunch, he responded to the various telephone calls and letters that had come in and needed attention, negotiated the settlement of a case, and prepared a series of status letters to clients. He reviewed and modified some pleadings prepared by a younger associate, then had Judy revise them and send them to the client for approval.

In the middle of the afternoon, Tony got a phone call from Eric Dawson, the leader of Boy Scout Troop 5 in Wilmette. Eric was a neighbor of the Jeffries and worked for an ad agency in the Prudential Building. He was calling to see if Tony could accompany the Troop on a weekend campout in a couple of weeks. One of the other fathers had cancelled, and they needed a replacement. Tony's sons, Mark and Roger were troop members, so he always tried to do his fair share of the fathers' collective responsibilities.

He took a quick look at his calendar. "Okay, Eric, I'll do it," he said a with chuckle. "But only if you'll agree to make your world-famous chili one of the nights."

"That's not a bad deal," Eric agreed. "I'm kinda partial to it myself." They both laughed and said goodbye and Tony made a notation in his desk calendar.

At four-thirty, Tony attended a meeting of the firm's hiring committee to decide whether to extend offers to two "lateral" applicants, experienced attorneys in other firms seeking jobs with Wilson, Thompson & Gilchrist. The committee decided to reject one applicant and extend an offer to the other.

A little after six, Charlie came into Tony's office and handed him a stack of documents. "Here are drafts of our first series of interrogatories and our first request for the production of documents by the Academy as well as a parallel set of each to O'Coogan," he said. "Make whatever changes you think are appropriate."

"Fine, I'll do that tonight, Charlie, and get back to you first thing in the morning. Since Karen and the kids are out at the lake, I'll review these over dinner downtown."

"Sounds like a good idea to me. See you in the morning, Tony."

Tony finished drafting the memo he was working on, completed his time sheet reflecting his day's work, packed up his briefcase, including the stack of papers that Charlie had delivered, retrieved his Panama hat from the back of the door, and turned out his office lights. He left the office a little before seven, said goodbye to the evening receptionist, took the elevator down to the upper lobby, walked out of the building and headed south on Michigan Avenue. As he crossed the Chicago River, the site of the infamous Fort Dearborn massacre, he stopped to watch and listen to a street band of black kids pounding out some good Dixie. After enjoying their music for a couple of minutes he dropped a five in their collection can and stepped inside Morton's on Wacker Place.

Morton's was his favorite of the city's many good steakhouses, whose quiet, refined ambience made it particularly popular with the downtown business clientele. It was an island of unhurried fine dining in a sea of swirling activity. Tony rarely went there for lunch because it took longer than the customary hour to have a proper meal at Morton's. But when he occasionally dined downtown in the evening, under no compulsion to rush back to the office or home, he enjoyed having a relaxing dinner at Morton's. He also liked the place because its management had put on a magnificent surprise birthday dinner party for Karen two years ago.

As he often did at Morton's, Tony told the maître-d', Daniel, that he didn't need a menu; he'd have whatever soup Daniel recommended, a six-ounce fillet mignon, rare with bordelaise sauce, accompanied by a glass of Stag's Leap Cabernet. Tony had been dining at Morton's since it opened several years earlier and had never been disappointed. The soup that evening, minestrone, was excellent as was the rare fillet, just as Tony had anticipated. The delicate aroma of the bordelaise was as enticing as its taste was satisfying. Over dinner, he reviewed Charlie's drafts of the interrogatories and document requests. The work was good, and he made only minimal changes.

Toward the end of the meal, Tony recognized someone sitting with a small group at a table on the far side of the room. He was the dean of one of the local dental schools. They caught each other's eyes, smiled, and silently raised their glasses.

"That's Tony Jeffries," the dean whispered to his two dentist companions. "He's the lawyer who's handling the suit against the ADS filed by the Federal Dental Academy and that O'Coogan guy."

"How good is he?" one of the others asked quietly as he glanced across the room.

"He's good. He and his firm have done a lot of work for the dental profession over the years. They've gotten good results. We shouldn't have anything to worry about."

"I hope not. We went to a lot of trouble to keep that program from being accredited. The last thing we need in this town is another school churning out graduate dentists. It's getting harder and harder to keep a full schedule as it is."

"Damn right," the third man answered. "By the way, do you guys think many people actually believed those stories about the mob being involved?"

"I know they did," the dean said, laughing. "In fact, that was the main reason why at least two of the commission members voted against accreditation."

"Gentlemen," he continued softly, raising his glass, "I think we owe a large debt to Bob Kaminsky, dentistry's great gossip monger. He came in with his wild rumor about the mob's ownership of the Dental Academy at the best possible time. With a little help from us, Kaminsky's gossip did them in. The most amusing thing of all is that Kaminsky actually believes his own rumor."

They all chuckled, clinking their glasses.

When Tony left Morton's he was relaxed, knowing that he'd had a productive day. He enjoyed what he was doing. He glanced at his watch, saw that he'd missed the 9:35 train and decided to take a taxi to Wilmette to avoid the hour's wait for the next one. He caught a cab going northbound on Michigan Avenue, stepped in, and told the driver to take Lake Shore Drive to the north suburbs. He'd give him the specifics when they got closer.

"Good evening, sir, be happy to" the cabbie said quietly. As the taxi pulled away from the curb, Tony leaned back and quickly dozed off.

"Here you are, Cap'n Jeffries," the cabbie said quietly, "606 Tenth Street, Wilmette. Right on the corner"

Tony opened his eyes; he'd fallen deeply asleep. That deep, gravelly voice. It sounded familiar. *Do I know this guy?*

Tony looked at the driver through the rear-view mirror, saw his well-rounded brown face, but didn't recognize him. He also saw that they were parked directly in front of his house. He looked at the name on the Chicago taxi license. *George Torrance.* Tony was jolted into full awareness. Torrance was an airman charged with double murder and rape when they were both in the Air Force many years ago. Tony was appointed defense counsel.

The thoughts of that event came quickly tumbling back. The local Air Force commander wanted to give Torrance the max, death by firing squad, or at least life in prison, as a warning to other black airmen to not mess with the white women in the small northern Michigan town where their base was located. Torrance swore his innocence; Tony believed him, worked hard, and against all odds got him acquitted in the court-martial. But Torrance was apprehended again shortly thereafter in an attack on another woman; *he was guilty all along and played Tony for a fool.* Second time around he was tried in a civil court. He couldn't be charged or tried for the two crimes of which he'd already been acquitted, but the local court found him guilty of the third assault and sentenced him to twenty years. Yet here he was, parked in front of Tony's home. *How does he know where I live? Does he regard me as a friend or as a mortal enemy?* It all came back to Tony in a rush as his mind cleared and as he quickly reached into his pocket for cash to pay the fare.

"Good to see you again, Cap'n; been a few years. That court in Tawas City sentenced me to twenty years but time goes by fast when you got nothin' else to do but think 'bout things. Thought a lot 'bout you, Cap'n. And here we are, both in Chicago."

"Torrance! How'd you know where I lived?" Tony pulled a couple of twenties out of his pocket and thrust them over the seat.

"Why are you so jumpy, Cap'n? Ain't you glad to see me? It's been a long time."

"Yeah, it's been a real pleasure. Here's your fare. Now I'm getting out." Tony pushed against the door, but it wouldn't open.

"Hey, I thought we were friends!"

"You were a client, George. And you lied to me. Swore you were innocent, and I believed you, threw my heart and soul into that case."

"Hey, that was a long time ago. And the court-martial found me 'not guilty,' thanks to you." He smiled, then added "So I figure I owe you one or two."

"Yeah, okay. Now let me out of here," Tony said as he pushed his money toward Torrance again. "You made me complicit in those killings. I defended you, and thought you were innocent. In fact, I told the court that I *knew* you were innocent. I got you off, and then you attacked another woman. You were guilty from the start." Tony shut his mouth and pushed against the cab door; it still wouldn't budge. Anger and apprehension were building fast in him.

"Sorry you feel that way Cap'n," Torrance continued slowly, his thumb still on the cab's autolock. "But I was entitled to counsel, that ended up bein' you, and you did a hell of a job for me."

"I want to get out now George. Here's forty bucks, that should cover the fare."

"The fare's on me, Cap'n. You were sleeping, and I just took you home. I know where you live, 606 Tenth Street in Wilmette. So what?"

"Oh Jesus!" Tony said, now fearful. "You've been stalking me."

"No, I've driven you home three times already. You just didn't notice. I guess we all look the same to you, don't we?" he chuckled. "I just want to say thank you. You saved my life in prison. Maybe worse, which I can't forget." As he finished, Torrance turned, smiled and extended his open hand.

Tony hesitated, then slowly took and shook it. The lock clicked open. Tony pushed the door and jumped out of the cab, his briefcase in hand.

"I still owe you one Cap'n," Torrance shouted after him, as he pulled away.

Tony walked briskly up the steps to his house. He turned and saw the cab make a right on Central then head east toward Sheridan Road. On top of his professional worries, Tony felt uneasy, frightened; a serial rapist and killer knew exactly where he and his family lived.

Chapter 4

July 9

—mm—

It was a steamy hot day in the Midwest. The temperature everywhere hovered around a hundred. Meetings were held that day in two downstate Illinois cities, Springfield and Moline, both under the same stifling conditions but with different participants and involving ostensibly different matters. In fact, both meetings dealt with the same subject.

In Springfield, Charlie Dickenson had been waiting almost an hour for his 9:00 a.m. meeting with William Weaver, director of the Illinois Department of Registration and Education. When he scheduled the meeting, Charlie advised Weaver's secretary that he wanted to discuss the Federal Dental Academy. In retrospect, Charlie thought as he looked at his watch once again, perhaps he shouldn't have been so specific. He also wished Weaver would have had the decency to tell him he was going to be late.

Charlie had flown down to Springfield the previous night and had run across a charming lobbyist in the bar at the Ramada. He didn't leave her room until after two, he could've used the extra hour of sleep.

Not much of a trip, Charlie thought. *The guys assigned to Thompson's corporate work get New York. What do I draw? Springfield! Still, working for Tony isn't bad. He's not afraid to try a lawsuit.* He remembered when Tony had told him that one of the keys to being a successful litigator was in knowing when to take a risk, and when to create the fear of risk in others. *I'm learning things the firm's report writers never learn. Besides, what the hell, even if my trips are to mundane places like Springfield, there are always diversions.*

Weaver's secretary was a dowdy woman in her late fifties. She was wearing a loose-fitting floral-print dress that looked like a rummage-sale leftover. She brought Charlie a can of Coke while he was waiting and asked him to contribute fifty cents to the office kitty. She said she had no idea why her boss was running so late. Charlie took a swig of the Coke, then quickly put the can down. It was warm. He hated warm Coke.

At a little after ten, the reception-room door opened to a portly man in his early fifties. He hesitated as his eyes spied Charlie, then hurried through to his inner office, leaving the door ajar.

"Mr. Dickenson of Wilson, Thompson & Gilchrist to see you, Mr. Weaver," his secretary said, raising her voice.

"Yes, I know. All right, send him in."

Charlie walked into Weaver's office. As he sat down he glanced around at the artifacts of thirty years as a Springfield bureaucrat. William Weaver was one of those political functionaries who drift from job to job in state government as the governors change. They're never out of work, regardless of who's in power. They survive because they know how the system works, they know not be *too* greedy, and, most importantly, they know each other.

Charlie noticed that the wall to the right of Weaver's desk was covered with autographed photographs of the man with every prominent Republican politician of the past generation. On the wall to Weaver's left was an equally impressive collection of photographs of him with every major Democrat of the same period. And over each panel of photos was what appeared to be a rolled-up map of Illinois that could be pulled down at the appropriate time.

The rest of Weaver's office was filled with the drab furniture usually allocated to middle range bureaucrats. The only bright spots in the decor were a large TV on a table adjacent to Weaver's desk, with a magnificent Chinook salmon mounted on the wall above it.

"What can I do for you, kid?" Weaver said without looking up, shuffling through a stack of papers on his desk. "I've got a busy schedule, so I'd appreciate it if you'd make it quick."

"Thank you for giving me some of your time, Mr. Weaver. I'm one of the attorneys representing the

American Dental Society in a suit brought in Chicago by the Federal Dental Academy and its owner William O'Coogan. It's an antitrust case with an added defamation count. One of the issues..."

"Look, kid, I told you I'm busy," interrupted Weaver, looking up at Charlie. "I've heard about your suit; it was in the papers. Get to the point."

"I'll do that, Mr. Weaver," Charlie replied. He was calm and spoke quietly. "We'd like to know exactly how the Federal Dental Academy obtained state approval in the first place. Your department approved the Academy as a post-graduate educational institution in the State of Illinois. We'd like to see their application, talk to whoever on your staff inspected the school, and..."

"Like hell you will. I've got a ton of work to get out. I'm not going to waste time with you just because your client got its tit in a wringer," Weaver clenched the stack of papers on his desk as he spoke. "First of all, you sure as hell aren't here to do me any favors. Why should I waste any of my time on you? Besides, I don't remember anything at all about that school."

Weaver glared at Charlie for a long moment. When he resumed, he made no effort to mask his contempt for the young attorney. "Look, pal, we handle hundreds of applications for licensure or state approval every month, everything from community colleges to blacksmithing. Did you know that? Nobody can blacksmith in the State of Illinois unless they're licensed by this department. You want to ask me about one of those guys too? Get out of here! I can't tell you anything, and I'm damn sure I don't have any more time for you." Weaver stood up, sweating profusely. It was clear that he regarded the conversation as being over.

Charlie remained seated. He pulled a folded piece of paper from his inner coat pocket and laid it on the desk between them. "I'm sorry you feel that way, Mr. Weaver," he replied without raising his voice. "But this is information that we're going to obtain, one way or another. If you don't want to discuss this just between the two of us, I guess we'll have to subpoena you for your deposition and production of all the records we'd like to review."

Charlie looked down at the folded piece of paper between them on the desk, then looked up at Weaver. "This is a subpoena. If I serve it on you, your deposition will be taken next Monday morning at nine, with a court reporter as well as opposing counsel present. You'll be obligated to produce a number of documents. Your testimony will become a matter of public record. Also, of course, in a deposition the witness is under oath. If he gives false testimony he is committing perjury, which, as I recall, is a felony." He paused, then added coldly, "Which approach would you prefer?"

Weaver hesitated. He reached tentatively toward the folded piece of white paper on his desk. "If you pick it up, you're served," Charlie commented.

Weaver gave Charlie a long look, sighed and sat back down. His shoulders sagged, and he unbuttoned his shirt collar. He had lost. "If I tell you what I know, will you guarantee that my deposition won't be taken?"

"No, I won't commit to that at all," Charlie replied, now clearly in command. "But if you won't talk to me today then I'll guarantee that your deposition definitely *will* be taken."

"All right, I'll tell you what I know. But it really isn't much."

As Weaver spoke, Charlie took out his mini recorder, flicked it on, and laid it on the desk between them. "Do you mind?" he asked. Weaver quietly shook his head.

He sat back and took a deep breath, looking at his young interrogator. "We received this application for a dental institute," he said. "It was different from most institutions because it was only going to have one program, dentistry. There's nothing wrong with that, mind you, but it was different. They had space rented, lab facilities already set up, faculty members under contract, and appeared to be financially solvent. In fact, they were already operating informally as a continuing education school for foreign dentists who wanted to sharpen their skills before they applied to transfer to an accredited U.S. dental school for their final year of education. To be licensed as a dentist here you must have graduated from a U.S. accredited dental school. I recall meeting the president of the school. He was a very impressive dentist."

"Would that be Dr. Jack Roberts?"

"Yes, that was him. First-rate guy. He's the dentist who organized the whole thing. Anybody who meets him would have confidence in what he was doing. It's coming back to me now. As I recall, his number-two man was also pretty sharp. A Swede named Swenson or maybe Sorenson, I think. He was an accountant, managing the financial side of things."

"Then I take it that you handled this matter yourself, you didn't delegate it to one of your staff investigators?"

"Absolutely. This was an important matter. We don't get new school applications every day, you know. I wanted it handled by the best man in my department," he smiled. "Me."

"Were you aware of the fact that Dr. Roberts had previously been expelled from the American Dental Society?" Charlie paused. Weaver started to say something but stopped. His only response was to repeatedly click his ballpoint pen.

"Did you know that a complaint to revoke Roberts' dental license was pending in your own department at the time the school's application was processed a couple of months ago?" Charlie pressed, raising his voice. "Or that his dental license has in fact since been revoked?"

"Hey, look, I don't want to get involved in dental politics," Weaver replied defensively. "To me, the question was whether the man was licensed as a dentist in Illinois at the time, which he was. Everything was in order; there was no reason to deny their application. We approved it as a licensed post-graduate school. Beyond that, it's up to the ADS to evaluate their dental program."

Weaver stopped to light a cigarette. The tremor in his hands betrayed his anxiety. "Remember," he stressed, "professional schools like this have to go through a two-step approval process. First, the institution has to be approved by the state as a legitimate post-graduate educational institution. Secondly, they have to obtain approval for any particular program from whatever professional agency or association is delegated responsibility in that area by the U.S. Department of Education. With dental schools, the ADS has been delegated that responsibility through its Commission on Dental Accreditation – CODA, they call it. It's the same with law schools or medical schools or whatever. When their application for state approval came before us, we did our review and it was in order, so we approved them. We didn't look at the details of their dental program; that's CODA's responsibility. That's all I know, except for what I've read in the papers about the suit that was filed." Weaver leaned back in his chair, smiled nervously, adding, "That's all I know."

"I see," Charlie said, taking notes. "By the way, you mentioned foreign dentists who want licensure to practice here. How do they go about getting that approval?"

"Well, to be licensed in Illinois, first they have to be a graduate of an accredited U.S. dental school, which in the case of transfer students might mean attending one or two semesters of dental education here. Then, for prospective dentists in that category they have to file an application and pass a test."

"Who processes those applications and administers those tests?" Charlie pressed.

"Why, this department. With the assistance of our

Dental Advisory Committee, of course."

"Who appoints the members of the Dental Advisory Committee?"

"I do, counselor, who else?" Weaver answered with his biggest smile.

"Thank you. You have been very informative," Charlie replied. He put his yellow pad into his briefcase, picked up his recorder, turned it off while putting it in his pocket, and stood up. "While I'm here," he added, "could I obtain a copy of the Academy's application for state approval as well as your department's response?"

"Sure, I don't see why not. After all, counselor, they are public records, aren't they? Give me your card, and I'll have my secretary make copies and mail them to you this afternoon." Weaver paused. He lowered his voice. "Now, look, I've been cooperative, so no deposition, right?"

"We'll see. Maybe, maybe not," Charlie answered. "If you don't mind, though, I'll wait in your reception room for your secretary to make me copies of those documents. We wouldn't want them lost in the mail, would we?" As he turned to leave, Charlie placed one of his business cards on Weaver's desk and picked up the folded piece of paper that he placed there earlier. It was his travel itinerary; it would be helpful in getting home.

At nine that same morning, a dark-blue Buick sedan pulled into the parking lot of the American Tractor

Company plant on the south side of Moline, Illinois. Two men in open-collared, short-sleeved shirts got out and walked in the door leading to the administrative offices. Both were carrying briefcases; they were the local union negotiating team.

They were met inside the air-conditioned building by the three negotiators representing American Tractor. After the usual foreplay, the five sat down to resume their negotiations, which had been going on for a month. The talks were reaching a critical stage, with a contract termination date of August 31st looming.

"Gentlemen," began Ben Crenshaw, the company's general counsel and chief negotiator, "we all know that they've reached agreement on the basic wage package at the national level, but our local issues still have to be finalized. We've gone over your revised list of demands, dividing them into three categories: those that we're prepared to accept now; those that we feel are subject to some negotiation; and those we feel that we cannot grant under any circumstances." Crenshaw took off his suit coat and hung it over the back of his chair. His two colleagues did the same.

"Fine, let's hear what's on your lists," replied the union's chief negotiator Vince Black, a stocky, deeply tanned man in his early forties with curly black hair, graying at the temples. "We've got our priorities too. Maybe we won't be too far apart."

"All right," responded Crenshaw. "We'll accept your demands that the company provide safety shoes, goggles and gloves for any employee who requests them, and for each employee's birthday to be an additional paid holiday. The middle category, which we consider negotiable, consists of your requests for increased overtime pay, and shorter hours in the summer. The items that we're not prepared to accept or negotiate further are two: guaranteed bonuses tied to the profitability of the company as a whole, and a fully paid dental plan for all our employees and their families."

"That won't fly," Black quickly replied, shaking his head. "We've got to have the dental plan sponsored by the union welfare fund. Our members feel very strongly about that; so strongly that I think it's a strike issue."

"Vince, you can't be serious," Crenshaw replied. "That plan's too expensive! You're asking for a program that will pay for 100 percent of all dental expenses if your members use the designated clinic. The premium for that plan is thirty-five a month for single employees and ninety a month for employees with dependents. With our thirteen hundred employees, that would cost us about a hundred grand a month. That's more than a million bucks a year! If we were to agree to that, we couldn't give you any of the other items that are still on the table."

"Well, maybe that's the way it's going to have to be, because the dental plan is very important to us." Black paused for a moment, "Tell you what, Ben. If you give us the safety equipment we've asked for plus the Union sponsored dental plan, we'll drop everything else."

Crenshaw considered the proposal for a moment, held

a whispered conference with his two fellow team members, took a deep breath, nodded and responded, “We’ll accept that. So, that’ll be the deal, right? Nothing else.”

“Right, that’s what we’ll recommend to our members,” Black answered. “What we recommend, we get approved,” he added with a smile. “You can start drawing up the contract extension. We’ll look at the language you come up with. If it matches what we’ve agreed on today, we have a deal. We’ve had a good day gentlemen.”

The parties stood up and shook hands, and the union representatives walked out to the parking lot. When they had left the building, Black turned to the similarly stocky man walking next to him. “Okay Mike, make a call to Chicago. Tell them it’s set; and they’ve got to have a dental clinic operating down here within six weeks. We’ll get them a location and the equipment, but they’ve got to supply the dentists. We’re going to need three. Tell them it’s a rush deal.”

“You got it, Vinnie,” said the other man donning his sunglasses. “Hell, that was a can of corn.”

“Mike,” Black chuckled, “when you’ve got your priorities straight, you can accomplish anything.”

When they reached their car, he turned and added, “On second thought, Mike, tell them to line up just two dentists, not three. We don’t want to have docs with spare time on their hands.”

They both laughed.

At eight o'clock that evening a large crowd was gathering for a formal banquet in the Grand Ballroom of the Ritz Carlton Hotel, just off Chicago's North Michigan Avenue. Unlike the stifling heat that blanketed most of the Midwest, the Grand Ballroom's temperature was a quite comfortable seventy-two. Magnums of chilled champagne sat in ice buckets beside every table.

As dinner ended, a distinguished gentleman in a tuxedo took the speaker's dais. The crowd slowly hushed as he began his address.

"Cardinal Bernardin, Mayor Daley, distinguished members of the City Council, and honored guests, it gives me untold pleasure to be with you this evening to honor one of this city's greatest citizens. We are here to present the Civic Foundation's Citizen of the Year Award to the person who has contributed the most during the past year to peace and goodwill in the greater Chicago area. His contributions are well known to all of you. No one more richly deserves this award."

Turning to his right, he gestured down to the front table, raised his voice and proclaimed, "I give you Chicago's Citizen of the Year, William O'Coogan!"

Three thousand people stood in tumultuous applause as a smiling, debonair Bill O'Coogan strode up the stairs to the dais to accept his award.

Chapter 5

July 24

The plaintiffs' answers to the defendants' written interrogatories included a list of all current and past officers and employees of the Federal Dental Academy. Tony reviewed it and decided that the first witness he would question in a deposition would be the Academy's treasurer. Tony picked him for two reasons; he was placed highly enough to know about the school's finances, and of all the current Academy employees he had the most obscure background. If anyone was a possible link to the mob, it was Leonard Battaglia. Tony would save O'Coogan's deposition for later.

The deposition was set for ten a.m. in Wilson, Thompson & Gilchrist's conference room A. The room had paneled walls, a thick oriental carpet, subdued recessed lighting, and a fifteen foot polished oak table surrounded by a dozen leather swivel chairs. It was designed for intimidation.

Tony and Charlie arrived first and chose their places deliberately. They took the two chairs nearest to the door. It would be difficult for Battaglia to walk out if he didn't like the way the deposition was going.

The court reporter was next to arrive. She was from Lake Shore Reporting, a reliable firm that Tony had been using for years. Tony had her sit to his left at the head of the table. The witness would be sitting directly across from Tony.

At a few minutes past ten, Judy brought two men in from the reception room. One of them was David Epstein, Jack Harrington's associate; Tony recognized him from their recent encounter before Judge Katsoris. Epstein was in his mid-to-late twenties, tall and well-dressed in a light brown summer suit with a thin dark mustache that matched his hair. The other man, in his late-thirties it seemed, was about five-nine and stocky, with a prominent mole on his right cheek. After the appropriate introductions, they all sat down, and the court reporter swore in the witness.

"Would you state your name for the record?" Tony began.

"Leonard Battaglia." He was younger than Tony had expected and looked overdressed in his dark custom-made silk suit, with a white carnation in his lapel and a large diamond ring on his left forefinger. There was something familiar about him that Tony couldn't place.

As Tony asked his questions, Charlie organized a series of papers in front of him on the table; the documents received from the plaintiffs, files of newspaper clippings on all the major mob figures in the Chicago area, and all the material he had received from Weaver at the Department of Registration and Education. He also had the secretary of state's registry of all foreign and domestic corporations. As Battaglia gave each answer, Charlie would quickly sort through his documents to determine whether it squared with information they already had and whether any follow-up questions were appropriate. During the course of the deposition he would be handing Tony a continual stream of documents and notes.

"What's your business or occupation, Mr. Battaglia?" Tony asked.

"I'm the chief financial officer of the Federal Dental Academy here in Chicago."

"How long have you held that position?"

"About five months. Before that, I was with the Buchanan Finance Company on the west side." He pulled out a pack of Camels, lit one, and blew a circle of smoke into the air.

David Epstein leaned back in his chair, relaxed; Lenny Battaglia was doing fine. Epstein, just a year out of law school, had attended only a few depositions. Jack Harrington had told him that since they had nothing to hide he should let Battaglia answer whatever questions Jeffries asked. His main responsibility in the deposition, Harrington said, was simply to "hold the client's hand." This was easy work.

Tony continued with a series of questions about

Battaglia's educational and professional background. He said he grew up in the south-west suburbs and worked his way through high school and college as a clerk at the Sears store on Twenty-Second Street in Cicero.

"Is Cicero where you grew up?" Tony asked.

"No," Battaglia answered with a slight smile. "Riverside. I grew up in Riverside."

That's where I know him from. Tony had grown up there too.

"I got an accounting degree from Chicago City College," Battaglia continued. "After graduation I held a series of clerical jobs before getting a job with Buchanan as an accountant." He denied ever having been convicted of anything more serious than a traffic violation. Charlie checked, the denial was accurate.

"What sort of business is Buchanan Finance Company engaged in?" Tony continued.

"Well, Buchanan acts as a mortgage broker. It finds investments for its clients and arranges all the paperwork to put the loans through. It also collects the payments from the debtors after the loans are made. For a fee, of course."

"Are the repayments made to the investor or Buchanan Finance?"

"Buchanan Finance, usually."

"Even when some other party, an investor, is the real lender?"

"Yes, that's the way the investors usually want it. After the loan is made and the papers are signed,

Buchanan assigns its interests to the investor. Buchanan stays involved to the extent that it collects the payments and forwards the funds on to its client, after deducting its service fee."

"So, the debtor never really knows who loaned him the money, is that right?"

"That's generally the case. As far as the debtor is concerned, he's dealing with the Buchanan Finance Company. But that's standard in this business."

"Now how, exactly, did you move from Buchanan to the Federal Dental Academy?" Tony queried.

"Well, I was working as an accountant at Buchanan, keeping track of the investments of some of their major clients including, William O'Coogan, when one of those loans started going bad. It was a sixty-thousand-dollar loan that Mr. O'Coogan made to the Federal Dental Academy through Buchanan. They were getting a little late in their payments; Mr. O'Coogan was concerned. He felt their finances weren't being very well handled. So, he made a deal with the Academy, through Buchanan, of course, that he wouldn't accelerate the loan and demand immediate payment if he could have someone who he trusted working for the Academy to watch their finances. That turned out to be me. I was really flattered! The deal was that I'd leave Buchanan Finance and be hired by the Dental Academy. Buchanan would pick up the difference in pay. I was the assistant treasurer at first."

"Who was the treasurer when you began working there?"

"His name was Sorenson. Rolf Sorenson."

"When did he leave the Academy?"

"About a month after I got there. When I began working with their books I found some *serious* irregularities. Naturally, I reported to Mr. O'Coogan what I found. That was when he decided that he had to take an active role in the company's operations in order to save his investment, so he called his notes. Neither Sorenson nor the Academy's president, Dr. Roberts, cared for that. They both resigned at about the same time."

"So Mr. O'Coogan took over the Dental Academy in order to secure his loan?"

"That's right. At that point he owned the place, since the stock in the Academy was the collateral for his loan."

"How much had Mr. O'Coogan loaned to the Dental Academy through Buchanan Finance by then?" asked Tony.

"I really can't remember." Battaglia's attention was focused on the wisp of smoke spiraling up from his Camel.

"Come now, Mr. Battaglia. You were intimately involved in those transactions. I'm not asking for the exact amount, but you must know the approximate amount of the loans. Give me a ball park figure."

Battaglia looked at Epstein, who nodded, then shrugged his shoulders. "With interest and fees over one hundred thousand dollars but I'm not sure exactly how much."

"Was it over a hundred and fifty thousand?"

"No, I don't think so."

"So the Dental Academy owed O'Coogan between a hundred thousand and a hundred and fifty at the time he took it over, is that your testimony?"

"Yeah, I guess so."

"That's better. By the way, who owned Buchanan Finance while you were working there?"

"Some investors in Arizona, I think. Never met them."

"Well, who was your immediate supervisor at Buchanan?"

"I worked for the president of the company directly," Battaglia paused, "But you know, I can't remember that guy's name; long name. I really can't help you."

"Was it Bustamante - Alex Bustamante?" Tony asked, glancing down at a note that Charlie had handed him.

"Yeah, that's it. Thanks for reminding me."

"How did you first meet Mr. Bustamante?"

"My uncle Al introduced us; helped me get the job."

"What's your Uncle Al's full name?"

"Pontico. Al Pontico."

"Would your uncle be the Alberto Pontico, who has a business on Clark Street?" Tony asked, looking at another piece of paper that Charlie had slipped him.

"Sure, that's him" Battaglia answered defensively, leaning back in his chair. "My mother's brother."

"How long were you with Buchanan Finance, Mr. Battaglia, before there was this arrangement for you to go over to the Federal Dental Academy?"

"I'm not sure; a couple of months maybe. Things started happening pretty fast after I got to Buchanan Finance."

"By the way, was there a 'Mr. Buchanan'?"

"Why, sure," responded Battaglia with a broad smile as he leaned back. "He was the president of the United States once, wasn't he?"

That set the tone for the balance of the deposition. Battaglia's answers were either evasive or barbed. He never answered directly unless required to. It was apparent that while he was going to avoid giving the defendants any useful information, he wouldn't lie if confronted with a question he couldn't evade. Often Tony had to repeat or rephrase questions in order to get an answer. But he was prepared to be painstaking in his approach. With the help of Charlie's data, they were slowly able to extract from Battaglia most of the information they wanted about the Dental Academy's current operations.

They learned that, notwithstanding the ADS's denial of their accreditation, the Dental Academy was apparently doing quite well. Since O'Coogan and Battaglia had taken over, they had greatly expanded the school's program of refresher courses for foreign dentists seeking licensure in this country. For a fee of $6,000, payable in advance, a foreign dentist would receive a package of material and tapes that he or she could study at home, and if they wished, personally attend any of the courses or lectures at the Academy. The package also included a series of self-administered tests that covered the basic curriculum of American dental schools. Many of the student/dentists enrolled while still in their native countries, a practice that the Academy encouraged through foreign advertising. Once the academy received U.S. accreditation as a dental school, when they complete the academy's program they'll graduate with a DDS, eligible to apply for licensure anywhere in the U.S. Over a thousand student dentists were enrolled, but they attended very few of the lectures at the Academy, doing most of their studying at home.

The professional program was run by a dentist from Brazil, Dr. Maria Henriques, "Dr. Maria" as Battaglia said all the staff and students called her. The individual lectures and lab courses were given by a group of younger dentists on a part-time basis. Each received thirty dollars an hour for their time. It was this group that would comprise the full-time faculty of the Academy when it received ADS accreditation. Battaglia acknowledged that a "full-time" faculty member would be free to maintain a private dental practice two or three day a week when that time came.

William O'Coogan had an office at the Academy and drew a salary as its president but stopped by only from time to time to oversee the operations. Battaglia was in charge of all the financial operations of the business.

When Tony noted that O'Coogan seemed to be making a tidy return on his investment, Battaglia was quick to point out that the Academy's expenses had risen sharply the past few months. The program wasn't nearly as profitable as it appeared. Their printing, mailing and maintenance expenses had gone up sharply with the increase in enrollment. They were also buying expensive lab equipment in anticipation of accreditation as a full dental school. In addition, Battaglia explained, Dr. Roberts had only signed a one-year lease when he started the Academy. When that lease expired on April 30th, the landlord, seeing that they had a growing business on the site, raised the monthly rent from $2,500 to $10,000. Because of their extensive advertising campaign, he and Mr. O'Coogan concluded that they couldn't change the Academy's location; reluctantly agreeing to the increased rent as part of a long-term lease. That rent, Battaglia insisted, was eating up a lot of their cash flow.

"Who *is* your landlord anyway?" Tony asked. "Who owns the building on Lake Street where the Academy is located?"

"Some bank." Battaglia answered casually, as he tapped his cigarette butt out in the glass ashtray.

"Which bank, Mr. Battaglia? Who do you write your monthly rent checks to?"

Battaglia paused a long time as he lit another Camel. "It's the Lafayette National Bank as trustee. The same trust has owned that building for years."

Tony glanced at Charlie, who quickly scanned a series of real-estate tract searches that he had in front of him, before nodding in the affirmative.

Tony decided at that point to move into a new line of questioning. "I see from your advertising," he began, "that you run a placement service for dentists. Is that correct?"

"That's right," Battaglia responded. He blew a cloud

of smoke in Tony's direction. "We try to find jobs for them. For an additional fee, of course."

"Of course. What is that additional fee?"

"Five thousand bucks. Half when they get the job; the other half three months later if they're still there." He paused, "That's pretty damn reasonable for a placement fee, by the way!"

Tony ignored the remark. "How many dentists have you placed in jobs so far?"

Battaglia shifted uncomfortably in his chair. "Well, this is a new part of our program, so we haven't had the chance to put too many numbers up on the board yet. We placed two last week in a new clinic in Moline. It's a clinic that's going to service the employees of the American Tractor Company. Two fellas from Pakistan." He leaned forward again and continued, "We expect this to be a very big part of our program in the months to come."

They broke for lunch at twelve-thirty, ate and caucused separately, having agreed to resume an hour later. Tony and his team had lunch brought up to another conference room so that they could continue to concentrate on Battaglia's testimony. When they returned to conference room A, Tony knew that the afternoon session would be more volatile than the mornings had been, based on the questions that he planned to ask as well as the alcohol on Battaglia's breath.

He began by attacking directly. "You told us something this morning, Mr. Battaglia that we didn't know previously; that Alberto Pontico is your uncle, your mother's brother. Your uncle Al has spent some time in jail, hasn't he?"

"What the hell does that have to do with anything?" Battaglia exploded, slamming his hands on the table. "I'm not going to answer a fuckin' question like that!"

David Epstein suddenly came to life. "Objection! That question's highly improper." Turning to Battaglia, he added quietly, "If a question's improper, like that last one, I'll object. You can't object, understand?"

"All right," answered Battaglia loudly. "But I'm not going to let this asshole ask me questions about my family!"

Tony directed his response to Epstein. "counselor, your clients have sued the American Dental Society and its officers for libel, among other things. You are claiming that it's libelous to state that your clients, Mr. O'Coogan and Mr. Battaglia, are connected with organized crime. The last time I looked, you were suing my clients for fifty million dollars, tripled, plus punitive damages. Now, the witness, Mr. Battaglia, is the chief financial officer of the Federal Dental Academy. We know from his own testimony that he got his job there through the intercession of his uncle, Mr. Alberto Pontico. We're entitled to know exactly who Alberto Pontico is, his background, and whether *he* has any connection with organized crime."

Tony's voice rose. "If your client won't answer these questions, I'll adjourn this deposition right now and go to Judge Katsoris for a ruling. Her office in the federal court house is only a five-minute cab ride away. I'll also ask for, and expect to receive, an award of costs." He paused and sat back in his chair. "Well, do we proceed, or do we adjourn the deposition and see Judge Katsoris?"

Epstein sat quietly for a long time, shuffling the papers in front of him. He had not been prepared for this sort of confrontation. He was terrified by the thought of having to argue this issue before Judge Katsoris without any preparation.

"Well, which is it?" asked Tony. He pulled out a copy of *Sullivan's Law Directory* from his briefcase beside his chair. "I'll get the judge's number, so we can phone her, tell her we have a problem and are coming over."

Epstein stopped shuffling his papers and turned to his client. "Lenny," he said, "you're going to have to answer his questions. I've objected for the record, but basically, he's right. This is a relevant area of inquiry."

"Son of a bitch," Battaglia muttered, shaking his head in angry disbelief. He raised his voice, "All right, what was the question?"

Tony had the court reporter read it back.

"Yeah, I think he's spent some time in the cooler. What of it?" Battaglia said icily. He stared at Tony. "Lots of people have relatives who've gotten in trouble somewhere."

"Actually, he's been sentenced to prison twice, hasn't he?" Tony continued calmly. He was looking over a police rap sheet that Charlie had handed him. "Alberto Pontico was sentenced to five years for armed robbery in 1965; paroled after two years. He was sentenced again for extortion in 1976. I believe he served three years on that last conviction. Isn't that true?"

"Could be. You've got the rap sheet. *You* tell *me*."

"No, Mr. Battaglia. *You* tell *me*. I'm going to have this document-marked as Battaglia Deposition Exhibit Number One." Tony paused as he gave the court reporter time to put the exhibit number on the sheet of paper. Then he pushed the paper across the table to the witness, "I want you to tell me, Mr. Battaglia, if the man described on this police rap sheet is your uncle, Alberto Pontico. Please note the photograph of the man on that sheet, as well as his home and business addresses. You'll also note several other arrests over the years that did not result in convictions. Is that your uncle Al, Mr. Battaglia?"

"Can he do this?" Battaglia hissed to Epstein. "I mean, asking personal questions about my relatives?"

"In this instance, yes, he's tied it in," responded Epstein in a stage whisper. "You've got to answer his question."

Battaglia shook his head in disgust. His face was flushed with anger. Finally, he looked at Tony, pushed the rap sheet back across the table, and responded. "Yeah; that's my uncle."

"Are you aware of the rumors, Mr. Battaglia, that your uncle Al is a lieutenant in the Outfit, the mob, here in Chicago?"

"That's a bunch of bullshit!" Battaglia jumped to his feet, toppling his chair. "Sure, he's made some mistakes," he shouted at Tony, "but he's paid for them. Guys like you will never let a guy up. Any Italian who's ever had a problem is in the mob as far as you're concerned. Well, that's pure bullshit. I'm not answering any more personal questions about my family!" He picked up his chair and slowly sat down, his eyes fixed on Tony. He turned to his young lawyer and added under his breath, "No matter what you say!"

Epstein picked up the cue from his client. "Mr. Battaglia is absolutely right. Questions like this are insulting and highly improper. It was bad enough for you to defame Mr. O'Coogan initially, but to now insinuate that Mr. Battaglia and everyone in his family are members of organized crime is irresponsible. There's not a thread of evidence to support that. I can see that it was a mistake for me to try to be a gentleman and cooperate with you earlier. Mr. Battaglia worked hard to put himself through college and start a professional career. He's here in his capacity as the treasurer of the plaintiff corporation, you have no right to inquire beyond that area. I'm instructing my client not to answer any more questions about his family."

Tony knew he had pressed the issue about as far as he could. Battaglia's personal record was clean, and even though his uncle Al was a convicted felon, there was nothing to link Battaglia himself to the crime syndicate. Still, it was interesting to learn that Alberto Pontico was Lenny Battaglia's uncle.

After Tony had explored several other areas of inquiry, the deposition ended at about four o'clock.

As everyone was getting ready to leave, Epstein turned to him, "You know, you guys are really hung up on this mob business. That's what got your client, the ADS, into trouble in the first place. I can tell you that we looked into it before we took the case and there's nothing to it. You and your clients just can't go around claiming that everyone whose last name ends in a vowel is a member of the Mafia."

While Tony was trying to decide how best to respond, Epstein went on.

"Look," he said, "at first I found your questions about the mob really offensive. After all, Lenny Battaglia is the CFO of a respected corporation. But in retrospect, I've got to admit that it's actually amusing." Turning to Battaglia, Epstein joked, "Lenny, this guy thinks you're a mobster. Just remember, his name is Jeffries and he lives in Wilmette. Why don't you put a contract out on him?"

Battaglia joined Epstein's laughter for a moment as he rose. He looked at Tony when he reached the door. "You know Jeffries," he said, "I remember you growing up in Riverside. You were a little bit older, but I remember you. You and your buddies always seemed to be too good for us. Didn't want to talk to people on our side of town."

What the hell is he talking about?

"Now you think you're better than anyone," Battaglia continued, raising his voice, "just because you've moved to the North Shore. Well, you're not!"

Tony leaned back and looked at him with a tight smile.

After a pause he quietly replied, "Well, Mr. Battaglia, I guess we'll be in court the next time we meet."

That evening after dinner, Karen and Tony enjoyed some Chardonnay in their living room, bringing each other up to speed on the events of the day. The lengthening shadows of the trees in their north-suburban neighborhood made this a very pleasant time of day. It was unusually quiet for the Jeffries' household. Their two older boys, Mark and Roger, were out with some of their neighbor friends; Billy, who would be entering first grade in the fall, was upstairs playing a video game, while their daughter Debbie, who at five was the youngest child, was visiting her friend next door.

Karen and Tony had dated at DePauw and married after Tony's first year at law school. Karen taught school the next two years to finance his tuition. After his tour of duty in the Air Force, required at the time, they returned to Chicago and moved to Wilmette. They had both settled comfortably into the suburban lifestyle and, five years ago when Debbie arrived, and Tony was doing well in the law firm, they bought a larger home in the same community.

Karen had always been active and energetic. She got involved in the PTA as soon as Mark entered grammar school. By the time Debbie started kindergarten, six years later, Karen was president of the Village Wide PTA. She had a successful term on the school board, personally intervening to prevent a threatened teachers' strike. When their state representative died suddenly in a plane crash without leaving a political heir, several of her friends urged her to run for the office. Tony, too, encouraged Karen to go for it. She won a close race in a three-way Republican primary, running on an education platform, followed by a convincing win in the general election. She was in the midst of her first term in the State House, and although the pace could be grueling, Karen loved it.

In the summertime, the Jeffries family alternated between Wilmette and their summer house in New Buffalo, Michigan. This year, though, their travel logistics were more complicated than usual with Karen having to spend much of the early summer in Springfield dealing with state budget issues. She had brought the kids in from Michigan that day for their school-required medical exams. From long experience, Karen knew that it was close to impossible to get an appointment with a North Shore physician in the two weeks just prior to school reopening.

"Look at this, Tony," said Karen with a laugh as she thumbed through her political mail. "They've already started having fund raising parties for candidates in next year's election. We've been invited to three of them." She tossed the invitations on to the couch between them.

"I think you should sponsor a bill; anyone who has a cocktail party or reception for a political candidate prior to ninety days before the election should have an eye poked out."

"Isn't that a bit harsh? The ACLU might have a problem with that."

"Perhaps; but just think, there would be very few second offenders."

"You might have something there," Karen replied with another laugh. "I'll give it to the Legislative Drafting Committee to work on."

Tony took a quick look at the three invitations and shook his head as he dropped them all into the waste basket. He poured them each another glass of Chardonnay before turning more serious. "You know, this case I'm handling for the ADS, the one I took this deposition in today?" Karen nodded that she did. "Well, it could take a nasty turn."

He took a sip of his wine, pausing to pick out a tiny piece of cork. "Some of these characters might be a little unsavory. I still don't know if they're part of the mob, or even if the mob still exists. They may not be, but they're on the tough side. It's possible that someone might try to intimidate us." Karen put her glass down and listened, he had her full attention. "We don't need to worry about anyone's safety," Tony continued, "because this isn't that kind of a case. I mean, we're not actually threatening anyone. But someone might give us a phone call to try to scare us or to get even for some rough questions in a deposition. If that happens the best thing to do is to just hang up. Don't give them the satisfaction of thinking they've intimidated or scared you. Do you know what I mean?"

"Sure," replied Karen calmly, "I'm glad you warned

me. But I really can't believe that something like that is likely to happen." She stood up to turn on the living-room lights and began to shut the curtains, then continued with a smile, "You know, you might be just looking for adventure and drama. I still think you have a secret desire to be a soldier of fortune without giving up the income of being a partner in a large law firm."

"You may be right," Tony said. He returned Karen's smile as he got up and helped her close the curtains.

Across the street, a block to the east, a large dark sedan pulled out of the shadows on the edge of the church parking lot. It turned onto Greenleaf Avenue without its lights on, slowly driving west. The lone man inside paid particular attention to the Jeffries' house at the corner of Tenth as he passed it.

Chapter 6

July 25

At ten the next morning Karen was standing in the kitchen chatting with her mother-in-law, Dollie, who had stopped by, and their cleaning lady, Essie, who had been coming to the Jeffries' home once a week for the past seven years. Everyone else was out; it was quiet except for their small talk. Suddenly the stillness was broken by the shrill ring of the telephone on the kitchen wall.

"Hello," answered Karen as she continued sorting out the silverware.

"Is this Mrs. Jeffries?" a husky male voice asked.

"Yes, it is." Karen put down the rest of the silverware.

"Well, Mrs. Jeffries, I just wanted to let you know I've got your daughter."

"What?" Karen froze. The other two women stopped chatting and looked at her.

"I've got your daughter, Mrs. Jeffries. I picked her

up a few minutes ago. She's wearing a blue-and-white dress."

"Who is this?" Karen demanded, straining to keep her voice under control. Dollie and Essie, alarmed by her obvious anxiety, stood speechless, staring at her.

"Let's just say that I'm someone who knows your husband and doesn't like the way he does business. You know what I'm going to do, Mrs. Jeffries? I'm going to take this pretty little girl of yours and fuck her brains out, that's what I'm going to do." The caller paused, then continued, "Your husband gets his kicks one way; I get mine another way. But I gotta tell you something, my way's a hell of a lot more fun." The caller laughed, adding, "Yeah, I'm going to fuck her brains out. Maybe you're going to end up with a little dago in the family! What do you think about that, Mrs. Jeffries?"

"I don't believe you for a second," Karen answered coldly. "My husband warned me that you might be calling like this. Goodbye!" She slammed down the phone, and stood shaking, her eyes shut.

"Karen, dear," Dollie said as she put her arm around her, "what's going on? Is there anything I can do?" Karen quietly shook her head, trying to decide what to tell them.

"Mrs. Jeffries, anything happens to one of the children?" Essie asked, stepping closer. Over the years she had become almost like a second mother to the Jeffries children. "Anything I can do to help before I leave?"

"No, it's nothing," Karen said, straightening up and shaking her head. She didn't want to tell them what she had just been told; they'd panic, giving her another problem to deal with. "No, it's nothing at all," she repeated, brushing her hair back. "But I do have to leave for a few minutes to get something done." She gently pushed them away, grabbed her purse off the counter, and walked quickly to the front door. "I'm afraid I'm going to have to leave for a while," she said to them, forcing a smile as she left.

"Well, I guess I'll be going too, dear," Dollie said. "I hope it's nothing serious."

Karen sped straight to Wilmette's Centennial Swimming Pool, barely avoiding two accidents as she ran lights. That's where Debbie had been taken earlier that morning by their neighbor, Cindy Nelson, along with Cindy's own daughter, Becky. Cindy would do some shopping, then pick them up after their swimming lessons were over. That was the routine that the two mothers had worked out for the summer, alternating responsibility. There would be over a hundred little girls at the pool, and Karen hoped that she could readily spot Debbie among them. *What is going on here? How did Tony get involved in something like this? Gangsters kidnapping our daughter? This is madness!*

As Karen crossed Skokie Boulevard she glanced over at the pool, coming up on her right. She couldn't make out any one there. As she turned sharply into the pool parking lot, she looked again. *There's no one there, no one!* The deck was completely empty! Karen was stunned. Where had everyone gone? Where was Debbie?

She skidded to a stop, jumped out of the car, and dashed up the five stairs to the pool deck. Empty! She pushed open the door to the girls' locker room, on her left, and stepped inside. There was some noise below. Karen ran down the steps and pushed open the door. There they were, all the girls and their instructors. Sounds of girlish chattering and laughter abounded. She stood still, trying to catch her breath as she looked for Debbie in the swirling mass of young girls.

"Can I help you, Mrs. Jeffries?" one of the instructors asked as she walked up with a smile.

"Yes, yes. I need to find Debbie to take her home now. There's been…an incident."

"Sure," the instructor replied, "Debbie," she shouted above the din. "Debbie Jeffries." Turning back to Karen, she added "We were just having a lesson on water safety and decided to have it down here."

"Hi, Mommy," Debbie answered as she scampered out of the crowd. "You're early."

"Oh Debbie!" Karen whispered in relief, wrapping her arms around her little daughter. "Change into your clothes. We have to go now." She turned to the instructor, who looked concerned. "Please tell Cindy Nelson when she comes that I've taken Debbie home." As the instructor nodded, Karen added, "In the future don't let anyone, *anyone,* pick up Debbie except me or Ms. Nelson."

Minutes later, Debbie stepped outside onto the pool deck with her mother. "Oh, look at my flower, Mommy. A friend of Daddy's was here a few minutes ago and he gave it to me. Isn't it pretty?"

Karen looked down and saw a fresh white carnation in her daughter's hand. She stared at it in horror then grabbed it and stuffed it into her pocket. She pulled Debbie down the stairs and into the parking lot. Debbie looked on the verge of tears.

Karen regained her composure as she drove home. "Debbie," she said, glancing back and forth between her daughter and the road, "listen carefully. Some bad men may be trying to hurt Daddy, and us too. I want you to stay in the house the rest of the day while I call Daddy and do some other things. Don't go out and don't answer the door for anyone, understand?"

"Okay Mommy." Debbie answered quietly, still looking confused. "But can Becky play with me later? In the house?"

"Yes, sweetie, but no one else; not today."

When they got home, Karen was relieved that both Dollie and Essie had left. She quickly locked all the doors, then put her hands into her pockets as she stopped to catch her breath. She felt something in her right pocket, it was the white carnation. Her hands trembling, she picked up the phone and called Tony and told him what had happened.

Tony was seething with anger as he hung up the phone. He immediately called the offices of Jack Harrington and demanded to speak to David Epstein.

"Mr. Epstein is in conference, and isn't available right now," he was told.

"Tell him it's Tony Jeffries," he shouted, "and that I need to speak to him immediately."

Within seconds Epstein was on the line. "What the hell is the problem, Tony?"

"I'll tell you what the problem is, Epstein. Your smart-ass client Lenny Battaglia called my house this morning and told my wife that he had kidnapped my daughter and was about to rape her. Did his best to intimidate and terrorize her. Luckily, my daughter's safe; but this is the direct result of your stupid suggestion at the end of the deposition yesterday that Battaglia do something like that to me. You even told him that I live in Wilmette. I'm holding you personally responsible for this!"

"Now wait a minute, Tony," Epstein answered defensively. "I'm really sorry if someone made a threatening call to your wife, but you can't assume that it was Lenny Battaglia. I'm telling you that he's not that kind of guy. This idea that he's part of organized crime is…"

"Bullshit!" Tony cut him off. "As far as I'm concerned he's a smart-ass thug. There's no doubt in my mind that he made the call and tracked down my daughter. The things that were said on the phone, the timing of the call, the fact that my daughter was given a carnation, his signature calling card, plus the fact that you encouraged him yesterday to do something to me - how can there be any doubt? And let me tell you something, if you don't get your client under control and anything like this happens again

I'm going after your law license. I'll personally have you disbarred."

"Okay, Tony," Epstein quietly responded. "I'll talk to Battaglia. If it was him, and I still don't think it was, it won't happen again. But I've got to tell you, I think you're dead wrong."

Tony hung up, still worried about his family's safety. Battaglia had given him a warning: mess with my family, and I'll mess with yours. It really couldn't be clearer. If Tony expanded his inquiry into the Battaglia family's possible involvement with the mob, he could expect the pressure on his own family to intensify. This was only a warning, he thought; next time could be the real deal. He felt a sudden chill; if Battaglia and O'Coogan actually were part of the Outfit, the danger to Tony and his family would surely increase dramatically with every successful development in his case.

Tony shut his office door and told Judy to take all his calls. He had to think this through. *What in the hell have I gotten my family involved in? What right do I have to expose them to these dangers? I'm not a cop or even a prosecutor. I stopped that kind of work years ago when I left the Air Force. I'm a corporate litigator now. Should I drop this case, get someone else to take it? Should I back off the defamation part of the case; forget about the mob connection?* Tony knew that he was a good enough lawyer to be able to pull his punches on discovery, and no one would ever know. Except Battaglia, of course, who'd see that his message had been understood.

But how could I try the case then? Without that evidence, my clients will almost certainly be hammered with a huge judgment. No, I can't do that - that would break every ethical principle I've ever learned.

The more Tony thought about it the clearer it appeared that he should get off the case. He should get someone else in the office to handle it, someone without a family to worry about; or, maybe even refer the entire case to another law firm ignoring the substantial fees that would be lost. His partners would understand when he explained why he just couldn't go on. But any new attorney would face the same pressure. Tony would have to warn him what he was getting into. *How many rational attorneys would take over a case under those circumstances?*

Tony paced around his office. He stopped at the window to look out over the city's sprawling South Side. He thought of all the millions of people who live and work there, the thousands of shop owners and small businessmen who struggle to make a living. How many of them are touched everyday by the mob or simply some crooked politician demanding a piece of the action. They always have to go along with the deal, whatever it is. Nobody can fight these guys; not private citizens anyway. It's never worth it when you consider the risk. It's always better judgment to back off. That's why the mob apparently still exists and is so powerful. The thought struck Tony like an icy blast off Lake Michigan in January. *Everyone always backs down, just like I'm doing right now.*

Tony looked down at the city and knew what he

should do. *I'm not going to back down.* The Outfit was trying to move into an area where they had never been active before. They had two or three things going on simultaneously here, and Tony wasn't sure exactly what their objective was, but it was clear that they were trying to grab a chunk of the dental profession. By the luck of the draw, Tony Jeffries was the person to either fight them or to quietly acquiesce. *I'm going to fight!* he resolved. But how could he protect Karen and the kids at the same time?

Tony picked up the phone and called Chief Fred Robinson of the Wilmette Police Department. He'd come to know the chief through some civic committees that they served on together and he trusted the man's judgment. Tony gave the chief all the details of the threatening call, including his belief that it had been made by Leonard Battaglia or someone working for him or for William O'Coogan, both of whose addresses he provided. The Chief was very helpful; he said that he would instruct village squad cars to make regular patrols around Tony's neighborhood, both day and night. The police would be instructed to stop and question anyone who looked even slightly out of place.

The chief also said that he would arrange with the telephone company to put a trap on Tony's telephone to automatically record the origin of all incoming calls, a procedure that the telephone company implements whenever there is a bona fide telephone threat and the local police requests its use. If another such call was received, all Tony or Karen had to do was report it, along with the time it came in. The Chief said that he would ask that the telephone trap be maintained for thirty days, extended after that if it was necessary. And he reassured Tony that very few telephone threats result in actual harm. Usually the intimidation was all the caller wanted.

"But hey," he added, "if you really want to play it safe, think about sending your wife and kids out of town for a few weeks."

Well, we've got a summer home in New Buffalo," Tony said.

"That would be perfect," the chief said. "I know Chief Hruby in New Buffalo and am confident that he could arrange extra police protection and a telephone trap there as well."

Tony thanked Robinson for his help, hung up and pushed a speed-dial button on the phone, Karen answered immediatcly.

"Karen, I've just talked to Chief Robinson. We think you should take the kids out to the lake house. Today, if you can." Tony recounted his conversation with the chief and emphasized that there would be extra police protection in New Buffalo. "This is serious business, Karen. I don't think it's something that we can just walk away from. I'll take the South Shore out this evening, let you know when I'll arrive, and we can talk it through tonight. I want to be sure that you agree with what I'm doing." Tony knew, even before talking to Karen, that she'd support his decision. Under her beautiful exterior, she could be one tough cookie.

"Okay," Karen said. I'll feel safer in New Buffalo. I'll meet your train this evening in Michigan City. Love you."

"Love you too."

Tony then got Charlie on the line and relayed what had happened. "Charlie, I'm convinced after the last two days that Battaglia might very well be part of the mob. I want to learn everything we can about him *and* his family. Let's also get Jake Wysocki involved; he has ways of digging out information that nobody else has."

"Wysocki! Are you sure that's a good idea?"

"Damn sure! Let's see if he can stop by tomorrow morning. I want to give him the whole story. Let's also see if he can locate Dr. Jack Roberts or his finance guy, Sorenson. If they're anywhere around Chicago, he ought to be able to get a lead on them."

"Do I somehow sense that you're turning up the heat?" Charlie asked, a smile in his voice.

"You bet your sweet ass I am! I want to go after these guys with everything we've got. We're defending a defamation case, and truth is still a complete defense. This has become personal, very personal. I've got a gut feeling that if we dig deep enough we can produce compelling evidence that O'Coogan is somehow connected to organized crime. I also want you to arrange a meeting with the FBI. Maybe there's something they'll tell us off the record about O'Coogan or Battaglia, or *their families*," he added with emphasis.

"You got it," Charlie asked after a pause, "Tony, do

you own a gun?"

"No," Tony hesitated, pausing before continuing, "Actually I do, it's an old handgun that my dad brought back from World War II. I've got it tucked away in some box in the attic. I've been reluctant to get it out in the past because I didn't want to bring more danger into our home than already is there."

"I understand, Tony, but under the circumstances you might consider getting it out, cleaning it up and registering it."

"Thanks, I will."

Tony put the phone down and turned in his chair to look out again at the city. He thought about the day's events and the possibilities of the days ahead. Suddenly, another thought struck him. He felt like a player in a high-stakes poker game who'd just pushed all his chips into the center of the table.

Chapter 7

August 9

Wrigley Field was packed that afternoon. The Cubs were still in the pennant race, only four games out. They were playing the Mets and the game had been sold out for a month, even though it was being played on a Friday afternoon. Starting time was 1:20. Tony worked through his lunch hour then caught a cab from the office just about the time the game began. He rationalized that he wasn't really ditching work, and besides, this was client business.

Tony arrived at the ballpark at 1:40. The giant scoreboard over the center field bleachers, which he could see from the street, told Tony that he'd missed only the first inning; the game was still scoreless. He entered the ballpark through the main gates at Clark and Addison, under the red-and-white scrolled sign that proudly proclaimed, "Home of the Chicago Cubs." As soon as he was under the cavernous grandstand he was enveloped by the sensations he'd associated with Wrigley Field since his boyhood days: the smell of sizzling hotdogs on the grills; the sight of vendors hawking scorecards and pencils; the bronze plaque honoring the immortal Frank Chance, who'd captained the Cubs' last world champions in 1908; the unending swirl of eight-to-ten-year olds in their Cubs caps or T-shirts; and the muffled voice of the field announcer outside. Tony loved this place. No matter how busy he was, he still managed to attend ten to fifteen home games a year. He and four of his close friends in the firm had four season tickets about twenty rows above third base, trading them among themselves as their schedules permitted.

It had been over a week since Tony met with Jake Wysocki, filled him in on the background of the case and asked him to start working on it. Wysocki had called that morning and said that he wanted to give Tony his preliminary report. It was a beautiful day, the Mets were in town, and since both of them were Cubs fanatics he suggested that they meet at the ballpark. That was a masterstroke. Tony arranged for one of the office messengers to meet Wysocki with his ticket at the Cubby Bear Lounge across from the ballpark at twelve-thirty.

Jake Wysocki was a retired Chicago police sergeant who ran a detective agency and security service on the northwest side. His greatest asset was that he knew every old-time cop and con man in the city. Tony had worked with him several years ago and called on him for help from time to time on "special projects." Wysocki had a questionable reputation in some circles because of suspicions that he used unconventional methods. But that was precisely the reason Tony liked him. When he was on a case, things always seemed to get done; Tony didn't want to know exactly why or how.

He walked up the stairs into the sun-drenched grandstand and was immediately engulfed in the noisy enthusiasm of the crowd. Everyone was enjoying himself. As Tony worked his way through the crowd in the aisle he recognized a number of regular fans. He didn't know their names, but he had seen their faces at the ballpark many times before, always in the same seats. He saw the gray-haired woman with her old hand-made sign of support for the Cubs. Everyone in both the grandstand and the Stadium Club beneath it, called her the Duchess. A few rows back was the Foghorn. Norman Rockwell would have loved him; his insults could be heard across a hundred yards of clipped sod. His daughter, the Screamer, was here today too. They sat, as always, in the reserved grandstand seats about ten rows behind Tony's. Tony had watched her grow over the years from just another kid at the ballpark into a natural cheerleader who could quickly galvanize thousands of fans into a frenzy.

Jake Wysocki was already in his seat when Tony arrived. He was a big man, about six feet two and built like a fortress. He had graying black hair and the hard, craggy face of a man who had been through it all. He had survived five reported street shoot-outs; there were probably more. Jake's friends sometimes affectionately referred to him as "the Polish John Wayne." Although he had retired from the police department five years ago, he still carried a .38 in a shoulder holster. He did so partly out of habit, partly for self-defense. His twenty-five years in the department had earned him many friends, but even more enemies, several of whom were released from prison every year. His license as a private detective sanctioned the gun. Wysocki was wearing a light-brown jacket, to cover his holster, even though the temperature was up in the eighties.

"How are you, Jake?" Tony said as he sat down and laid his suit coat on the empty seat to his right. Tony had all four tickets that day, even though he and Jake were using only the two middle seats. Although they were at the ballpark with thirty-five thousand other fans, Tony wanted to have a modicum of privacy at their meeting.

"Doing fine, Tony. How about a beer?" Wysocki responded as he signaled the passing beer vendor, Maxie, who had been peddling Bud in this section of the park for as long as Tony could remember. Jake finished off the beer he was drinking with a single swig and bought two more. "You missed a great first inning. They had two men on, and Sutcliffe struck out Strawberry, swinging, to end it."

"Terrific," Tony replied. He took his Bud from Maxie and relished his first sip. *Nothing like a cold beer on a hot summer day at the ball park.*

There was a light breeze blowing out toward left

field. *That should help Dawson and the other right-handers*, Tony thought. The rippling ivy covering the walls merged into the constant movement in the packed bleachers to give a sense of living excitement to the outfield. Sunbathing fans filled the rooftops of the buildings beyond the left and right-field bleachers, including the three-story apartment building rumored to have been hit by Babe Ruth's legendary "called" home run in the 1932 World Series. Tony settled back to watch the Mets bat in the second. He knew that Wysocki would tell him what he knew when he was ready.

It didn't take long.

"I found your dentist friend, Roberts," Wysocki said after the Mets made their third out in the second inning.

"Is that right?" Tony replied, casually, watching the Cubs jog in from their field positions. "Where is he?"

"Over in St. Joe, Michigan. It really wasn't very hard to locate him. After all, the guy's been a dentist all his life. What else is he going to be doing?"

"Are you saying that he's practicing dentistry?" Tony asked incredulously, turning to Wysocki. "His Illinois license was yanked just a couple of months ago. Don't tell me he got a Michigan license in the meantime!"

"No, of course not. He was working under an alias in a public-aid dental clinic in St. Joe. Still is, in fact. I have a hunch that the guys who run the place suspect that he's not licensed, but they don't give a damn as long as he does decent work and keeps his mouth shut and his patients' mouths open."

Wysocki paused to watch Mark Grace punch a sharp single over the third baseman's head into left field to lead off the Cubs' second inning. The hit caused the constant murmur of the crowd to erupt into a sharp cheer. "He's agreed to meet with you and tell you what he knows."

"How the hell did you get him to agree to that?"

"Very simple," Jake said and paused for a swig of beer. "After I found out where he was, I told him that I wouldn't blow his cover if he cooperated with us. He didn't like the idea; he's been trying to keep a very low profile lately. But he finally agreed to meet with you and answer any questions he can. Once. Strictly off the record and he won't testify in any court."

"Well, that will certainly be a help," answered Tony. "When can I meet him?"

"Tonight, at seven o'clock," Wysocki's eyes never left the playing field. "At The Billy Goat Tavern."

"Under the bridge?"

"Under the bridge."

Tony leaned back. He smiled as he took a healthy swig of his beer. Wysocki certainly had a way of finding things out and making things happen. While Tony was wondering exactly how he'd located Roberts, the irony of going from Wrigley Field to The Billy Goat Tavern struck him.

It was Billy Goat Sianis, a local saloon keeper, who placed a curse on the Cubs in 1945 when Cubs' owner P.K. Wrigley ejected him and his pet goat from the World Series, even though Sianis had two front-row box-seat tickets for them. Sianis vowed that the Cubs would never be winners again until he and his goat were welcomed back to the ballpark. A subsequent effort to lift the curse failed because of the untimely demise of the goat, thereby dooming the Cubs, in the eyes of some sages, to an eternity of losing.

Tony returned his attention to the game. It was still scoreless. It remained that way until the Mets scored a run in the top of the fifth. In the bottom of the seventh, however, Ryne Sandberg hit a screaming shot into the left-center-field bleachers to give the Cubs a three-to-one lead. The crowd went absolutely crazy. Sutcliffe gave the Mets a consolation run in the top of the ninth, but the Cubs still hung on to win three to two. It was a great afternoon, notwithstanding the curse.

The Billy Goat Tavern is hidden in the bowels of Lower Michigan Avenue, on the north side of the double-deck bridge over the Chicago River. Outside, the dusty brick walls never see the light of day; while the inside walls never see darkness. In token deference to the city's liquor code, drinks aren't served from four to six every morning. But the grill never closes, the doors are never locked, and the Billy Goat has never been empty since it was opened in 1934.

The most divergent clientele imaginable is found at the Billy Goat: well-dressed executives and shoppers from upper Michigan Avenue, cabbies and truck drivers, newspaper people from the nearby Tribune Tower and Sun-Times Building; street people from the rivers' edge who've begged enough money for a cheeseburger and maybe, in the wintertime, some warmth; and every type of person in between. The walls are covered with yellowed newspaper articles written by some of the bar's regular customers over the years, along with photos of prominent Chicagoans who've stopped in to indulge from time to time.

Tony pulled open the heavy wooden door, stepped in, and walked down the five steps into the tavern a little after seven. He scanned the crowd to see if he could locate Roberts. None of the three men at the bar nor any of the eight or ten people seated at the tables looked right, and none was paying any particular attention to Tony. He paused a moment to get used to the smoky atmosphere, then walked through the main bar toward the small room behind it, a room that had been added a generation earlier to handle the occasional overflow crowds.

The musty back room was empty except for eight sets of tables and chairs, and one man, seated at a table in the far corner watching the entrance. He was dressed casually, had thick white hair and a deeply lined face that betrayed anxiety and apprehension. A glass of draft beer rested in front of him next to an ashtray full of cigarette butts.

Tony walked over, pulled out a chair and sat down across from him. "Dr. Roberts, I presume," he said quietly.

"That's right," the man replied nervously. "You must be Tony Jeffries."

"Right. Good to meet you." Tony extended his right hand. Roberts hesitated, before taking it. "I appreciate your meeting with me, Doctor." Roberts looked much older than he had expected, in his late sixties, though Tony knew he was ten years younger than that.

"Look, Jeffries, I don't know what you've been told; but I'm not here voluntarily. Your man Wysocki put some pressure on me that I couldn't resist. So, I agreed to meet with you once to answer your questions. But believe me, I'd rather not be here at all, and I want it understood that whatever I tell you is strictly off the record."

"I understand, and it will be. But *you've* got to understand that I'm in a very tough case, and I need some information from you in order to do my job. As a matter of fact, the case I'm defending is the case that you set in motion. So, you're not exactly uninvolved." Tony was leaning forward, speaking quietly. "First of all, how the hell did Bill O'Coogan and his flunky Lenny Battaglia take over your dental academy? What happened?"

Robert swirled his beer in his glass for a moment, before looking up at Tony. "Are you sure this is really necessary?" he asked. "Dealing with those guys was the biggest mistake I ever made. And I've made several, as I'm sure you know."

"Yes, I *do* know, Doctor," Tony nodded, sipping his beer. "And yes, it's necessary that you tell me what you know and what happened." He wasn't going to let Roberts off the hook, now that he had him.

Roberts sighed, then nodded.

"What happened was this," he said quietly. Tony pulled a small note pad from his jacket pocket and began taking some notes. "When I began organizing the school I realized that I'd need some interim financing. I've had some financial problems in the past, so I had a little trouble getting a loan. Finally, someone suggested that I try Buchanan Finance Company. They were supposed to be more flexible than many other lenders. I applied for a loan there, and I got it. Sixty thousand bucks. I pledged all my stock in the Academy as collateral."

He hesitated as the thin black waiter came over. "I'll have another beer," he told him. "And bring a drink for my….friend. What are you drinking, Jeffries?"

"A draft beer will be fine, whatever you have." Tony leaned back in his chair, waiting for the waiter to leave.

Roberts leaned forward and continued, "Buchanan was charging murderous interest rates; I had trouble making the payments. Simple as that. So twice in the first six months I refinanced the loan to cover the interest and penalties that had accumulated. Before I knew it, I was into them for over a hundred grand! I didn't know what to do. I had a good start on getting the school organized, but the costs were getting away from me. Plus, my applications to the State of Illinois and the ADS were both hung up on technicalities, almost as though nobody was really looking at them. Finally, someone at Buchanan called me. He said that they were concerned about their loan and would hold off foreclosing *only* if I agreed to hire someone new to handle our finances. Someone they had confidence in. I already had an accountant, Rolf Sorenson, but what could I do? I agreed, of course. The next day Lenny Battaglia shows up, says he was sent by Buchanan." Roberts paused to take a deep drag on his cigarette while the waiter served their beers.

"Actually, Battaglia got some good things done initially," he continued. "He got our application to the State of Illinois off dead-center and got it approved within a couple of weeks. I don't know what he did, but after he went down to talk to the people at the Department of Registration and Education, the approval came right through. Maybe something passed between them; I don't know. But it was a success. Battaglia just took over our bookkeeping office, changed suppliers and contractors without consulting anyone else. He began negotiating with our landlord to renew our lease. Sorenson tried to object to some of it, but what could he do? To be honest, I didn't object. I thought that maybe Battaglia was a little more savvy than Sorenson so I should probably give him a free hand. After all, he had obtained the State of Illinois approval that Sorenson had been messing around with for six months. He also pumped some life into our course for foreign dentists, which began generating a little income. So, I put Rolf off; and told him I didn't want to talk to him about his concerns." Roberts ground his cigarette butt into the overflowing ashtray, then nervously lit up another.

Tony took a sip of beer, waiting for him to continue.

"Finally, one day toward the end of April last year, Battaglia comes into my office and tells me that somebody from Buchanan is coming over that day to discuss our loan. I wasn't worried. I figured that Battaglia would give them a report and that would be that. I couldn't have been more wrong."

Roberts looked hard into Tony's eyes. "The person who showed up that afternoon was O'Coogan. I had never met him before. Big, well-dressed Irishman. We had a meeting at the Academy, with O'Coogan, Battaglia, Sorenson and me. O'Coogan had all our promissory notes to Buchanan, along with Buchanan's assignments of those notes to him. He told me that actually he had been our lender all the time. He also told me that the notes were overdue, that he was foreclosing on them, and that unless we paid off the loans on the spot he was taking over the Academy. I was absolutely dumbstruck. I remember turning first to Rolf, then to Lenny Battaglia, and asking whether he could do that. Rolf was as speechless as I was, but Battaglia spoke right up and said that he had examined the documents and that, yes indeed, O'Coogan was entirely within his rights. It was only then that it was clear to me that Battaglia had been working for O'Coogan all along and that this was all part of a prearranged plan."

Tony was listening quietly but intently, taking occasional notes. For all his faults, Roberts appeared to be genuinely naive in business matters, and Tony couldn't help feeling a twinge of sympathy.

"I didn't care what Battaglia said," Roberts continued. "I wasn't going to just let them take over my school that easily. I told O'Coogan that I was going to see my attorney immediately, perhaps the state's attorney as well. He wasn't going to get away with that. I'll never forget what happened next. O'Coogan unbuttoned his suit coat, reached inside, and pulled out a pistol! He was carrying a gun. He placed the gun on the table in front of him, with the barrel pointing directly at me and said that perhaps he hadn't made himself clear. He was taking over the Academy right then, and if either I or Sorenson gave him any trouble at all it would be a very serious mistake. I remember looking at him, glancing at his gun, then back at him for a long time. It was the first time in my life that I felt that I was facing a truly evil person. I had this gut-wrenching feeling that my life was actually on the line. Finally, I got up, didn't say a word, and just walked out. Rolf followed me. There was no point in seeing an attorney or anyone else."

Roberts took another sip of beer, turned a little and looked away toward the collection of faded sports photos on the wall. When he resumed talking, Tony thought he detected some moisture in his eyes. "That weekend I moved out of my apartment and went over to Michigan where I'd spent some time in the past. This is the first time I've been back in the city since that day. Rolf didn't even wait until the weekend. He went down to the street, caught a cab to O'Hare and took the first plane he could catch to the West Coast. His family followed him a couple of weeks later." Roberts sat back in his chair, took a deep chug of beer, and looked at Tony. "And that, Mr. Jeffries, is how William O'Coogan took over the Federal Dental Academy."

Tony hesitated before asking his next question, "From what you said earlier, Doctor, I don't suppose that you're willing to repeat that story in a court of law, are you?"

Roberts just laughed. "Are you kidding? No way! Jeffries, I don't think you understand the kind of people you're dealing with. These are evil, vicious men. Are they part of organized crime? Probably, although I didn't know it at the time. I've learned more about these guys since I left. I'm convinced that they'd just as soon kill you as say hello."

"Okay, I understand your concern," Tony responded. "But I still have this question in my mind. Whether O'Coogan and Battaglia are involved in the mob or not, why would men like that want to get involved in your school? I've heard a rumor that dental insurance is involved; is that what this is all about? Some arrangement between the mob and some unions to set up dental clinics, with kick-backs to the mob? With dentists from the Dental Academy staffing the clinics?"

"That's part of it," Roberts answered. "I realize that now. But there's more, much more. I think that's what Rolf had figured out at the end. He kept trying to explain things to me, but I didn't want to listen. Remember that Rolf was still involved in the financial side of the business even after Battaglia got there. He'd be in a position to spot things that I'd never notice. I was preoccupied with trying to get my school going, writing a curriculum, getting faculty members lined up, things like that."

"How can we reach Rolf Sorenson? I'd really like to talk to him, too. We've tried but can't locate him."

"That's not surprising, he's been trying to stay under the radar as much as possible."

"So, you've been in touch with him."

"Well, yes; we've kept in touch. But I promised him I wouldn't tell anyone else where he was."

"Doctor, our deal was that you'd tell me what you knew and answer my questions tonight. If you won't tell me how to reach Sorenson, as far as I'm concerned I'm going to tell Jake Wysocki that you haven't been fully cooperative." Tony hated to put that kind of pressure on Roberts, but he figured that this might be his only opportunity to find Sorenson, who, it was clear, was going to be crucial to building a case against Bill O'Coogan.

"Damn." Roberts looked down at his half-empty glass for a few uncomfortable seconds, while he slowly ground out his cigarette in the ashtray. "All right, I'll tell you how to find him," he finally said, looking up. "But I don't want him to learn that it came from me. He's in the Ingleside district of San Francisco. Operates a small accounting practice from his apartment. His wife and daughter live with him. After he flew out there, they sold their house here for whatever they could get and followed him. His phone number is listed under Rolf's Accounting Service, or something like that."

Tony scribbled a few more notes before looking up at Roberts. “Thank you very much, Doctor. I appreciate your help; I really do. If you think of anything else that might help us, please give me a call.” Tony took one of his business cards from his inside coat pocket and placed it on the table.

Roberts nodded, picked up the card and slipped it into his shirt pocket. “I rather doubt that we’re ever going to meet again, Mr. Jeffries.”

He hesitated a moment, then added, “When these guys get involved in something, it’s like a cancer. It infects everything around it, and the infection spreads. As a doctor, I can tell you that it’s almost impossible to contain a metastasized cancer. The patient almost always dies. Do you understand?”

“I think I do. That’s one reason why I’m involved in this case.”

Roberts finished his beer, got up and walked out through the smoke-filled front bar without saying anything more. Tony waited a few minutes finished his beer, slipped his note pad into his pocket and mulled over Roberts’ comments as he got the tab and paid it. Whatever else he thought, he certainly now had a clearer, much more ominous, picture of William O’Coogan.

Chapter 8

August 15

The phone rang three times before it was answered by a pleasant-sounding woman's voice. "Rolf's Accounting Service," she said.

"Hi, is Rolf there?" Tony asked, hoping to sound friendly enough to lower any defenses she might have.

"Just a minute."

A few moments later a man's voice came on the line, "Rolf here."

"Rolf, my name is Tony Jeffries. I'm an attorney in Chicago representing the American Dental Society. We're defending a lawsuit brought by William O'Coogan and the Federal Dental Academy. I need to talk to you about some matters that you may have run across while you were working at the Academy." Tony paused for a moment to let it sink in. "What I'd like to do is to arrange some time in the next week or so when we can get together in the San Francisco area, in a place of your choosing. This will be a discussion just between the two of us."

There was a long silence on the line. Tony finally broke it. "Did you hear me, Mr. Sorenson? I said that I'd like to arrange a time for the two of us to get together in your area to discuss the Federal Dental Academy. There's some information that we need to get from you."

Another long silence. The only sound that Tony could hear was nervous breathing. Finally, Sorenson spoke; his voice was little more than a whisper.

"How did you find me?"

"Well, that doesn't matter, Mr. Sorenson. The real question is, will you meet with me to discuss the Dental Academy?"

"No! Absolutely not! I have nothing to say!"

"I can understand your reluctance," Tony answered, "but I want to assure you that we're on the same side in this matter. I believe you may have some information that's very important to me and my client. I'd like to discuss these matters with you privately. If you simply refuse to meet with me, then we'll have to subpoena you for your deposition. If that happens, the other side will receive a copy of the subpoena along with the right to attend. Is that what you want?"

"Listen, mister, you do whatever you want to do, but I'm not meeting with you to discuss the Dental Academy. Is that clear?" The next sound Tony heard was the soft buzz of an open line. Sorenson had hung up.

Okay, Rolf, Tony said to himself, *have it your way. I'll have a subpoena issued this afternoon and served on you tomorrow morning. We'll advise Harrington's office that we're taking your deposition in San Francisco.* He checked his pocket calendar, *next Wednesday afternoon. It should be interesting.*

Six days later Tony took the 7:40 a.m. Trans American flight to San Francisco and checked in to the Fairmont Hotel a little after noon. His room wasn't available yet, but he had reserved a small conference room on the second floor for the deposition at 2:00. He grabbed a light lunch before settling into the conference room to organize his documents and his thoughts.

David Epstein showed up a little before two, the court reporter, an attractive blond named Glenda, moments later. They made small talk until two-twenty when the door opened slowly and a thin, graying man walked timidly in, clutching a subpoena. He stopped just inside the doorway, looked nervously at the three-people seated at the conference table, and said, barely audibly, "My name is Sorenson."

Tony rose to greet him. "Good afternoon, Mr. Sorenson. I'm Tony Jeffries."

Rolf Sorenson took the proffered hand and shook it limply. "I'm sorry I'm late. I..." His voice trailed off, then picked up, "I wasn't sure that I was going to come, even with this," he said, glancing down at the subpoena. "But I finally decided to get it over with."

Sorenson was in his late forties, of medium height and looked almost frail; his shuffling walk was that of a much older man. He was unsure in almost everything he did, including picking a chair.

Tony introduced him to Epstein and offered him a cup of coffee, which was declined. He then introduced him to Glenda, who swore him in.

"Would you state your name for the record, please?"

"Rolf Sorenson" was the almost whispered reply.

"Mr. Sorenson, you're going to have to speak up, so that we can all hear you and so that the reporter can make an accurate transcript, all right?

"All right," Sorenson answered, slightly louder.

"Mr. Sorenson, what's your business or occupation?"

"I'm a certified public accountant." There was a touch of pride in his voice.

"Mr. Sorenson," Tony asked, "have you ever had occasion to work for the Federal Dental Academy in Chicago?" He leaned back in his chair and watched the witness.

"Yes. I was the Academy's chief financial officer from the time it was founded until about a year ago." His voice dropped as he answered. He looked down at the subpoena in front of him on the table, then folded his hands-on top of it. *It's like he's praying*, Tony thought.

"What were your duties as the Academy's chief financial officer?"

"I was completely responsible for the business side of

the operation," Sorenson answered without looking up. "Dr. Roberts, the school's founder, concentrated on the professional side, the dental side. I handled all the books and records, prepared the tax returns and applications for approval of various agencies, paid all the bills, things of that nature."

"Did you do all that yourself?" Tony asked.

"Yes, with the help of my secretary, of course." He paused, then continued, "At the end I had an assistant, a Mr. Battaglia."

"Leonard Battaglia?"

"Yes. My wife and I had been thinking of moving out here to the Bay Area ever since our daughter, Sara, entered college at Berkeley a year ago. When Mr. Battaglia joined the Academy, that gave me an opportunity to make that move. He was a very bright man; after about a month I decided that he'd do just fine. I told Dr. Roberts that I was resigning to move out here. My wife couldn't have been happier."

Tony kept his eyes on Sorenson as he spoke, but Sorenson's eyes were focused on his folded hands. He refused to look at Tony. "Mr. Sorenson," Tony pressed on, "did you ever meet a man named William O'Coogan in Chicago?"

"No, I don't believe so. The name doesn't ring a bell." He answered quietly, keeping his eyes down.

Damn! Tony thought. *He's going to stonewall me*.

"Would it refresh your recollection, Mr. Sorenson, if I told you that you attended a meeting late last April at the

Dental Academy with Mr. O'Coogan, Mr. Battaglia, and Dr. Jack Roberts? Does that refresh your recollection at all?" Tony's voice rose slightly as he spoke, reflecting his growing frustration.

"No, it really doesn't. Of course, I attended many meetings at the Academy with Mr. Battaglia, Dr. Roberts, and other people. Mr. O'Coogan might have been at one of those meetings and I just didn't catch his name, or maybe I knew it then but have forgotten it."

"Well, do you recall any such meeting, Mr. Sorenson, when someone pulled out a gun, laid it on the table, and said that they were taking over the school that day?"

The forcefulness of Tony's question finally caught Sorenson. He looked up, hesitated a moment, then said softly, "No, I think you must be mistaken."

"Wait a minute!" interrupted Epstein. "What kind of a question is that? That's outrageous! There's not a shred of evidence that such an event occurred. I don't want the transcript of this deposition to be salted with suggestions of improper conduct on my clients' part that are pure fantasy. I'll move to strike that question if this transcript is used in the trial of this case. Furthermore, counsel, we find the defendants' entire approach to the defamation aspect of this case distasteful, if not unprofessional. If you have actual evidence that our clients are connected with organized crime, then present it. There isn't any such evidence, and you know it. The entire defense on this issue seems to be one of character assassination and dirty innuendo. William O'Coogan is an upstanding and distinguished member of the Chicago community. Personally, I find this line of questioning despicable."

It was clear that the young attorney was speaking from his heart and was making every effort to protect his clients from having their good names dirtied any further. He was being more assertive than he'd been during the Battaglia deposition; it was very likely that when Harrington had read the transcript, he'd berated Epstein for letting Tony push him around.

"You're entitled to your opinion, Mr. Epstein," Tony retorted evenly. "And we're entitled to develop the evidence that your clients aren't the white knights that they've portrayed themselves as in the lawsuit they filed in Chicago."

Sorenson's eyes were riveted on Epstein. While the attorneys continued arguing, he put his right hand into his suit coat pocket and fumbled for something.

"Well, do you have any questions left?" Epstein asked. "Any legitimate questions?"

Tony shuffled through his notes. He had prepared a number of additional questions, but they were all based on the premise that Sorenson would be reasonably truthful in his responses. Now, Tony thought it best to end the deposition right there. Any further questions would only make the record worse.

"No," he finally answered. "Under the circumstances, I have no further questions."

"Well, I certainly don't have any questions for Mr. Sorenson," Epstein added. "That makes it a short afternoon. Glenda, if Mr. Jeffries has this typed up, we'd like a copy. Although, frankly, Tony, I can't imagine why you'd even want it typed up. It was pretty much a waste of time and money all around."

They all rose to collect their papers, getting ready to go. While Glenda was packing up her machine, Sorenson came around the table to Tony, extended his hand, and said softly, "I'm sorry."

Tony took his hand, nodding silently, more frustrated than angry. Suddenly, Tony felt something in the palm of his hand. Sorenson held Tony's hand for an instant, caught his eye, then turned and left.

"Tony, can I buy you a drink if I promise not to talk about the case?" Epstein asked. "There's a decent-looking bar down the street."

"No, I don't think so, but thanks," Tony responded. "I can use this time to make some calls."

"I understand. Well, I'll see you back in Chicago." Epstein snapped his briefcase shut, nodded to Tony, and left, followed by Glenda.

Tony was alone in the conference room now. He looked down to see what Sorensen had handed him so discreetly. It was a book of matches from the Tadich Grill. It took him a moment to catch its meaning. Suddenly, it dawned on him. Sorenson was willing to meet with him privately, perhaps tell him more. He would be waiting for Tony at the Tadich Grill.

The restaurant was crowded when Tony got there. Tadich's afternoon cocktail hour had already begun; the area around the bar was packed. Tony worked his way through the crowd to the left, checking the tables by the window as he passed. He figured that Sorenson was more likely to be at a table or a booth than simply milling around the bar.

The darkly paneled lower walls and dark wooden booths gave the Tadich Grill a character unique among the bars and restaurants at the foot of California Street, nearly all of them housed in one of the newer office buildings that dominate the area. It traced its history back to the Gold Rush days. During the intervening one hundred and forty years, even though it had moved its location several times, it had always stayed in the same neighborhood, always kept its unique nineteenth century ambiance, and was always under Yugoslav ownership. During the past generation the little two-story building housing the restaurant has been dwarfed by the forest of glass-and-steel skyscrapers that had grown up to surround it.

Tony found Rolf Sorenson sitting alone in one of the back booths on the left. He had ordered a half-dozen cherrystone clams in order to appease a waiter who insisted that the booths were only for people having meals. He was half-way through a glass of white wine. Tony sat down on the bench across from him and moved in toward the wall. "Hello, Rolf," he said quietly.

Sorenson waited a moment before he spoke, looking down at his clams while he collected his thoughts. "You know, I wasn't going to talk to you," he began. "I almost didn't go to the deposition. But I realized that if I didn't show up, you'd both be after me. You'd be trying to force me to come in and tell what I knew, while the other guys are trying to make sure I wouldn't. So, I figured that the best thing to do was to show up and say that I didn't know anything."

"But now you've changed your mind?"

"Yes. I don't know what it was…something that Epstein said during the deposition. I think the way he was sanctimoniously going on about what fine, upstanding citizens his clients are. Fine upstanding citizens. Baloney! They're hoodlums. Then the unfairness of the whole thing struck me. What right do men like that have to destroy someone else's life, like mine? It's not as though I was an insider who turned on them, and this is their way of punishing me. I had a happy life back in Chicago. We had a decent home and were involved in the community. My job with the Dental Academy didn't pay that much, but it was exciting. We were trying to put a new school together. I liked what I was doing. I also had built up a nice accounting practice on the side." Sorenson paused to catch his breath; it was as though, once he'd decided to talk to Tony, he wanted to get everything out.

"Then these bums show up; first Battaglia, followed by O'Coogan. They end up driving me out of my job and even my city. I was afraid for my life when I ran out here, and I've been hiding ever since. And there they are, back in Chicago, living off the school that I helped put together; suing people who question their sainthood. It's wrong, wrong. That's when I decided to tell you what I know. Now I'm not as brave as you must be, so don't ask me to appear in any court. If you do, I'll do the same thing I did this afternoon; play real dumb. But maybe I can give you some information that you can use against these guys. All right?"

"That would be very helpful, Rolf. I really appreciate whatever you can tell me." Tony paused to allow several people milling in the aisle nearby to pass; he caught their waiter's eye and ordered a glass of Chardonnay for himself. After the waiter left, Tony leaned forward and asked, "Now, you were at that meeting at the Academy where O'Coogan pulled a gun, weren't you?"

"Of course, I was. It happened just the way you suggested in your question. O'Coogan showed us the notes we had signed to Buchanan Finance, together with Buchanan's assignments to him. He told us that he's the one who's been loaning us the money right along. Then he said we were in default and that he was taking over that day. When Dr. Roberts tried to challenge him, O'Coogan casually pulled out this gun and laid it right on the table facing me and Roberts. I've never been so terrified in all my life. He was telling us in the clearest possible terms that if we interfered with him in any way, he'd kill us. I'll never forget the look on Lenny Battaglia's face. He was grinning like the Cheshire Cat."

"Was that the first time you realized that you were dealing with thugs, possibly gangsters?"

"No, it wasn't; not really. I'd slowly become aware of the fact that Lenny Battaglia was cooking the books, playing games with our income and expenses. He seemed to have his own agenda. I tried to talk to Dr. Roberts about it, but he was always too busy to listen. I saw increasing income from our foreign dentists, but I also saw expenses going up just as sharply. I saw Battaglia negotiating new contracts with suppliers, but the expenses never went down. Finally, it dawned on me what was going on." Sorenson sat back, looking at Tony with a wry smile. He was relishing this moment.

"Well, what is it?" Tony pressed.

"It's a money-laundering operation, that's what it is. They're running millions of dollars through there, taking income from illicit sources and funneling it out as legitimate income to dozens of shady figures in the Midwest. People who had absolutely nothing to do with the dental school, and some of it to companies they control. Oh, they'll make some money from the school itself if they ever get it accredited. They're already getting some kickbacks from the dental clinics. But it's basically a money-laundering operation. What could be a better, more innocent front than a dental school? I finally figured out who this money was for. It reached the point where it was millions of dollars. Then I knew it had to be for organized crime, the mob. At least that's what I figured was going on. My mistake, after I figured it out, was in asking too many questions to try to prove my theory. Once Battaglia sensed that I knew, he and O'Coogan moved quickly. Dr. Roberts and I were out of there the next day."

"That's incredible," Tony said quietly as he sat back, trying to sort out everything he had just heard. "Wait a minute," he finally said. "I've seen their books, at least what they say are their books, and I didn't see the cash flow that you're talking about. They've got good income now from their foreign student program, and they've also got a lot of expenses directly related to that..." Tony stopped in his tracks, then asked slowly, "Are you saying that they're laundering money through the foreign-dentist program?"

"Mr. Jeffries, there aren't *any* foreign dentists," Sorenson replied with a slight smile. "At least not very many. I'm convinced that the whole program is a front." He paused to take a sip of wine letting his comments register. Tony's mind was bursting with questions, but he decided to wait and listen.

"I first became suspicious," Sorenson continued, "when the enrollment in our foreign program jumped suddenly. We hadn't spent a dime for advertising. How did all these people hear about us? All at once! I also found it a bit odd that virtually all the tuition payments were made to the Academy by wire transfers that left no paper trail. Also, all of the foreign dentists had post office boxes for their addresses. The post offices, by the way, were always in cities like Bogota, Colombia or Portobelo, Panama. Those are places that just happen to be centers of the international drug trade, from what the newspapers say. Also, the Bahamas. Why were all those dentists in the

Bahamas suddenly interested in our program? Of course, none of them ever showed up to attend classes in person."

Sorenson finished off one of his clams, took another sip of wine, then continued with a question. "Tell me, Tony, how many foreign dentists does the Academy say they have enrolled now? Do you know?"

"Well, we took Battaglia's deposition a few weeks ago. He said that they had over one thousand foreign students at that point in time."

"How much are they currently charging per student?"

"Six thousand dollars each, as I recall."

"I'll bet the tuition is still always payable in advance, isn't it?"

"That's what Battaglia said in his deposition."

"It sounds to me like they've moved a cool six million bucks through their laundry in less than six months of operation and they're just getting started." Sorenson paused to make some mental calculations. "And I'll bet that 90 percent of that money was passed on as ostensibly legitimate income to mob figures in the Chicago area."

"What about their suppliers?" Tony asked. "Are you saying that their suppliers are also just conduits for moving the money? They aren't really providing the goods or services that the Academy appears to be purchasing?"

"Exactly," Sorenson answered, leaning forward. "I didn't see any proof of that, but I'm sure that's the case. If you could somehow get a look at the payrolls of those companies, their suppliers, I'll bet you'd see some pretty interesting names."

The bar had filled by now as the businesses in the surrounding buildings emptied. Scores of well-dressed professionals filled every available seat, bar stool, and standing area. No one paid any attention to the two men engaged in their intense discussion in the back booth. None, that is, except a man seated at the far side of the bar, sipping a beer and reading the sports section of a newspaper. His open collar and swarthy complexion set him apart from the well-dressed yuppies around him. From time to time he would glance up from his paper at the two men in the back booth. Finally, he finished his beer, laid a ten on the bar, folded his paper under his arm, and left, melting into the late-afternoon crowd.

"What about their rent?" Tony continued, "It quadrupled after Battaglia got there, from twenty-five hundred to ten thousand a month, beginning the first of May. But the landlord, the building owner, didn't change. It's still the same bank as trustee."

"I know. But there was something awfully funny about that. It's true that we only had a one-year lease, which was up, but we also had a one-year option to renew at a 10 percent increase in the rent. So, it didn't make any sense at all for Battaglia to agree to such a huge increase. He negotiated the new lease just before I left. The rent went to the same bank as trustee, but I'll bet anything that the beneficiaries of the trust holding that property changed when the rent went up. In fact, that was one of the things that really made me suspicious about Battaglia. There was something going on concerning the building, but I don't know what it was. I'm sure, though, that someone in the background got the benefit of that huge rental increase."

"Well, we're going to have to go back and take a look at their books from an entirely new perspective," Tony said, partly to himself. "And we're going to have to subpoena the records of their major suppliers to see who really profited from those transactions." He looked across the table at Sorenson and added, "Rolf, you've been incredibly helpful. This is exactly the breakthrough we were looking for. Thank you very much."

"I feel much better now myself," Sorenson answered. "This has been all bottled up inside me for months. I was afraid that I couldn't do or say anything about it. But I'm confident that I've given the information, whatever it may be worth, to the right people." He smiled again, and Tony noticed that he suddenly looked ten years younger.

Tony paid the tab and they walked through the crowded bar to the street.

"My car's handy," offered Sorenson on the sidewalk, gesturing to an old Chevy across the street. "Can I drop you off somewhere?"

"No, thank you, Rolf," Tony answered. "I'm going to walk up to Grant Street and wander through Chinatown for a while. Could use the exercise. Then hop a cable car to the Fairmont." The men shook hands and parted.

Tony walked about ten steps when a thunderous blast knocked him forward. He barely had time to cover his head when a shower of glass splinters covered him and the surrounding sidewalk. Although dazed, he could hear women's voices crying out nearby. Tony struggled to his feet, looked around, trying to grasp what had happened. Several other people were on the ground, dazed and bleeding. Greasy smoke filled the air. He turned and looked back. Across the street from the Tadich Grill the wreckage of a car was blazing furiously. Inside the car, surrounded by intense white flames, was the writhing shape of a person. Tony watched in horror as the movement stopped. As he stared at the grisly scene, another wave of horror swept over him. He knew that car. It was Sorenson's Chevy.

Chapter 9

August 21

Tony had a difficult time on the flight back from San Francisco. He was still in shock from Rolf Sorenson's horrible death – a death for which he was responsible. If he hadn't subpoenaed Sorenson for his deposition, revealing his location, the man would be alive right now. In trying to accomplish something good, Tony had inadvertently done something terrible. He had caused the death of a good man. No amount of rationalizing could bury that thought. He had experienced that feeling only once before; the George Torrance case. He'd successfully defended Torrance, thinking he was saving an innocent man from unjust punishment. But Torrance had been guilty all along and was apprehended during another violent rape. The victim survived, but the crime had seared into Tony's psyche the Law of Unintended Consequences. And now, it had happened again! Just as Torrance had surfaced again in Tony's life.

He stared out the window at the billowing white clouds beneath him. They rolled on like a gentle field of softly tossed cotton as far as he could see. Tony knew, though, that beneath that inviting white fluff were the rugged peaks of the Rockies. It was like the peaks of lemon meringue over a pile of broken glass. How easy it is, Tony thought, to miss the terrible dangers hidden under a thin veneer of innocence - or naiveté. He suddenly shivered. *Is that what really killed Sorenson*, he wondered. *My own naiveté?*

Still, Sorenson had known there was danger in meeting with Tony. He accepted that risk because he'd decided that the trial was important, and he'd died virtually in the act of telling Tony what he knew.

Those thoughts dominated Tony on his flight back to Chicago. They merged into a single conclusion as the plane began its descent. *Rolf Sorenson's life is not going to be wasted.* Whatever else happened, Tony would bring his killers to justice. He knew that was inexorably linked to proving in a court of law that William O'Coogan was an integral part of the criminal underworld.

During the next two weeks, David Epstein took the depositions of nine ADS employees and CODA members who had been involved in the decision to deny the Dental Academy's application for accreditation. He pressed them all on the reasons for the denial. Charlie attended those depositions, doing everything he could to protect the witnesses and the ADS. But there was no refuting that, as witness after witness testified, one of the principal reasons was that everyone "understood" that the Dental Academy's owner was connected with organized crime. It became clear that there were many discussions and internal memoranda to that effect within the ADS. There was no question now. The libel and slander had been made public and had materially damaged the reputations of both the plaintiff, the Academy and its owner, William O'Coogan.

At the same time, the defendants pressed the discovery into the Dental Academy that Sorenson had suggested. Tony took the lead on that. The Dental Academy's financial records, which had already been produced, were carefully scrutinized to determine its real cash flow. Major suppliers had the records of their transactions with the Academy subpoenaed. As each set of documents was produced and analyzed, like peeling an onion, new facts were discovered, which led to the issuance of further subpoenas. Jake Wysocki was also working on his own, digging out whatever information he could find about the Academy and O'Coogan.

Chief Robinson reported that since the telephone threat to the Jeffries the Wilmette police had picked up six young men who appeared out of place, walking around the Jeffries' neighborhood late at night. All were residents of Chicago, but had clean records, weren't armed, and had plausible reasons for being there. After checking out their stories and finger-printing them, they were advised of Wilmette's 11:00 p.m. curfew and escorted to the Linden Avenue el station and sent back to the city. Nothing of apparent relevance to the Dental Academy case, however.

Tony set a meeting with Charlie, Carol James and Jake for eight o'clock on the morning of September third to analyze what they had obtained. He hated early-morning meetings, but this was the only time they were all available.

They met in the conference room adjacent to Tony's office. He'd picked up a dozen fresh donuts at the train station when he got downtown. When he arrived at the office, Judy already had a pot of fresh coffee brewing.

They talked for a few minutes about Mike Harkey's shutout over the Reds at Wrigley Field the night before, until Tony directed the conversation to the business at hand.

"All right, we know that Harrington and Epstein have covered a lot of ground over the past two weeks; dug up some damaging evidence against the Academy. What have we accomplished over that same period?" Tony asked, filling his coffee cup. "I'll begin. I went back over the Academy's records and identified every supplier who received at least ten thousand dollars from the Academy, for whatever reason, over the past six months. There were eleven such suppliers, including the landlord. That was my starting point. I subpoenaed the records of each of those suppliers for any documents relating to the Dental

Academy's transactions with them during that period. We've now received all those documents. In reviewing them with Carol, there are several interesting things that have come clear."

Both Charlie and Jake were giving Tony their full attention. They knew he'd been digging into these matters, but not where his investigation had taken him. They were about to learn.

"First of all," Tony continued, "we found that within thirty days of his arrival at the Academy, Lenny Battaglia bought fifteen large-screen television sets, at a total wholesale cost of twelve thousand dollars. He bought them from Acme Electronics on the north side, paying for all fifteen sets in advance. We have a copy of the Academy's check. We subpoenaed the records of Acme Electronics and confirmed that they received an order for fifteen sets from the Dental Academy on the same day that the Academy's check was dated. They shipped them out on April tenth."

"They're probably TV sets for individual classrooms," commented Charlie as he dug another donut out of the box on the table. "Closed-circuit teaching aides. That sounds pretty straightforward."

"It does until you look carefully at the shipping records of Acme Electronics," Tony responded. "When we did that, we found that thirteen of those TV sets were delivered to the Dental Academy's offices on West Lake Street in Chicago, and two sets were delivered to the Academy in Springfield. The shipping memos, by the way, also include the serial numbers of each set and the address where each set was delivered."

"Where in Springfield were those two sets delivered?" asked Charlie.

Looking at the subpoenaed shipping invoice of Acme Electronics, Tony responded, "One was sent to the Federal Dental Academy at suite 801, 320 West Washington." He paused, looked at his colleagues, and asked, "Do you know whose address that is?"

"Not offhand," Charlie responded, "but it sounds familiar." He took a sip of coffee, keeping his eyes on Tony.

"It ought to," answered Tony. "That's the office address of your old friend, William Weaver, director of the Department of Registration and Education. The delivery date is four days *before* the department issued its approval of the Academy. How's that for being pretty raw!"

"Damn!" Charlie exclaimed. "Weaver sold out the State of Illinois for a lousy television set! In fact, I remember seeing that TV set in his office. I thought it looked too good for a hack like Weaver to have." The four exchanged glances for a moment, then Charlie asked, "Where was the last TV set delivered in Springfield?"

"It was delivered to the Federal Dental Academy in care of Adriane Lockridge, suite 1810, Lincoln Tower, Springfield."

"Who the hell is she?" Charlie asked, looking confused.

"She's Bill Weaver's girlfriend," Jake spoke up nonchalantly as he lit a cigarette. "Has been for years."

"Are you sure of that, Jake?"

"Absolutely, Tony. Everyone in Springfield knows that. Weaver supposedly lives in Peoria with his wife; but in fact, he spends maybe ten nights a year there. The rest of the time he's in suite 1810 of the Lincoln Tower in Springfield. The apartment's in Adriane's name. It's a very nice place." When he saw the looks the others were giving him, he quickly added, "Hey, I was there a couple of times as a bodyguard for the mayor. The old mayor."

"So, Weaver's price to sell out the State of Illinois wasn't one, but *two*, television sets; is that what we're saying?" asked Charlie.

"That's the only logical reading of this evidence," answered Tony. "I wasn't sure about the last TV set; but you've answered that question, Jake." He thought a moment as he slowly turned to Charlie. "That's part of what we've learned. Mainly thanks to Carol's spade work," he added, giving her a nod. "Have you been able to come up with anything new, Charlie?"

"As a matter of fact, yes." He pulled a manila folder out of his briefcase. "Sorenson was right about the landlord. The building effectively changed hands right after Battaglia arrived at the Academy. Someone new got the benefit of the big rent increase. I blew that one originally. I really apologize."

"What do you mean by "effectively changed hands?" Tony asked.

"I originally ran tract searches and they showed the building as being owned by the Lafayette National Bank as trustee all through that period. I rechecked yesterday to confirm that the bank is still the title holder. What I hadn't considered was that someone might have purchased the beneficial interest in that trust, which wouldn't affect the title."

"And now you think that's what happened?"

"I'm sure of it. Land titles are maintained in the recorder of deeds' office; but the Cook County treasurer keeps the records of where real estate tax bills are sent." As Charlie was talking, he pulled some additional documents out of his briefcase. "Last April second, counsel for the Lafayette National Bank filed a notice with the treasurer's office that all future tax bills for that trust should be sent to suite 21-A, 5401 West Lawrence Avenue. Still in the Bank's name as title holder, mind you, but to this new address."

"What's at that address?" Tony asked.

Charlie grinned. "I thought you'd never ask."

"It sure as hell isn't an office of the Lafayette National Bank. That's my neighborhood. I know it." Wysocki interjected.

"Right," Charlie answered. "It's the office of a company named Nonno's Health care, Inc. I have no idea what they do, but the secretary of state's records show that its president is our old friend William O'Coogan."

"Well, what do you know!" Tony leaned back in his chair, mentally distancing himself from the others as the disparate facts began to coalesce. "That's quite a coincidence." The others looked at him quizzically, waiting for him to drop the second shoe.

"That ties right in with something else we discovered this past week," Tony continued, turning back to them. "To follow up on Rolf Sorenson's suggestion, I subpoenaed the payroll records of all of the Academy's major suppliers. Nothing of consequence showed up. No known mob figures; no apparent phantom employees. That was a dead end. But, when Carol subpoenaed the books of those suppliers something very interesting showed up. Over and over again we found payments to the same company for consulting and management services. A company up on Lawrence Avenue. Guess who those payments were to?"

"Nonno's Health Care, Inc.," said Charlie confidently.

"Bingo! Give the man a prize."

"Then if Sorenson's premise is correct," Charlie continued, thinking out loud, "it's the payroll of Nonno's Health Care, Inc. that should be the mother lode. That's how the payments are being made to mob figures. Sorenson had the right idea, but O'Coogan set up an extra layer of corporations to shield what he was doing. What do you think, Jake?"

"I think you've probably hit it," the old cop answered in his gravelly voice. "What you've got to get now is Nonno's payroll. But if it really is a front, they're not going to just turn it over to you, even if you do lay papers on them."

"You're right on that," Tony responded. "We did subpoena Nonno's payroll--two days ago. Yesterday a courier delivered a motion to quash our subpoena. It was filed by some sole practitioner, and guess what? His office in the same building where Nonno's is located. His name is Malone, Jack Malone. Never heard of him before, but I spoke with him on the phone late yesterday afternoon. He insists that Nonno's records are irrelevant to our case and that they have no intention of producing them. We agreed that his motion to quash will be dealt with when Judge Katsoris has her status call in our case on September eleventh, which is a week from tomorrow. Of course, Malone never mentioned that the president of Nonno's is William O'Coogan. That should make our hearing on the eleventh very interesting."

"Well, it looks like the fat's really in the fire, doesn't it?" Wysocki smiled as he leaned back in his chair. "But if you're really interested in the other side's bank accounts, let me tell you about an old trick you might use."

"That's all right, Jake," Charlie answered. "We've already subpoenaed the Academy's bank records and have received copies of all their checks and deposit records. There's nothing more to get."

"Tony, where did you find this guy? At a Cub Scout meeting?" He turned to Charlie, "How do you know, Charlie, that they don't have another bank somewhere? Their *real* bank?"

"Well, I guess I don't know that. But we haven't seen any evidence of that."

"That's what I'm trying to tell you. There are ways of double-checking these things."

"Go ahead, Jake," Tony interjected with a slight smile.

"Charlie, we're all learning things here. Just listen for a while. We have to be smarter than they are."

Jake took a sip of his coffee. "What you do is this," he began, putting his cup down. "You need someone who works for you and you trust. Someone whose name the other side won't recognize. Have them write out a personal check for some small amount, payable to the Dental Academy, and mail it to them. The check should be for something like twenty bucks. Stick a note in the envelope thanking them for the loan for the cab fare. They'll cash it; everyone always does. When it comes back, you can see if it was cashed at a bank you didn't know about before."

"That's pretty cute, Jake," Charlie admitted. "It's a good idea. I'll have my secretary send them a check of hers today and ask for copies of the front and back when it's cashed and cleared."

"Maybe the kid's not hopeless after all," Jake said. "He seems to learn fast. Actually, you guys have found out quite a bit. Who knows, Charlie, maybe when you grow up, you'll make something of yourself and become a cop."

"Thanks, Jake," Charlie responded. "We *have* made a lot of progress. But it wouldn't have happened without Rolf Sorenson's information. That's what broke open the log jam."

"That's right," Tony replied quietly. He turned in his swivel chair and looked out the window for a long moment. After an uncomfortable silence, he turned back with a hardened look. "That's damn right," he said forcefully. "Rolf Sorenson gave up his life giving us this information. Let's not forget that." He stood up and turned to Wysocki, "Jake, I appreciate your stopping by this morning. You added a lot. Keep working on it, look into every angle you can think of and let us know what you come up with." He moved toward the door. "I've got an appointment with the FBI at ten this morning. I'm very interested to see what they'll tell us about Lenny *and his family.*"

The meeting broke up and the four left Tony's office and strolled toward the reception area. "Tony," Charlie said, turning toward him, "is this the weekend you're having your office party over in New Buffalo?"

"Yes, it is," Tony answered, "Karen and the kids have been over there most of the summer; they're anxious to get back. This will be a nice way to wind-up the summer season."

"So, you've got a place in New Buffalo." Jake said casually, glancing at Tony. "Nice area. Get over that way myself once in a while. Where about is your place?"

"On the beach, about half a mile north of town."

Jake nodded approvingly and kept walking.

They walked into the reception area oblivious to the khaki-uniformed young man they passed in the hallway. He was trimming the rental plants that were scattered along the halls of Wilson, Thompson & Gilchrist. He had begun working there just that week.

"I understand there's been some sort of a lawsuit filed in Chicago that's causing some people to look into our affairs," the raspy voice on the phone said.

"Nothin' to worry about. It's something that O'Coogan started, but we're taking care of it."

"Good, Lenny, O'Coogan's a good man, but sometimes he doesn't think things through." The voice paused, then continued with a harder, steelier tone. "You know we don't like people looking into our affairs. I don't know anything about this God damn lawsuit, and I don't wanna know. But Lenny, do what you have to do to make it go away."

"I understand, and we will. Like I said, you got nothin' to worry about."

"I hope not; for everyone's sake. By the way, you ought to come down to visit sometime. Being here without a lot of my friends around is like being in the middle of the God-damn Sahara Desert. In fact, it is the desert. It *is* a dessert. It sure as hell ain't New York. I like to see my pals once in a while, just to be sure I keep in touch."

"Okay. Thanks for the invite; I'll do that. How is it these days in Tucson?"

"Another day in fuckin' paradise."

They both laughed as they hung up.

The FBI's offices in Chicago are located on the ninth floor of the Dirksen Federal Building, seat of the United

States District Court for the Northern District of Illinois. Tony arrived at ten o'clock for his scheduled meeting with John Ellington, one of the senior local agents. He was ushered by a receptionist into a windowless conference room that was furnished with only a metal table and two chairs. The walls were bare except for a framed photograph of the Capitol in D.C. Ellington arrived a few moments later, introduced himself and sat down across the table from Tony. He was in his late thirties, thin, sandy hair; cordial but reserved.

Tony explained the case he was working on, with its growing underworld implications. After he gave an overview, he asked whether the Bureau would be willing to make any comments or suggestions that would be helpful to them.

"No, I'm sorry, Mr. Jeffries," Ellington answered crisply. "The Bureau has a policy against getting involved in any civil litigation. It would really be inappropriate for us to provide you with any information."

"I thought that might be your position," Tony replied. "But what if, during the trial of our case, evidence is uncovered that federal crimes have been committed by one party or another? Would the Bureau be likely to follow through with a criminal investigation under those circumstances?"

"Well, in that case, of course," Ellington said. "Anytime that the Bureau learns that federal crimes may have been committed, we have an obligation to look into the matter."

"That would be true, I take it, if someone presented you with evidence that had been uncovered during civil discovery that a federal crime had been committed? Before the civil case went to trial, that is!"

"Of course. We wouldn't have to wait for the civil trial to be completed before we began a criminal investigation, if that appeared to be warranted."

"Well, Mr. Ellington, let me show you this." Tony pulled a file out of his briefcase, laying it on the table between them. "A gentleman named William Weaver is currently the director of the Illinois Department of Registration and Education. He has been for the past three years. In February of 1990 a newly formed school named the Federal Dental Academy filed an application with Weaver's department for State of Illinois approval as an accredited post-graduate educational institution. The application got mired down in technicalities. Subsequently, a man named William O'Coogan gained control of the Academy under circumstances that I would not describe" Tony paused, "as friendly."

As Tony spoke he began taking documents out of his file and laying them before Ellington. "No action was taken on the Academy's application for several months. But, on April fifth, 1990, a new employee of the Academy, Leonard Battaglia, visited Mr. Weaver in his office in Springfield to discuss the pending application. Five days later, a large-screen television set, paid for by the Academy, was delivered to Mr. Weaver's office. Another identical set, also paid for by the Academy, was delivered that same day to the apartment of a Miss Adriane Lockridge in Springfield. Miss Lockridge is Mr. Weaver's longtime mistress; he lives with her while he is in Springfield." Thirteen other sets were delivered to the Academy's offices in Chicago."

Tony paused to allow Ellington to scan the Academy's application, its purchase order of the fifteen sets, and Acme Electronics' shipping memos showing where the sets had been delivered. And had he detected a flicker of reaction when he'd mentioned Lenny Battaglia's name.

After a moment, he continued, "Two days after the television sets were delivered in Springfield, Weaver himself conducted his department's review of the Academy's application. The following Monday the state's approval was mailed by his department. Here's a copy of their approval form, dated April fifteenth, signed by William Weaver personally." Tony sat back waiting for Ellington to digest the material that had been laid before him. "Is this the sort of material, Mr. Ellington, that the Bureau would have some interest in?"

"You'd better believe it!" said the agent, looking slowly at the document in front of him. "This looks to me like either bribery of a state official or extortion by a state official. If it's indicative of how Weaver operates on a regular basis, it also has income-tax implications. Those are federal offenses. How did you get this evidence?" Ellington looked up at Tony.

"Through the discovery process in our civil suit," Tony responded, leaning back. "A request for the production of documents we served on the Academy; a subpoena of Acme Electronics' business records, a deposition of Battaglia and an interview with Weaver. We've also learned that the Dental Academy may be part of a money-laundering operation for the mob. The man who passed that information on to us was murdered immediately afterwards." Tony's voice took on a touch of steely hardness as he made the last point.

"You see, Mr. Ellington," he continued, "the scope of discovery in a civil suit is very broad. In this case, one of the central issues is whether or not it was defamatory to say that William O'Coogan is connected with organized crime. Our defense is based on proving the truth of those allegations. The possibilities for discovery are practically unlimited." Tony paused again, "I suspect that there is a variety of information that we can obtain through our civil discovery that the Bureau cannot currently obtain, at least not without exposing the fact that an investigation is underway. Isn't that correct?"

Ellington quietly nodded.

"Just as there's data," Tony added, "that you can obtain through court authorized wire taps that we can't obtain."

The agent stroked his chin and stared off into space for a long moment, before looking back at Tony. "Yes, you're right on both counts," he said quietly. "Maybe there would be a value in cooperating with each other. But if we do, it has to be understood that this is absolutely off the record, is that clear?"

"That's the understanding." Leaning forward, Tony

repeated the question he had asked Ellington at the start of the conversation; "Now, what can you tell us that would be helpful to our case? While you're thinking about that, you might take a quick look at these documents as well, which we also obtained through our discovery process." With that, Tony pushed a stack of well-chosen documents across the table.

Ellington poured over them intently, occasionally pausing to make notes on a yellow pad. Tony leaned back and crossed his legs, just watching. He knew that he had Ellington's full attention now and wanted to give him enough time to absorb the impact of the material Tony had presented.

After a few quiet minutes Ellington looked up. "This is very interesting material, Mr. Jeffries," he said quietly. Then, lowering his voice still further, he continued, "I can tell you this, you may be onto something big. We know about William O'Coogan; the suspicion here is he's the financier of the Bruni family. We believe it, but we've never been able to prove it. Strictly speaking, he's not a member of the family, because he's Irish. But he's extremely bright, and we believe that he's been masterminding their money movements for at least the past five years."

Tony was incredulous. "Are you talking about Angelo Bruni, who's supposed to have headed up one of the Mafia's Five Families?"

"That's exactly who I'm talking about. Don't kid yourself; he's *still* head of one of the Five Families. He moved down to Tucson about fifteen years ago when things got a little crowded in Manhattan. The word on the street was that he was going into semi-retirement. Nothing could have been farther from the truth. In the past few years, he's rebuilt his organization around the South American drug trade, making a fortune in the process."

Tony began taking notes as Ellington went on; this was much bigger than he'd envisioned.

"One of Bruni's keys," Ellington continued, "is that he maintains iron discipline and doesn't tolerate any second-guessing of his decisions. Another key to his resurgence has been your nemesis, William O'Coogan. You mentioned money laundering; you hit it right on. By laundering Bruni's money and channeling it as legitimate income to whoever they choose, O'Coogan has been able to build Bruni a powerful network of allies centered around Chicago."

"Let me tell you something we've learned on that point," Tony interjected. "We've concluded that a company named Nonno's Health Care, Inc. is the end of the laundering pipeline here. They're on Lawrence Avenue. We're in the process of trying to subpoena Nonno's payroll records."

"We'd be extremely interested in seeing what you come up with there," Ellington replied. "We've had our eye on that outfit for some time, but we're not ready to tip our hand yet. While you're at it, you might also take a look at Lydian Associates, Inc. It's also owned by O'Coogan. We believe that it's the end of another laundering pipeline."

"Very interesting," Tony said, making some notes. "What we have to do now is turn these leads into hard evidence that O'Coogan is actually part of organized crime. Anything else you can tell me?"

"No, I don't think so, not now anyway. But let's keep in touch," Ellington replied. "And let me know what you learn from your subpoenas of those employment records. Here's my card. Let me write some additional numbers on the back, my direct line here at the office plus my cell and my home number in Oak Park."

As they exchanged cards, Ellington added as an afterthought, "Let me give you the name of someone else you might want to contact. An investigative reporter in Phoenix. Her name is Christina Anderson, everyone calls her Chris. She's working on a series of articles about the spread of mob activities in Arizona, and she may be able to give you some additional information. Nothing's been published yet; but she's collected a lot of data."

Ellington paused. He gestured at all the papers on the table between them. "Can I get copies of any of this," he asked.

"Of course, John, these are all yours," Tony answered, feeling comfortable enough now to use the man's first name. "I appreciate your help." Ellington escorted him to the outer reception room, where they shook hands before parting.

On the elevator down, it hit Tony what he was getting into. These were not peripheral thugs he was dealing with; they were major mobsters. He was involved in a matter that was undoubtedly very important to them. A moment of panic seized him. He fought it off, and steeled himself; he was going to see this through. He'd already made that commitment. *I am not going to back down.*

Chapter 10

September 7

That Saturday was Tony and Karen's annual party for all the firm's attorneys, interns and their families at their summer home in New Buffalo, Michigan. If the weather held up, it was usually a great day.

New Buffalo is a quiet little hamlet on the southeast corner of Lake Michigan, about a ninety-minute drive from the Chicago Loop. It's an old village that had blossomed as a popular resort area as successive generations of Chicagoans discovered it. Its prime attraction is its wide sandy beach. Seasoned travelers have long contended that the three-hundred mile-long beach stretching up the eastern shore of Lake Michigan is one of the finest in the world. It remains a secret to most of the world though, which is just what the residents of New Buffalo would like it to stay.

The first guests arrived about noon. Karen had set up

a buffet in the dining room so that anyone could wander in for a sandwich or a snack. Drinks of all kinds were on the patio. Although no one was ever asked to bring anything, a number of the families who had been coming to the party for several years brought casseroles or desserts to add to the buffet table. As a result, the table was a kaleidoscope of food, constantly changing during the afternoon as one dish was finished and replaced by something completely different.

Tony and Karen had begun having these parties years ago when Tony was new with the firm. Back then, only the younger lawyers and their dates or families were invited. As time passed, Tony became a partner and he and Karen decided to invite all the attorneys and their families. Finally, three years ago, the party had become such an institution that the management committee decided that the firm should underwrite its cost, invite the entire staff, and recognize it as the firm's official summer party.

The old-timers in the firm never attended. They still thought of it as Tony Jeffries' party for the younger people. Of course, many of those "younger" attorneys were now in their forties. By three o'clock close to two hundred people had arrived, at least a third of them small children. Most of the guests were on the beach enjoying the eighty-five-degree sun and clear blue sky that the day had brought. Some were swimming near the shore or floating in the dozen inflatable plastic water chairs that Tony had provided. Others were farther out on the lake in Tony's Hobie Cat or the two canoes he'd borrowed from neighbors. A large group was playing volleyball at one end of the Jeffries' stretch of beach. But most people were simply lying in the sun, relaxing and enjoying themselves.

Tony was strolling around the beach, chatting with his guests, particularly his good friends Cal Cizma and Rasheed Collins, who joined the firm about when he did and had been attending these parties from the beginning. He occasionally refilled his plastic cup of beer from the iced keg of Michelob resting in the shade of a beach umbrella. Carol James and her boyfriend, Bill Tuttle, who was with one of the accounting firms in town, came up to Tony and talked for a while, then ran down to the shore to lay claim to the incoming catamaran. The light but steady breeze made sailing perfect, even for neophytes.

"Great party, Tony," Charlie Dickenson said as he walked up to the keg. "You should do this every Saturday!"

"Actually, we do, but we've missed you the past six or eight weekends. Where have you been?" Tony laughed.

"I've been into something very interesting," Charlie answered. He smiled as he filled two cups of beer, "which I'm about to return to." Tony watched as Charlie walked over and sat down on a beach towel next to a beautiful young woman in a white bikini. *Good judgment, Charlie.*

A few minutes later, his fellow partner, Sid Johnson, walked up to Tony and several others who were discussing the Cubs. Johnson was a few years older than Tony, but was still considered somewhat of an outsider, he'd joined the firm just two years back as a lateral transfer from another firm. His value to the firm wasn't just the corporate business he brought, but also his deep political roots; his grandfather had been governor of Illinois and his father was a sitting member of Congress. They chatted a few minutes then Sid pulled Tony away from the others. "Tony," he said quietly, "some of us are interested in bringing Bill Fremont and his group from the Cronin firm. He's expressed some interest to a couple of us, off the record, of course. What do you think?"

"I know Fremont; he does good work," Tony answered. "How much business could he bring with him?"

"Enough to pay for himself and his people, plus about a hundred grand a year. The Cronin firm's having some problems, and Fremont would like to make a move. You should be aware, though, that some of our old-timers, including Thompson and Gilchrist, don't care for the idea. I think they're worried about their positions being threatened."

"Well, *I* like the idea," Tony responded. "A firm like ours has to keep growing to stay healthy. If you're looking for my support, you've got it."

"Thanks, Tony. I'll keep you informed. In the meantime, though, can you keep it quiet? This is all very, very confidential." Johnson refilled his beer then walked off into the crowd.

Dinner was served at six in the yard, overlooking the beach. The main course was a hundred-pound pig roasted on a spit. There were thirty folding chairs around tables on the patio and twenty others clustered in conversation groups in the yard. Some people took their food and drinks back to the beach; but the preferred venue for eating was the grass where guests were sitting in groups of four or five.

People began to leave around seven, especially the families with small children. Others waited to watch the sunset across the lake. It was a crystal-clear evening with the sunset outlining the towers of the distant Chicago skyline.

By nine-thirty everyone had gone. The two women Karen had hired to help with the kitchen chores and clean-up were gone too. The four Jeffries children had settled down to a game of canasta, the traditional lake-house card game. Karen and Tony decided to pour themselves glasses of wine and take a walk on the beach.

This was one of Tony's greatest pleasures; walking on the beach at night under a star-filled sky, a glass of wine in hand. Lapping at his feet, the cool water of the lake washed away all his worries. Karen shared Tony's love for these late-night walks.

They talked about the day, and what a great party it had been. They also talked about the family returning to Wilmette tomorrow.

Karen reached for Tony's hand and squeezed it as they walked in the cool sand.

"Tony," she said after a few minutes. "I don't want the kids to be afraid when they go home."

She walked a bit farther, the water swirling around her ankles, then stopped and looked up at her husband. "I was very proud of you when this Dental Academy case began. You were standing up for what we both knew was right. But after a while, after I told all the kids for the tenth time that they couldn't go somewhere or couldn't do something because it was too dangerous, I began to wonder. What kind of a life is it, when you're always looking over your shoulder, always afraid? I don't want our children to have to live that way, Tony, when we get back to Wilmette."

"It won't be," Tony said, squeezing her hand gently. He was lying but didn't know what else to say.

"Promise?" she asked.

"Kinda."

"That's what I thought," she sighed, looking away.

They walked quietly up the beach for a few minutes. The only sounds around them were the gentle splashing of the low waves washing across the sand and the occasional chirping of crickets in the grass on the dune.

"I figured out how to solve the problem," Karen said, raising her head.

"What's that?"

"The next time I'm in Springfield, I'll arrange with the Attorneys' Registration and Disciplinary Commission to have your law license yanked. Then you won't have to mess around with that case anymore." Karen laughed as Tony put his arm around her, fondling her butt.

"Always the loving wife. By the way, you know you've still got a pretty neat little ass."

"You probably say that to all the state representatives you know."

"Only the cute ones; and only gals."

Tony turned to Karen and gave her a kiss. She wrapped her arms around him as the lake water swirled around their ankles. Tony still loved the feeling of Karen's body pressing up against him.

"I've got a wonderful idea," he said softly.

"What's that?"

"Ever make love in the lake, late at night?"

"Yes, as a matter of fact, I have," Karen smiled. "Years ago. And if you say you've forgotten, I'll bite your ear." She looked into his eyes, dropped her wine glass in the sand, and began unbuttoning her blouse.

Tony let his glass slip from his fingers. "I can't think of a better way to end a very nice day," he said, as he ran both his hands down to her ass and pulled her close.

"Neither can I," Karen whispered. "You're a dirty old man, but I still love you."

"You probably say that to all the lawyers you know."

"Only the cute ones, and only guys."

Three hours later, long after the lights had gone out in the beach house, a dark sedan pulled up at the bottom of the hill just past their home. Its lights turned off, it coasted to a stop under the overhanging branches of a large willow tree about ten feet off the road. For about fifteen minutes, the two men inside watched the house for any sign of life. When they were satisfied that everyone was asleep, each screwed a silencer onto his revolver and got out, easing the doors quietly shut. Again, they waited, listening for any sound of activity from any direction. The only sounds they heard were crickets and far-away owls.

With their dark long-sleeved shirts and jeans, they were practically invisible in the midnight shadows. After another two or three minutes, they pulled dark ski masks down over their faces, walked across the quiet country road, and began slowly climbing through the grass and shrubs on the slope toward the beach house, ignoring the stairs. The house was about a hundred feet from the road; the hill was thick with foliage.

Suddenly, the distinctive metallic click of a revolver being cocked behind them froze them in their tracks.

"You boys are a little out of your neighborhood, aren't you?"

Behind the two gunmen a hulking figure slowly stepped out of the bushes. "Don't move, boys, not an inch!" a husky voice commanded. The moonlight first caught a steel-blue snub-nosed .38 leveled at the backs of the gunmen, then revealed a slowly advancing Jake Wysocki. "Drop your iron, boys, really carefully," he ordered. Both guns fell quietly into the grass.

"Keep your hands up high, where I can see 'em," Wysocki ordered as he came in close behind the two. "Make a move and I'll blow your fucking heads off." Pressing his revolver hard against the back of one of the gunmen, Wysocki reached around with his left hand and found another gun tucked under the man's belt. He deftly removed it with his gloved hand and slipped it into his own coat pocket.

"You," he said, poking that gunman hard with his .38, "lie flat, face down, arms out." The man complied. Wysocki repeated the process with the other, keeping a careful eye on the first, patting his lower legs, and finding his second gun, which he tucked under his belt. After patting their pants pockets and pulling out their wallets, he knelt down and quickly ripped off their ski masks, keeping his gun poised and ready to shoot.

Standing and stepping back a pace, Wysocki pulled a flashlight out of his back pocket and turned it on. "Now, let's see who we've got here. Roll over, boys; carefully, like nice little doggies," he ordered. After a moment of hesitation, they both did. "Well, well," the old cop said, half to himself, "Weasel Frattio and Turk Escevada. You boys really are out of your neighborhood!"

"Who is that?" one of the men of the ground asked, holding a hand in front of his face while trying to see the voice behind the flashlight's glare.

"It's Wysocki," the other said quietly, raising his voice slightly he added; "Wysocki, I thought you were supposed to be retired. What the hell are you doing over here?"

"Private work, Turk, just like you. Only difference is that I've got a license for what I'm doing." He paused a moment, "Now get up, boys; real slow, and start walking down those stairs. We're going to get in your car and take a ride."

The two men got up and started down the concrete

steps in the center of the slope. As they did, Wysocki picked up the revolvers they had dropped. He wore thin black leather gloves and was careful to not smudge any possible fingerprints.

"Where are we going, Wysocki?"

"The Michigan State Police station. It's only about a five-minute drive from here; out on the highway."

"What the hell are you going to charge us with, trespassing? You know, we didn't actually do anything, except dress up in Halloween masks." The two men ahead of Wysocki both chuckled at that.

"Maybe," answered Wysocki, keeping his .38 leveled at their backs. "Or maybe you'll be charged with unlawfully carrying firearms. As I recall, you're both convicted felons. It's a serious offense for you to be carrying any type of firearms. You just may get some time for that. I understand that the court over here doesn't regard that as a bailable offense. I've got a hunch you boys aren't going to be seeing Chicago for at least a year."

Their chuckling stopped. "Shit," muttered one of them under his breath.

Up in the house, Karen tossed and woke up. She thought she heard some noise in the yard, listened for a minute, then decided that she'd been dreaming. She snuggled up to her husband in bed, peacefully falling back to sleep.

Chapter 11

September 10

Jack Harrington scheduled the deposition of Dr. John Schofield, executive director of the American Dental Society, for the day prior to the status hearing before Judge Katsoris. Harrington had already taken the depositions of all the staff and committee people at the ADS and CODA involved in the denial of the Dental Academy's application, in preparation for his final deposition of the ADS' chief executive officer. He also wanted to be able to tell the Court tomorrow that the plaintiffs had completed discovery and would like the earliest possible trial date. He accurately perceived that the defense case had not been pulled together yet. An early trial date would give the plaintiffs a decided advantage.

Tony and Charlie spent the entire day before the deposition preparing Dr. Schofield for the rigorous interrogation that he could expect. They role-played the deposition, with Charlie aggressively asking questions as though he were Harrington and Tony objecting and counseling Schofield the way he would do in the actual deposition. Schofield, like most people who rise to the top of major associations, was a quick study. He was also very perceptive. Once he understood what the issues in his deposition would be, he immediately identified the areas where he needed to be careful in his testimony.

John Schofield was a dentist by education, but he had spent most of his professional life as an administrator in organized dentistry. In his mid-fifties, tall and urbane, he was the perfect representative of the dental profession. That was a role he'd often filled testifying before Congressional Committees or civic groups on issues of interest to dentistry. As the executive director of the ADS for almost ten years, he headed a staff of over four hundred people and enjoyed a reputation as a skilled administrator.

"Remember, Doctor, you're not going to win the case by giving such brilliant answers tomorrow that plaintiffs' counsel will throw his hands up in despair, abandoning his suit," Tony advised Schofield. "That just isn't going to happen. The trial is the time for that kind of testimony, where you'll be playing to an impartial judge and jury. Your deposition tomorrow is purely for the benefit of plaintiffs' counsel so that he can learn what your testimony will be if you are called as a witness in trial."

"I get the picture," Schofield smiled as he took a sip of coffee. "I'll save my speeches for the trial."

"Good," Tony continued. "Let me tell you something else. *Do not* volunteer anything, and don't add anything to your answers unless it's required to truthfully answer the question asked. Do you understand? Volunteer nothing!"

"Yes," Schofield answered confidently. "Don't worry; I'm not going to give him any information except what he asks for."

"Let's see about that," Tony continued. "I'm Harrington. Let's see how you'd answer some questions. First of all, what's your name?"

"Dr. John Schofield."

"Think about what you just said," Tony said, leaning forward. "I didn't ask you for your profession. I only asked for your name. By telling me that you were a doctor, you gave me some information that I may not have otherwise known. Do you see what I mean?"

"Yes, I do," said Schofield soberly. "I'll have to really listen to what he asks, won't I? All right, try another question."

"Are you married?"

"Yes, I'm married to…" Schofield caught himself, exchanged glances with Tony, then restated his answer, "Yes, I am."

"Good; that's exactly what I mean. Keep your answers tight and strictly to the point when Harrington is questioning you. The same principle will hold true during the trial. Don't add *anything* unnecessary when you're being questioned by the other side. When we're questioning you, however, that will be a different story. In the trial, we will be serving you soft lobs so that you can slam home one good point after another. But in the deposition tomorrow, we're probably not going to be asking you anything unless it's necessary to let you clarify something you may have said earlier, so keep your answers short and sweet." Schofield nodded his understanding.

"One other thing I should tell you, Doctor," Tony continued, "is that we've learned some information about the plaintiffs during the past few weeks that we've consciously not shared with you yet. We were concerned that if you knew it all, something might inadvertently slip out during your deposition, especially if things get heated. We don't have real evidence of mob involvement by O'Coogan, mind you; just leads. But some good ones. We plan to get together with you *after* your deposition to bring you fully up to date. Do you have any problem with that approach?"

"None at all; I think that's a wise thing to do. Now, let's go back over some of those earlier questions."

They went on until about six in the evening. When they broke, Tony gave Schofield transcripts of the earlier deposition testimony of several ADS staff and commission members to review. They agreed to meet at eight-thirty the next morning at Wilson Thompson & Gilchrist's office to answer any last-minute questions that Schofield had.

"Hello, Dr. Schofield, so good to meet you." Jack Harrington strode into his reception room at ten the next morning, extended his hand and gave Schofield his biggest, toothiest smile. "I've heard so much about you." After pumping Schofield's hand, Harrington acknowledged his attorney. "Jeffries, isn't it? Good to see you again. This is my associate David Epstein; I believe the two of you have already met. The court reporter's already here. Are you folks ready to begin, or would you prefer to have some time to talk?"

"We're ready whenever you are," Tony responded.

"Fine. Well why don't we get started, then?" Harrington took Schofield by the arm and walked him down the hallway. Tony followed a step behind.

"You know, Doctor," Harrington continued, talking quietly to Schofield, "we have several mutual friends. Nathan Benoit is one who comes to mind. Nathan and I have served for years together on the board of the Chicago Symphony. He's a great admirer of yours."

"Why, thank you, that's very flattering. Nathan's a fine man," Schofield responded. He was obviously charmed.

Just before they walked into the conference room, Tony gently pulled Schofield aside and turned his back to Harrington. "Don't let this guy fool you," he whispered. "He's trying to destroy the ADS. Don't let him con you!"

Schofield touched Tony's arm. "Don't worry about a thing," he answered quietly. "I know how to deal with people like this."

The conference room in Harrington's office had a

polished hardwood floor, rich oriental carpets and dark oak paneling. In the center was a ten-foot-long solid-glass conference table surrounded by Chippendale chairs. Three walls were covered with paintings that could have been hanging in the Art Institute. All were reminders that this was the office of a man who had won vast sums of money in litigation over the years. The fourth wall, on the east side, had large windows overlooking the Loop, with the blue-green water of Lake Michigan beyond. Harrington directed Tony and Dr. Schofield to their seats, which Tony quickly recognized would be directly facing the late-morning sun; a tactic calculated to make the witness uncomfortable just as he was likely to be tiring and letting his guard down. Tony had them take two other seats away from the direct sunlight. Harrington didn't say a word but moved his papers so that he'd be directly across the table from Schofield when the deposition began.

Harrington's secretary, whom he introduced as Miss Shaw, served coffee while they were taking their seats. An attractive blonde, dressed in a tailored white linen suit, she maintained a bright smile throughout. Harrington continued his intimate chatter with Schofield, recalling experiences with several other mutual friends. Epstein took the chair next to Harrington with various documents already spread out in front of it. Her duties discharged, Miss Shaw left as the court reporter completed setting up her equipment. When everyone was seated, Harrington had her swear in the witness, and he began.

"Now, Dr. Schofield, just for the record, why don't

you give the court reporter your name."

"Certainly. It's John Schofield," the witness responded. He sipped his coffee and returned Harrington's polite smile.

"What's your current position, Doctor? Again, just for the record."

"I'm employed by the American Dental Society."

"Yes, of course, but what's your position at the ADS?"

"I'm the executive director."

"Just to save a little time here, and putting aside some of the formalities," Harrington continued, giving Schofield a big smile, "wouldn't it be fair to say that you are responsible for running the ADS?"

"No, I wouldn't say that," Schofield said carefully, taking another sip of his coffee. "It would be more accurate to say that I have certain responsibilities related to the management of the ADS."

Harrington waited for Schofield to continue or expand on his answer. Schofield did neither. *Good*, Tony thought. *He's being careful. He hasn't been conned.* Harrington went on for several more minutes, dealing with preliminaries, before getting to the main subject.

"Now, Dr. Schofield, let's talk a bit about this unfortunate business regarding the Federal Dental Academy. What really happened here?"

"Objection," Tony interjected. "That question's vague and ambiguous. I don't see how anyone could intelligibly answer it."

"Your objection is noted, counselor," responded

Harrington with a condescending smile. "But if Dr. Schofield understood the question and can answer it, I'd like to hear his answer."

"I'm afraid that I can't answer that question as asked," the witness replied. "It seems terribly vague and ambiguous." Tony smiled to himself; Schofield was holding his own.

"Let me rephrase the question," Harrington continued, his voice taking on a harder tone. "Why, exactly, was the Federal Dental Academy's application for accreditation denied by the American Dental Society?"

"It didn't meet our standards," Schofield replied easily.

"Who made that determination?"

"Our Commission on Dental Accreditation. It's actually a semi-autonomous body."

"Did you review their decision before it became final?"

"Yes, I did."

"What conclusion, if any, did you reach?"

"I concurred in the decision of the commission. The school did not meet our normal accreditation standards, even for initial or provisional approval."

"In what ways, Doctor? Could you be more specific?" Harrington leaned forward as he asked his question.

"Certainly. As I recall, the professional head of the school, Dr. Roberts, had very questionable credentials. In fact, a proceeding to revoke his dental license was underway. The only other full-time member of the professional staff was a woman who had never attended dental school in this country, nor practiced dentistry here. It seemed rather anomalous to have people with that limited a background overseeing a dental-education program. All the rest of the prospective faculty members were young dentists, part-timers who had never taught previously. In addition, the finances of the school appeared to be terribly tenuous. It wasn't at all clear that the school would survive the coming academic year, much less the five years necessary for someone to graduate. All in all, I regarded it as a very weak application, and agreed that the application for accreditation was properly denied." Schofield spoke with the confidence of a naval captain who had just fired a broadside into his opponent. It showed that he had recently reviewed the file on the Dental Academy's application.

"How could all of that possibly be true, Doctor?" Harrington pressed, now clearly an adversary. "The Department of Registration and Education of the State of Illinois approved the Academy only a few months before the ADS rejected it. Many of the areas that you just referred to are items that the State of Illinois would look into before granting their approval, such as the school's finances. Isn't that correct?"

"I don't know what the Department of Registration and Education looked into or what their decision to approve was based on," Schofield answered forcefully. And, of course, they were only reviewing the Academy as an institution, and not the details of this dental program.

"I can tell you that the Academy's dental program clearly did not meet ADS standards when it was reviewed by our commission."

"But you'll admit, Doctor, that the State of Illinois, and the American Dental Society came to diametrically different conclusions regarding the same school within a few months of each other, won't you?"

"Yes, that's true. But, as I said they were reviewing the institution itself and our commission was reviewing the institution's specific dental program."

"But since the Academy's only objective was to offer dental programs, there must have been a great deal of overlap between what they reviewed and what your commission reviewed. Without giving Schofield time to respond Harrington went on. "Is it possible, Doctor, that the State of Illinois' evaluation of the Dental Academy was accurate and objective, while the ADS' evaluation was biased?"

"I find that exceedingly unlikely," Schofield asserted. "The Illinois Department of R and E rarely reviews applications for dental schools, while our Committee on Dental Accreditation evaluates applications for all fifty states on a regular basis."

"Are you saying that it is absolutely impossible for there to have been bias in the ADS' evaluation?"

"Well, no, there aren't many things that I'd say are absolutely impossible."

"So, you'll admit that it's possible?"

"Possible, but very unlikely."

"All right, now that we've established the fact that the ADS' evaluation of the Dental Academy may possibly have been biased and unfair..."

"Objection!" Tony interjected quickly. "That's not what the witness said; I don't want his testimony mischaracterized."

"Oh, but that is what he said, Mr. Jeffries. He specifically testified that it was possible that the ADS' evaluation of the Academy and its dental program was biased. He equivocated on the likelihood of that happening, but he clearly admitted the possibility of bias. Isn't that true, Doctor?"

"Yes, I guess I did, but...," Schofield answered unsurely.

Harrington cut him off before he could further qualify his answer. "As I was saying, now that we've established that the ADS' evaluation of the Dental Academy may have been biased and unfair, let's see if we can determine what may have caused that bias and unfairness. Doctor, what is a proprietary school?"

Tony noticed that Schofield pushed his chair back slightly and crossed his legs before answering. "That would be a school that's owned by private parties," he said. "It's' proprietors, if you will. They operate the school to make a return on their investment. Unlike schools that are connected with colleges or universities, which are operated on a not-for-profit basis."

"The Federal Dental Academy is a proprietary dental school, isn't it?"

"Yes, I understand that it is."

"The old guard in the dental profession doesn't care for proprietary dental schools, does it, Doctor? Proprietary dental schools are considered somewhat improper, aren't they?"

"Why, no, I wouldn't say that. Oh, years ago some dentists felt that way. But not anymore. Today they're put to the same tests that academic schools are put to."

"Come now, Doctor, let's be honest with each other," Harrington responded. "How many dental schools in the United States are currently fully accredited by the ADS?"

"Fifty-eight, as I recall."

"How many of those are proprietary schools, owned by investors with the objective of making a profit?"

"Well, actually, dentistry's in a bit of a transition at the moment." Schofield cleared his throat before continuing. "I believe there are several applications of proprietary schools pending right now."

"That's not what I asked, Doctor." Harrington snapped. "How many proprietary dental schools in the United States are fully accredited by the American Dental Society right now?"

"None."

"None? None? Doctor, doesn't that fact just scream to you that there's a powerful bias in organized dentistry against proprietary dental schools? That the dental establishment, through the ADS, is doing everything within its power to keep dentistry and dental education a closed club, and to keep out all outsiders; outsiders like the

Federal Dental Academy?"

"Absolutely not," Schofield replied, "Not at all."

"Well, that's a question that's ultimately going to be decided by the jury in this case; whether the American Dental Society was guilty of restraint of trade, in violation of the antitrust laws, in refusing to accredit the Dental Academy." Harrington paused, before adding, "But Doctor, you'll surely admit that there's at least some potential for bias against proprietary schools such as the Dental Academy, won't you?"

"Yes, I suppose there is with some dentists."

"Fine, thank you for your honesty."

"Doctor, let's approach this from a different perspective," Harrington continued, and took a sip of his coffee. "How many fully accredited dental schools are there in the Chicago metropolitan area right now? By that I mean dental schools that are fully accredited by your organization, the ADS."

"Three. Northwestern, Loyola, and the University of Illinois."

"Doctor, there are ten members on the ADS's Commission on Dental Accreditation, aren't there?"

"Yes, I believe there are."

"In fact, this is a list of the ten current members of that commission, isn't it?" Harrington asked as he slid a piece of white paper across the table to the witness.

Schofield looked at the document for a moment before he responded. "Yes, it is."

"Doctor, how many of those ten commission members

are graduates of either Northwestern, Loyola, or the University of Illinois dental schools?"

Schofield took a longer look at the paper in front of him. Tony knew that Schofield sensed where Harrington was going, and he wanted his answer to be precise. "Four," he answered. Drs. McCarthy and Carlson are graduates of Northwestern, and I believe Drs. Svoboda and Smith are alums of the University of Illinois."

"In addition, isn't it true that Dr. Rosenthal, a member of CODA, just retired as dean of the Loyola University School of Dentistry?"

"Yes, he did."

"So, five of the ten members of the ADS's Commission on Dental Accreditation have a strong connection with one of the three dental schools here in Chicago, don't they?"

"Yes, I suppose they do."

"Applications for admission to dental schools have declined the past few years, haven't they, Doctor?" Harrington leaned forward and pulled a volume of the *ADS Journal* out of a folder in front of him. "In fact, there's been articles written in your own *Journal* about that subject, haven't there?"

Schofield shifted in his chair. "Yes, that's true. If you look at national statistics, applications for admission have dropped a bit in the past few years."

"And all dental schools are getting nervous about their enrollment and financial bases, aren't they, Doctor?"

"Well, I'm not sure I'd agree with that, Mr. Harrington.

That varies from school to school. And, I might add that Northwestern, Illinois, and Loyola are three of the strongest programs in the country."

"And three of the most influential, also, aren't they, Doctor?"

"Objection!" Tony exclaimed. "That's a totally inappropriate question!"

"I'll withdraw the question, counsel." Harrington smiled, then continued, "But surely, you'll agree with me, won't you, Doctor, that a new fully accredited dental school in this city would put certain competitive pressure on the three schools that are already here, wouldn't it?"

"Yes, I guess it might."

"And if five of the ten members of the Commission on Dental Accreditation have a close affiliation with the three existing schools here, will you admit that there's at least the possibility of some bias against a new dental school seeking accreditation here in Chicago?"

"I suppose that that's a possibility, but…"

"Fine." Harrington quickly interjected, "you've answered the question. Again, Doctor, thank you for your candor." Harrington leaned back in his chair and flipped through his notes, looking pleased with the admissions he was extracting from Schofield. Tony on the other hand, was uncomfortable with the way the deposition was going.

"Now let's talk about some other biases that may have been working against the Federal Dental Academy's application; biases of a more sinister nature. Are you aware of the fact, Doctor, that all ten members of the ADS' Commission on Dental Accreditation admitted in their depositions that they had heard rumors or saw memos that the Dental Academy was owned and run by gangsters?"

As Harrington asked his question, David Epstein pushed over to him a stack of bound transcripts of the depositions of the ten members of the commission. Slips of paper with handwritten notes protruded from each transcript. Harrington didn't need to see those transcripts. He had read his own copies the night before and knew what they contained. So had Schofield.

"Answer the question please, Doctor," Harrington pressed.

"Yes, I'm aware of that fact, but I don't think it had any bearing on their decision."

"Can you be certain of that, Doctor? Can you sit here today, under oath, and swear that the decision of the ADS' Commission on Dental Accreditation to deny accreditation of the Dental Academy wasn't based, at least in part, on the commission's belief that the Academy was run by gangsters and hoodlums? Can you swear to that, Doctor?"

"No, I suppose I can't. There's no way I can tell what's inside someone's head when they make a decision."

"Doctor, did you run any independent investigation of the Dental Academy, or did you rely entirely on the report that the Commission on Dental Accreditation put together for you?"

"I relied on the report and recommendation of the

commission. I did not conduct an independent investigation or inspection."

"Therefore, if the commission was biased, which you've already admitted was possible, and they based their conclusions on a dislike of proprietary schools, or a desire to keep another dental school out of Chicago, or on rumors that the mob ran the Dental Academy, or any combination of those biases, their report and its conclusions would reflect those biases wouldn't it?" Tony was desperately searching his mind for some legal basis for objecting to this line of questioning; he couldn't think of anything.

"Well, I guess it might."

"And in that case, your decision to support the commission's decision would have been influenced by the same biases and unfairness that influenced the commission's decision, wouldn't it?"

"Yes, I suppose so." As he answered, Schofield pulled out his handkerchief and wiped the perspiration that had begun to appear on his brow.

"Now let me ask you this, Doctor," Harrington continued, pressing forward for the kill. "With all this talk about mobsters running the Dental Academy, talk that quite possibly influenced both CODA and yourself into denying the Academy standing, have you seen one piece of evidence that the owners of the Dental Academy are in fact connected with organized crime?"

Schofield hesitated, "Well, no. But I'm not the one who would necessarily collect data like that."

"Don't evade the question, Doctor!" Harrington demanded, raising his voice. "I'm asking you, Dr. John Schofield, in your capacity as executive director of the American Dental Society, whether you are presently aware of any evidence, admissible in a court of law, that the Federal Dental Academy or its' owner William O'Coogan, is involved in any way in organized crime? Answer the question yes or no!"

There was a long silence. Then Schofield looked Harrington straight in the eye. "You don't need to raise your voice with me, sir. No, I am not."

"That's what I thought, Doctor," Harrington replied triumphantly, laying his pen on top of the yellow pad in front of him. "That's exactly what I thought. This deposition is over!" Harrington stood, turned and strode from the room. David Epstein hurriedly gathered up their papers and left a moment later.

The room was as silent as a tomb as the court reporter packed up her equipment and left. Tony and Dr. Schofield quietly collected their papers. Finally, Schofield turned to Tony and broke the silence. "Why do I feel like I've just had a wooden stake driven through my heart?"

"That's a natural reaction," Tony responded. "You'll do fine in the trial." He was lying. *Unless we come up with some compelling evidence to connect O'Coogan with organized crime, we're going to be hammered at trial with a massive judgment.*

That night was one of the rare occasions when the entire Jeffries family was home for dinner at the same time. Between Tony's evenings at the office, Karen's trips to Springfield, and the older boys' growing sets of commitments, there weren't more than two evenings a week when they were all able to have dinner together. Tony and Karen relished these moments, they knew that within a couple of years Mark would be in high school, wrapped up in all its commitments, followed a year later by Roger. These family dinners would one day be a thing of the past.

They talked that evening about the kids' events of the day. Mark and Roger were on junior soccer teams; Tony and Karen had strongly discouraged football. They knew too many people of all ages with lasting injuries related to playing football. Billy's and Debbie's after school activities mainly involved playing in the yard with other kids from the block.

After dinner, and the usual skirmish about whether the television would be turned on while the older boys had homework to be done. Karen and Tony retreated to the den. Tony poured two glasses of Chardonnay while Karen opened the day's mail.

"Here's something interesting," Karen said, looking at one letter. "Your sister's alma mater, Barat College would like you to serve on the search committee to find their new president. That's quite a compliment."

"The last thing I need right now is another obligation," Tony responded, taking off his wire-rim glasses and rubbing his eyes. "This Dental Academy case is smothering me. It's not going well. We don't have any hard evidence yet to link O'Coogan with the mob, and we're running out of time."

"Tony, you're letting this case consume you. I'm getting worried about you. Serving on Barat's search committee might be a good diversion. It wouldn't take that much time." Karen laid the letter on the couch between them. "Why don't you give it some thought? Who knows, you might make some good connections, too."

"Okay, you win," Tony said, putting his glasses back on and picking up the letter from Barat. In the back of his mind he already knew that he'd probably accept the invitation. He began mulling over ideas on how to choose a college president as he opened his briefcase, put the letter inside, and pulled out one of the Dental Academy subfiles.

Tony didn't sleep well that night. He was worried about the case and couldn't put it out of his mind. By now, the defense should be shaping up. Evidence should be falling into place. But it wasn't. For a case that was only a month away from trial there were too many unknowns. Tony was worried.

He'd have been much more worried if he'd known what the next month had in store for him.

Chapter 12

September Twelfth

The case of the Federal Dental Academy versus the American Dental Society was the last one scheduled on Judge Katsoris' calendar that day. Sometimes being last on a judge's call meant nothing. In this case, however, it was intentional, the Judge wanted to have time to discuss and resolve any discovery or other issues that had arisen in order to determine when the case could be set for trial.

"Gentlemen," the Judge began, as the attorneys approached her bench when their case was called, "I'd like you to give me a report on the status of this matter, particularly regarding the state of discovery." She thumbed through the pleadings, then added, "Also, it appears that there is a motion to quash a subpoena served by a company named Nonno's Health Care, Inc., is that correct?"

"That's right, Your Honor." A small dark-haired man

with a mustache pushed his way past the others. "I'm John Malone, counsel for Nonno's Health Care, Incorporated. My client is not a party to this litigation, but has had all its employee payroll records subpoenaed by the defendants. There is no conceivable connection between my client and this lawsuit, therefore we have filed that motion to quash that subpoena. The records involved are personal to our employees and former employees, who are entitled to have their privacy respected."

"Counsel," Judge Katsoris said, looking at Tony, "what's your response?"

"Your Honor, this case includes a defamation count. The plaintiffs have asserted that it is libelous to state that William O'Coogan and the Dental Academy which he owns, are connected with organized crime. The defendants intend to raise truth as a defense to that count. We have reason to believe that the employment records we've subpoenaed will go a long way toward establishing that defense. Your Honor, given the libel and slander allegations in the complaint filed by the plaintiffs we have no alternative except to pursue that aspect of the case. In that regard, if you will recall, at our prior status hearing you granted defendants' motion for leave to inquire into the personal investments and financial activity of Mr. O'Coogan."

"Yes, I do. As I recall, plaintiffs' counsel had no objection." Judge Katsoris glanced briefly at Jack Harrington, then looked back to Tony. "Mr. Jeffries," she asked, "what's Mr. O'Coogan's connection, if any, with Nonno's

Health Care, Inc.?"

"Mr. O'Coogan is listed by the Illinois Secretary of State as the president of Nonno's Health Care, Inc.," Tony answered. It's an Arizona corporation doing business in Illinois. He handed a certified document from the Secretary of State's office to the Judge's Clerk, who in turn handed it up to Judge Katsoris. "We have reason to believe that the payroll of this company will include a number of prominent mob figures."

The Judge looked over the page that had been handed to her. "If what you say proves to be true, counsel," she said, "that would certainly assist in proving your defense under the libel and slander count." Turning to Harrington, she frowned and asked, "Didn't you stipulate to this type of discovery, counsel, at the last status hearing?"

"Well, yes I did, Your Honor," Harrington replied. "But I was referring to discovery into Mr. O'Coogan's personal affairs, not corporations in which he happens to be an officer. This corporation as a separate entity is entitled to raise its own objections, which it has done through its own counsel, Mr. Malone."

"Mr. Harrington, I don't like the sound of this," the Judge countered sharply. "If this is a company that your client Mr. O'Coogan owns, in whole or in part, the prior order applies to it, as far as I am concerned. Now, are you prepared to tell me today, as an Officer of the Court, that Mr. O'Coogan has no ownership interest in Nonno's Health Care, Inc.?"

Harrington hesitated a long time before answering,

"No, Your Honor, I am not. I understand that Mr. O'Coogan has an ownership interest in this company."

"Then the prior order applies to it and any other companies owned in whole or in part by Mr. O'Coogan," Judge Katsoris replied crisply. "The motion to quash will be denied. Nonno's Health Care, Inc. is ordered to produce the subpoenaed payroll records within ten days. Mr. Malone, I want you to tell the people you deal with at Nonno's that I'm ordering them to cooperate in this document production, do you understand?"

"Yes, Your Honor, I will," Malone stuttered. He looked dismayed at the swift turn of events against him.

"Your Honor," Tony interjected, "can we assume that your order will also apply to any other corporations which list Mr. O'Coogan as an officer or director? I ask this question since the secretary of state publishes corporate officers and directors but not ownership interests."

"Yes, I think that's reasonable Mr. Jeffries," the Judge agreed. "Any company that shows Mr. O'Coogan as an officer or director is subject to your discovery of their payroll and financial records. If you subpoena the records of any corporation and its shown to my satisfaction that Mr. O'Coogan, even though an officer, has no ownership interest in that company, then I will consider a motion to suppress any documents produced in response to such a subpoena. But I want it understood that, under the circumstances of the complaint filed in this case, the defendants are entitled to very broad discovery rights. Now, what's the status of discovery? How close are we to a trial in this matter? Mr. Harrington?"

"I am pleased to advise the court that the plaintiffs have completed discovery. We are ready for trial and prepared to begin next week if that's the court's pleasure."

"Fine. Mr. Jeffries, from our exchange a moment ago, I take it that you have a few loose ends to complete before you have finished discovery, is that correct?"

"Yes, Your Honor. We could use two months to properly complete discovery," Tony answered. He knew that they hadn't come up yet with any real evidence to link O'Coogan or Battaglia with organized crime. Lots of leads, but no evidence admissible in any court. He needed more time.

"Two months?" the judge said, frowning as she leaned forward. "Surely, Mr. Jeffries, that isn't necessary. I'll give you one month. That should be sufficient. All right, gentlemen, discovery closes on Friday, October eleventh, with any pretrial motions due by the close of business that day. Responses will be due the following Wednesday, the Court will rule on them at the commencement of trial, which will be Friday, October eighteenth. We'll handle the preliminaries and choose your jury that day, and begin in earnest the following Monday. How long a trial are we talking about, so that I can reserve that time on my calendar?"

"I would estimate two weeks, Your Honor," Harrington replied.

"Given the number of witnesses that we expect to put on, you'd better allow at least three weeks, Your Honor,"

Tony said. He wanted Harrington to think about that.

"All right, I'll block out three full weeks. Gentlemen, I'll see you on October eighteenth, ready for trial."

The attorneys filed from the courtroom and took separate elevators down to street level. It was a hot, sticky day, and the edges of Tony's wire-rim glasses steamed up as they walked out onto Dearborn Street. Tony and Charlie took off their suit coats and caught a cab back to the office. The air conditioning in the cab wasn't working. On the way, they began discussing their last wave of discovery. Time was running out, all those interesting leads they had been collecting had to be turned into hard evidence within the next thirty days.

As they exited the taxi at the base of the Hancock Building, Charlie stopped suddenly when he glanced at the coin-operated newspaper box on the sidewalk. The afternoon edition of the Sun-Times had just come out. It was headlined "State Official Arrested for Income Tax Evasion." Under the banner was a photograph of William Weaver.

"Tony, look at this!" Charlie exclaimed. He dug in his pocket for a couple of quarters, dropping them in the slot as he pulled out a paper.

"Well, what do you know?" Tony exclaimed, reading over Charlie's shoulder. William Weaver, the paper reported, longtime state official and currently Director of the Department of Registration and Education, had been arrested that morning at the apartment of a female friend in Springfield. He was charged with evading over $100,000 in federal income taxes for the years 1986 through 1989 arising from his receipt of bribes while working for the State of Illinois.

"Well, Charlie, how do you feel about helping to make the news?" Tony asked, patting his younger colleague on the back.

"It couldn't happen to a nicer guy. I hope the creep gets ten years."

They walked out of the heat into the air conditioned building, crossed the lobby, and caught an elevator to the seventy-sixth floor. As they were riding up, Charlie turned to Tony "I wonder if we could get evidence of Weaver's arrest into the trial?"

Tony thought for a moment. "We probably couldn't get it in as direct evidence, because he hasn't been convicted of anything yet," he said. "But we might be able to get it in as rebuttal evidence if Harrington contends that the department's approval of the Academy means anything. In that case, we may be entitled to show that the department's approval was related to the two TV sets that the Academy gave Weaver. That doesn't really prove our basic case, but it sure as hell takes the Knight in Shining Armor image away from O'Coogan and the Academy." The elevator doors opened, "Yes, let's get that evidence ready to present in trial, but in rebuttal, not our case-in-chief."

As they walked back toward Tony's office, Sid Johnson passed them in the corridor and pulled Tony aside. "Tony, let me tell you what's happening on this

Bill Fremont matter that I mentioned to you out at New Buffalo," he said quietly. "Almost all the younger and mid-range partners are in favor of bringing the Fremont group of five attorneys in from the Cronin firm, but a couple of the old-timers are really resisting it. Do we still have your support, if it comes to a count of hands? You're a key guy on this."

"Absolutely," Tony answered. In the rush of activity in the Dental Academy case, he had almost forgotten about Johnson's proposed merger of the Fremont group into the firm. It was an exciting idea. "Fremont is a first-rate lawyer with a good reputation," Tony said. He'd be a great addition to the firm. What sort of timetable are you looking at?"

"The management committee isn't going to recommend the deal because the old guard's afraid that another strong partner like Fremont might, in the long run, take the control of the firm out of their hands. But a couple of us are determined to bring it before the full firm at our next meeting. It looks like we might have the votes to push it through."

"Great! Well, you've got my support; just keep me advised," Tony responded quietly.

"What was that all about?" Charlie asked as Johnson walked away.

"Oh, I really can't tell you, Charlie; it's partnership business. But I'm sure you'll hear all about it soon enough."

"It wouldn't have anything to do with Bill Fremont

and his group possibly joining the firm, would it?" Charlie asked with a smile.

Tony stopped and turned to him.

"How in hell did you hear about that?"

"Very simple. One of Fremont's associates was a roommate of mine at Duke. A couple of weeks ago he asked me what it was like to work here. We've talked about it a couple of times since then."

Tony laughed as he continued the walk toward his office. "Well, so much for secret negotiations. All right, Charlie, since you know about it, what do you think about bringing them in?"

"I think it's a great idea as long as they bring their business with them - and as long as my old roomie doesn't get paid more than I do when the smoke clears," Charlie answered with a smile.

"Well, those both sound like reasonable conditions. I'll keep them in mind." By then they had reached Tony's office.

"Judy, hold my calls for a few minutes," he said as they walked in.

Tony hung up his suit coat before sitting down. "All right," he began, "we're going to be getting the employment records of Nonno's Health Care, Inc. within ten days, based on the Court's order today. Why don't we simultaneously subpoena the employment records of Lydian Associates, the other outfit that Ellington at the FBI told us about? He thinks they're the end of another laundering pipeline."

"Fine, I'll take care of it," Charlie answered, taking some notes. "While we're at it, I wonder if there are any other companies that O'Coogan controls that we should be looking at?"

"Good point, Charlie. We should check that out. "It'll be a big job, but it would be worth doing. Let's get a group of paralegals -- about a half a dozen should do -- to look through the Secretary of State's list of corporations, making a list of all companies that show William T. O'Coogan as an officer. That's a fairly common name, so they'll have to cross check any companies they find with addresses we already have for our Bill O'Coogan. They should check both foreign and domestic corporations. Tell the paralegals it's a priority project and that we'll need the results in no more than a week."

"Tony, there's a much easier way to get that information," Charlie smirked. "Lexis has all the Secretary of State's corporate records in its data bank. All we have to do is punch in O'Coogan's name and some other data and we'll have a print-out in minutes of all the companies that list him as an officer or director. I'll have Larry do that in our library downstairs. Shouldn't take more than a few minutes. Welcome to the 1990's." Charlie added with a laugh.

"I didn't know you could do that." Tony thought for a moment, "Will the print-out include addresses of the officers? To be sure that we have the right O'Coogan?"

"Sure, if we ask for addresses."

"Well, let's do it; and see what other corporations

list Bill O'Coogan as an officer. And let's see if Lenny Battaglia shows up as an officer of any company as well."

"No problem," Charlie commented as he continued taking notes. "And if Larry runs across any such companies, I should also subpoena their employee records, I assume."

"Absolutely! We may find that there are more than two money-laundering pipelines that O'Coogan runs for the Bruni family into the Chicago area. Wouldn't that be something!"

Tony thought for a moment, there was a loose end out there that troubled him. "There's something else we need to do," he said. If some outfit characters show up on the payroll of any of these companies, which is what we hope will happen, how do we convince the jury that those people are part of organized crime? Think about that."

"Well, some names are pretty obvious," Charlie answered. "If one of them was Angelo Bruni, for example, you wouldn't need any further proof to convince a jury of Chicagoans that we're dealing with organized crime."

"But most of the names we're likely to come up with, guys we may know are mobsters, won't be that well known to the general public. What I'm getting at is that we may need an expert witness. Someone whose credentials will establish him as being knowledgeable on the structure of organized crime in the Chicago area. Someone who can testify in trial that particular people are in fact part of the mob. What do you think?"

"You may be right," Charlie responded. He thought

through the problem which Tony had just posed. "If our main evidence of mob involvement is going to be a list of names that appear on the payroll of some of O'Coogan's companies, we'll need that extra link of proof. The trial is only a month away, we need to get an expert lined up. Someone from the FBI would be ideal, of course. Do you think they'll come out of the closet to help us in the trial?"

"I'm sure they won't. I'll ask the Bureau, but I already know Ellington's answer. He'll decline. We need to come up with someone else; someone with a reputation for integrity who is clearly an expert in this area." Tony stood and looked out the window for a moment. There was a cloudburst over the far south side; it looked like it was moving toward the lake. Suddenly, an idea came to him and he turned back to Charlie. "What about Bill McNulty? He's chaired the Chicago Crime Commission for years, knows more about organized crime in this city than anyone else, and is a highly-respected guy."

"He'd be perfect," Charlie concurred. I've already talked to him about this case. I'll bet he'd be glad to do it."

"Great! Set up a meeting with him, explain the situation, and see if he'll agree to it." Tony began to pace around his office. "And try to reach that investigative reporter in Arizona that Ellington mentioned to us; Chris Anderson, I think that's her name. Since the other end of this pipeline is supposed to be in Arizona, maybe she can help us. See if she'll meet with you early next week. I'll be tied up all week taking depositions in the Consolidated

Steel case, so I'd like you to cover that. Tell her that we're willing to exchange information."

"Okay; I'll see if I can reach her."

"One more thing," Tony added, "We need to have a motion for summary judgment put together, with a strong supporting memo of law. I'll see if Carol can handle that. Her appeal in the Kinshaw case has just been filed so she should have some available time. She knows this area of the law damn well. We should move for summary judgment on all the antitrust counts on the ground that the plaintiffs haven't shown any losses resulting from the ADS' activities. It's worth a shot; if the judge agrees that the Rule of Reason standard applies, she could throw out all the antitrust counts prior to trial. I'll talk to Carol about pulling that together." Tony sat down and scribbled himself a note as he finished talking.

Charlie glanced over the notes on his yellow pad, then looked up. "I hope some of these things work, Tony. Our case is starting to shape up, but we're still awfully short on hard data. We've got less than thirty days left to turn some of our hot tips into admissible evidence that William O'Coogan, Chicago's Citizen of the Year, is a working member of the outfit. We're running out of time. I'm not sure we're going to be able to do it."

"To be completely honest, Charlie," Tony replied quietly, "neither am I."

It was nearing two in the morning when Tony awoke. He heard shuffling downstairs. Noises he couldn't recognize.

"Karen, did you hear that?"

Karen woke up, looking over at him in the bed, still half asleep.

"Karen, I heard something downstairs. Did you hear that?"

"I'm sure it's just Roger," she said scratching her eyes. "You know he's an insomniac. He watches TV in the middle of the night."

"Should I go down and get him?"

"No," she said, her arm around Tony. "Let's give him a few minutes…"

Suddenly there was a scream, it was clearly Roger's, followed by a series of shouts. One of the shouters was an adult man.

Tony shot upright, jumped out of bed and bolted down the stairs followed by Karen. They saw Roger pressed up against a wall in the front hallway, a swarthy, stocky man holding a knife to his throat while another man pointed a gun straight at Tony.

"Leave him alone!" Tony shouted, lunging forward.

The nearest man stepped forward and slammed him hard in the jaw. Tony dropped like a rock to the floor. It took him a few seconds to clear his head. *What the hell is going on?* When he looked up there was the barrel of a pistol pointed in his eye.

"Up against the wall. You too, bitch; get down here," the gunman shouted, waving his .38 at Karen. She hesitated a moment, then came down and stood next to Tony against the wall. The other man, short and wiry with a pocked-marked face continued to hold his knife to Roger's throat.

The front door, Tony could see, had slowly swung open.

The man with the switchblade then smiled and lowered it to Roger's groin. The boy was terrified, his eyes saucer-wide, his hands shaking as he was pushed still harder against the wall. Tony prayed that some unlikely passer-by would see or hear them. The door was wide open now, though the intruders paid it no attention.

"Leave him alone!" Tony shouted again, ignoring the .38 pointed at his face. The intruder was taller and stockier than Tony, with long black slicked-back hair. Tony was desperately trying to figure out what to do. Then he realized something, neither man was masked. They weren't worried about being identified later. *They're going to kill us!*

"We have some business to conduct with you, Jeffries," the younger gunman said with a low growl. "Where are your other kids?"

Before Tony could manage a response, two explosive shots shattered the scene in the hallway. Both intruders collapsed to the ground. Karen lunged forward, grabbed Roger and pulled him into the living room. Tony waited a long moment in shock then stepped carefully over the two lifeless bodies, blood pooling around them on the tile floor. He stared cautiously into the darkness outside, through the door onto the front porch, expecting to see a squad of policemen.

Instead he saw a lone African-American man standing next to a cab in the driveway; *George Torrance*. He was tucking his gun under his belt.

When their eyes met, Torrance gave Tony a salute. “We even now, Cap’n.”

Tony nodded, still in shock and returned a hint of a salute. “Thank you,” he whispered, almost inaudibly. Torrance got into his taxi and drove away, as two Wilmette squad cars, coming from opposite directions, pulled up in front of the Jeffries’ home.

The police carried off the two limp bodies, took Tony’s statement, and swabbed down the blood on the tile floor of the entry hallway. Tony thanked them as they left and walked back to the kitchen. Karen, sitting on the kitchenette bench, was holding her arm tightly around their shaking son. Tony sat down on Roger’s other side, put his arm around his son, overlapping Karen’s and held him just as tightly.

“How are you doing, Rog?” he asked quietly. “That was a hell of an experience to go through. You okay?”

Roger nodded quietly, then looked up at Tony. “Dad, who were those guys? And why did they want to do that to us?”

“It’s this lawsuit that I’m involved in, Rog. The one I’ve mentioned before. It’s gotten ugly and it turns out that the guys on the other side are terrible people, mobsters." Tony paused a moment, holding his son even tighter. "And I'm really sorry its come to this; that they dragged you and the family into it, threatened you like that. But I know it's going to end soon. I'm working with the FBI and we're not going to stop until those guys are all dead or behind bars for a long time."

"The FBI?" Roger asked, his concerns averted, looking up at his dad in awe. "You're working with the FBI?"

"Yes we are, very closely. And it's up to the good guys like us to drive those scumbags out and put them in jail. If good people like us won't fight them, who will? Do you understand?"

"Yeah. Wow, you're working with the FBI! Like on TV? That's really cool Dad." Roger wiped away the trace of tears on his cheeks and gave his dad a guarded smile as Tony pulled him close with a big hug.

"Why don't you sleep with me and mom tonight, Rog," Tony said softly. "We'll be right next to you to keep you safe."

"Thanks, Dad."

"Mom, Dad, what's going on?"

Tony turned quickly and saw three little heads peering at him from the stairs to the second floor.

"It's nothing, kids," Karen responded. "We'll tell you all about it in the morning."

"Is Roger in trouble?" Mark asked, looking at his brother being held tightly by their parents.

"No, not at all," Karen responded with a slight smile

as she rose. “Let’s all go on upstairs and go to bed; you too, Roger and we’ll talk about it in the morning.”

“Okay,” Mark responded, turning and scampering back upstairs. Karen followed, Roger in hand. As she reached the first step, she turned and whispered in a voice as tough as steel, “Tony, that is enough! This has got to stop. Now! Get us out of that goddamn lawsuit!”

Chapter 13

September 16

A dirty beat-up Jeep bounced along the potholed main street of Portobelo, Panama, scattering chickens and small children, leaving behind a dusty wake. Half of the buildings along the road were abandoned; the others looked like they should be. Vine-covered ruins of the old Spanish forts protruded from the jungle above the town.

Portobelo had been founded by the conquistadors in 1597, developed over the next hundred years as the major Spanish Pacific seaport in Central America, and was a key collection point for Spain's fabulous gold pipeline from the New World to the Old. Six forts were built in a crescent surrounding the harbor and its flourishing city. But repeated British sackings in the eighteenth century, coupled with Spain's gradual decline as a Caribbean power, led to Portobelo's corresponding deterioration. By the late twentieth century all that remained were a few hundred people who lived off the sea, a handful of one or two-story buildings that lined the harbor and remnants of countless homes that were being gradually recaptured by the jungle.

Nonetheless, Portobelo retained some assets that were valuable to certain people. It had a post office, a branch of the National Bank of Panama, and, most importantly, American dollars as the local currency. It also still had a sheltered harbor, too shallow for modern cruise ships, but very hospitable to private yachts that occasionally came in from other ports on the Pacific's vast eastern coastline. These attributes led to Portobelo's resurgence in the late 1980's as the nexus of another pipeline of gold. This time, however, the pipeline went not to Spain, but to multiple banks around the world.

The Jeep pulled to a stop in front of the one-story concrete-block bank. Two men got out, the one on the passenger's side, wearing a weathered sombrero and a faded red bandana tied loosely around his neck, carried a large battered briefcase. The driver, similarly attired, but shorter and stockier, carefully scanned the street scene around them before moving around the jeep to join his companion, who was also eyeing the nearby buildings. Both men wore sidearms and sunglasses. Manuel Ortiz and Angel Santiago had come in by boat from San Diego the night before; they knew the routine well. They had been doing this run twice a month for the past four years, even while the Americans were swarming into Panama City to oust the dictator, Colonel Noriega. No one interfered with the sleek sixty-foot yacht that had brought them into the old harbor during the night.

Inside the bank they were immediately escorted to a small private office in the rear, where they met the branch president and a colonel, the local military commander. This room, the president's office, provided privacy as they exchanged perfunctory pleasantries. It was also the only air conditioned room in the building. That was important; it was only nine a.m. but the temperature already exceeded one hundred.

As soon as the office door was shut and the interior shades drawn, Santiago opened the briefcase he was carrying and carefully transferred its contents to the banker's desk. The contents were neatly bound packets of United States' currency, all one-hundred-dollar bills. The bank president sat down and began passing the money through a counting machine while the other three took seats watching in silence. Santiago took off his sunglasses, folded them, and slipped them into his shirt pocket, his eyes never leaving the moving piles of money on the table. He knew exactly how much was there and what he was responsible for. He wanted to make sure that the banker came up with the same count. The banker did; an even ten million. It was two weeks' net income from street sales in the United States, the end-point in Angelo Bruni's cocaine network.

The banker sorted out two stacks of $250,000 each. The first he handed to the colonel, who nodded, putting it into the weather-beaten leather satchel that hung from his left shoulder. The second quickly went into the bankers' top desk drawer which he immediately shut and locked. He gave Ortiz and Santiago a polite smile which they returned. Few words were spoken. The two requisite fees having been paid, it was now time to deal with the bulk of the funds.

Santiago pulled a piece of folded paper from his shirt pocket and handed it to the banker. It contained instructions on where the money should be wired. The paper, damp with sweat was in handwriting that the banker recognized and listed accounts at various banks in the Caribbean, Argentina, Switzerland and South-East Asia, and the amounts to be transferred to each. One of the largest transfers was to the account of the Federal Dental Academy in Chicago. Those funds would be individually transmitted in the names of over four hundred local dentists who were remitting their $6,000 fees to the Academy to enroll in the foreign-dentist prep course, effectively laundering that money as legitimate business income to the Academy. Some local residents would have found that transaction rather amusing had they known about it. There wasn't a single dentist who currently either lived or practiced in Portobelo.

The banker gave Santiago a vaguely worded receipt, and the two couriers left. By noon, $9,500,000 had been deposited in the designated accounts around the world, and one ton of fresh, uncut cocaine was loaded into a hidden section of the yacht's hold in Portobelo's harbor.

If Tony hadn't realized it before, he certainly knew now that he was engaged in a mortal conflict with an enemy that he couldn't see and didn't fully understand. Complaints, restraining orders, injunctions and court sanctions, weapons that Tony had mastered and had successfully used in all his prior disputes, were of little value in this conflict. He had to fight this enemy at two levels; one, in the courts where Tony was confident and comfortable, and secondly, in the back alleys and dark crevices in the minds of evil men, where Tony just didn't know the rules of the game.

In the days following the shootings in his home, Tony took a series of steps to improve his family's safety as much as he could. He had an electronic burglar-alarm system installed, connected directly to the police station. He urged Charlie to do the same. Karen arranged for the kids to get rides to and from school, and she and Tony began adjusting their work schedules to ensure that one of them was always home at the end of the school day. Chief Robinson stepped up the police patrols in their neighborhood, and apologized profusely for his men having missed not only the two intruders, but Torrance as well.

Tony got out the old gun that his dad brought back from World War II. It was a German Walther 7.65 ppk, similar to an American .45. His dad had taken the gun off a Russian officer he killed at the end of the war in one of those little skirmishes with our Great Russian Ally that were never publicized, while both sides were feverishly trying to round up as many German missile and nuclear scientists as they could, or kill them if it appeared they would fall into the others' hands. Hoping that he'd never have to use it, but thankful for his Air Force training, Tony had the gun cleaned and loaded and put in a drawer next to his side of their bed.

Tony was in his office completing the gun registration form that Monday morning, when Charlie rushed in.

"Tony, look at this! I ran O'Coogan's name through Lexis and came up with five more companies that list him as an officer or a director!" Charlie laid a computer printout on Tony's desk. "You know what?" he asked excitedly, "they all have the same address; Suite 21-B, 5401 West Lawrence Avenue. That's the same building as Nonno's office; in fact, it's the adjacent suite. We were looking for a pipeline and we found a main goddamn pumping station!" Charlie stepped back, grinning triumphantly as Tony looked over the list. "One of those companies, you'll notice, is Lydian Associates, which Ellington at the Bureau mentioned to you."

"This is great!" Tony said excitedly, his mind racing through the new possibilities that they had just discovered. Nonno's Health Care, Inc. was first. All the other companies had innocuous names and appeared to be engaged in unrelated businesses. At the bottom of the sheet was one company that had been crossed out. Tony looked up at Charlie, but before he could even ask the question, Charlie provided the answer.

"That last one is O'Coogan's regular place of business, the Francis X. O'Coogan Contracting Company. It has a different near north address. I crossed it out because we already knew about it and it's probably straight. It does numerous government projects and is under a lot of scrutiny. The others, though, counting Nonno's, look as kinky as three-dollar bills, don't you think?"

"Absolutely," Tony responded as he stood. "Let's get subpoenas out as fast as we can. Let's see exactly who each of them has on its payrolls. This should be very interesting!" Tony savored this moment. *All right, O'Coogan, you son of a bitch. We've got you now*. Tony felt that they were very close to a major breakthrough in the case.

"By the way," Charlie said, "I hope that things have calmed down at your house since the other night. That must have been one hell of an experience."

"It sure was. I told the cops everything I know. They found Torrance, interviewed him, and let him go. There was no reason to hold him. He probably saved our whole family from being slaughtered, and his gun was registered."

"That's getting a little dicey, Tony. Be careful."

"I'm trying to be. But Karen hasn't been the same since it happened. She's nervous as hell. This thing is really getting to her."

Charlie began picking up the documents he had dropped on Tony's desk, "Oh yes," he added, "I almost forgot. I've made arrangements to meet that Arizona reporter Chris Anderson, and her editor tomorrow in Scottsdale. They were reluctant to talk to us at first; said they wanted to think about it. She called back about an hour ago and we set up an appointment. I'm flying out there this afternoon. I hope it'll be worthwhile."

"So do I, Charlie. We don't really have much of a perspective on that end of this whole business. I'd like to go myself, but these depositions in the Consolidated Steel case, along with everything else, are eating up my whole week."

Tony's phone rang. He picked it up, listened, made a few comments, then put it down. "See what I mean? Two of Consolidated's officers, whose deps are being taken tomorrow, will be here to go over their testimony in fifteen minutes. And Barton Thompson, who I speak to about once a year, insists on talking to me right now. Give me a break."

It was long past the point, however, when breaks were being given or received.

Tony was escorted into Barton Thompson's office a few minutes later by Thompson's secretary, Helen Flemming. "Miss Flemming," now in her eighties, had been with the firm since 1941 and had worked for Barton Thompson since her prior boss Nathan Wilson died ten years earlier. When Thompson assumed leadership of the firm on Wilson's death, she was one of the accoutrements that came with the office.

Barton Thompson was a tall patrician in his early seventies. He was seated behind his polished mahogany desk in a tailor-made dark-blue pin-striped suit when Tony entered. The desk was bare except for an ivory-and-gold desk set and a single sheet of white paper. Neither Thompson's demeanor nor the decor of his office was designed to set a person at ease. Tony had never worked directly for Thompson and always found him to be aloof and distant.

"Good afternoon, Anthony." There was a distinct chill in Thompson's voice.

"Good afternoon, Barton. What can I do for you?" Tony took one of the black leather seats across from Thompson's desk, without waiting for an offer that he sensed might not come.

"Something has come up, Anthony, that troubles me a great deal. One of my fellow directors at the First National Bank asked me the other day if I was aware of the personal attack that our firm has made against Bill O'Coogan. O'Coogan is a close friend of his. I was embarrassed, of course, because I didn't know what he was talking about, and because Bill O'Coogan is a highly-respected man in this city. I said that I would look into the matter. When I did, I found that you're the attorney involved. What do you have to say for yourself?"

"Barton, I'm simply defending a defamation suit that O'Coogan brought against one of Henry Gilchrist's clients. Henry asked me, personally, to handle the defense. That's what I'm doing."

"I've discussed the matter with Henry. He assured me that he never authorized you to level a vicious personal attack on O'Coogan, which is what I understand you've done. There's a difference, Anthony, between defending a libel or slander suit, and aggravating the situation by defaming the plaintiff even more. From what I've been told, you've crossed that line."

Tony was shocked. "Barton, believe me, I've only done what was necessary to defend a very difficult suit. To win this case, we have to prove that William O'Coogan has a rather unsavory background. I think that we're going to be able to do that at trial."

"You didn't run this by the management committee before you launched your attack on O'Coogan, did you?" Thompson was making a statement, not asking a question.

"Why, no. Of course not. Henry told me to handle the case as I saw fit. We don't usually ask for the management committee's approval of litigation tactics."

"This is not a usual case, Anthony. You've attacked a highly respected member of this community, employing unscrupulous tactics in the process. You've put the firm in an embarrassing position."

"Barton, I'm sorry you feel that way. Everything we've done has been not only proper but necessary. Besides, I'm optimistic that we'll win our case in trial by proving that Bill O'Coogan actually is involved in organized crime."

Thompson snorted and shook his head. "That's preposterous," he said under his breath. After a moment he continued, "Well, I suppose it's too late to undo what's already been done."

He looked at Tony coldly. "There's an old saying,

Anthony. 'If you strike at a king, be sure to kill him with the first blow.' We simply cannot have partners in this firm launching unwarranted personal attacks against prominent local businessmen. If at trial you can't prove these distasteful allegations that you've made against Bill O'Coogan, this firm will certainly be embarrassed and some of us may want to reconsider whether we want you to remain as our partner."

Further argument was useless, Tony knew. Barton Thompson had made up his mind.

When Tony left he was furious; angry at Thompson, and at Gilchrist too for not supporting him. He was shocked to see the extent of O'Coogan's influence; he'd badly undercut Tony in his own firm! Tony felt that he was under siege from every direction.

It was absolutely essential now, for a whole new reason, that Tony win the trial.

Chapter 14

September 17

Charlie arranged to meet Chris Anderson and her editor, Walt Landes, in the lobby of the Camelback Inn in Tucson, where he'd be staying. The Camelback had been highly recommended by the law firm's travel agent and was convenient to Anderson and Landes. It was a good recommendation.

He flew down via Trans-American, arriving in Tucson at 5:30 in the afternoon. It was hotter than he expected, in the mid-nineties. The moment he stepped out of the terminal into the blistering heat he realized that his business suit, white shirt and tie were completely inappropriate. Also inappropriate was any lingering outside. Charlie quickly learned that the principal rule of survival in Arizona was to spend as much time as possible in air-conditioned environments.

He grabbed the first cab in line, threw in his bag and

pulled the door shut behind him. He quickly noted one fundamental difference between taxis in Tucson and Chicago. The cab was comfortably cool. In Chicago, no matter how hot it was, few taxis had functioning air conditioners, or so the drivers would claim, but in reality, many of them were just trying to save a buck or two a day on gas. In Tucson, a cab with non-functioning air conditioning was a non-functioning cab.

When he checked into the Camelback, the desk clerk advised him that he had visitors. Mr. Landes and Ms. Anderson were in the bar. He also commented that it was unusually warm for this time of year; he didn't need to apologize. Charlie took his bag up to his room, changed into more casual clothing and quickly headed back downstairs to join them.

Not too bad, Charlie thought as he crossed the comfortably cool lobby. Scattered groups of deeply tanned guests, some carrying iced drinks, drifted leisurely around him. Somewhere in the distance was the sound of softly tumbling water. He suddenly realized that he was striding as though he were trying to beat a light on LaSalle, took a breath and eased back into a stroll. *No, not too bad at all. I could learn to live with this*.

When Charlie walked into the lounge at the far end of the lobby he noticed three white-haired ladies seated at one table, an elderly couple at another, and a twenty-something young man sitting at the bar hustling a red-haired bar tender. In the corner of the room adjacent to the bar a rather serious-looking man in his forties was seated with an attractive younger woman. That had to be them.

Charlie walked over to their table wondering exactly what he would say. Before he could mutter a word, the man rose and extended his hand, "I'm Walt Landes; you must be Charlie Dickenson."

"Yes, that's me, very pleased to meet you. So you must be Chris Anderson," he added, turning to the young woman.

"My pleasure, Mr. Dickenson," she responded with a smile. "But why don't we drop the formalities and just be Walt and Chris and Charlie? Have a seat, Charlie."

Charlie dropped himself into the third padded seat at the cocktail table and ordered a beer from the bartender when she managed to pry herself away from the young hustler. The three tablemates exchanged small talk about the weather and travel for a few minutes, kicking each other's tires.

Walt Landes was thin, graying at the temples with a leathery tan complexion. His shirt was open collared and, like all the other men there, he wore no suit jacket or sport coat. He was an Arizona native, Charlie learned, and pictured himself as a gentleman cowboy, spending as much time as he could outdoors. He had worked for newspapers in Arizona all his adult life, and had risen to the editorship of the *Phoenix Sun* seven years ago. The *Sun* maintained an office in Tucson, where Walt spent one or two days a week.

Chris Anderson on the other hand, was a transplanted

mid-westerner with a degree in journalism from the University of Iowa, who, she said, joined the *Sun's* Tucson office five years earlier because it was the best newspaper job she could find. She progressed rapidly through several positions at the paper and had been the *Sun's* chief investigative reporter for the past six months. Her blond hair was cropped short and she was dressed in a light-blue skirt and blouse, unbuttoned just far enough to be interesting.

"We weren't sure we should meet with you, Charlie," Walt said, turning the conversation more serious. Until Chris spoke to a friend of ours at the FBI here in town. He confirmed that Ellington had given you her name. It appears that we're both working on similar projects," he paused a moment, then continued with a slight smile, "as well as both having friends at the Bureau."

"We're basically interested in exchanging information with you," Charlie responded. "But let me begin by telling you what our case is all about, and what we're trying to do." The journalists nodded and leaned back.

Charlie gave them a concise overview of the facts surrounding the lawsuit, careful not to divulge any particular facts that he might want to barter later for information from the reporters. He concluded by mentioning that since the trial was only a month away, whatever additional evidence he and Tony, his boss, hoped to utilize had to be developed soon.

"That's fascinating stuff," Chris Anderson said. She took a sip of her margarita and leaned forward. "You guys have bitten off quite a piece. Most lawyers I know, who aren't prosecutors, would have backed off this kind of a confrontation." She paused, her light-blue eyes focused on Charlie. "Aren't you worried about your safety? Or your family's safety?"

"Not me. But I don't have a family to be worried about. I'm a bachelor," Charlie replied with a hint of a smile. "Hey, this is a very exciting case. As far as I know, it might be the biggest case of my life. Antitrust violations, libel, murdered witnesses, bribery of state officials, the mob, a major trial coming up; the most fascinating things in the practice of law are all wrapped up in this one case; and it's not over yet! It's hardly what I anticipated when I joined a blue-stocking Chicago firm, but it sure as hell is interesting!" He took a sip of his beer, "It's a little different, though, for my boss, Tony Jeffries. He's got a wife and four kids and they've already had some serious threats leveled at them. Frankly, he's more of a target than I might be, after all, he's calling the shots. But Tony gave it a lot of thought early on, and decided that he wasn't going to back off. He's taken some precautions to protect his family; but deep down inside I think he's worried sick. I honestly don't feel there's much danger to myself personally. Tony's the one who's put himself in the bullseye and, if anyone's at risk it's him, not me. At least I don't think so."

Charlie stared at his beer for a moment, then put down his glass. Walt and Chris were listening intently. "He's sure that organized crime is moving into dentistry right now with its mob-controlled dental plans, kickbacks, money laundering, and who knows what else, and by the luck of the draw he's the one person who's in a position to block them - or step back and quietly acquiesce. And he's decided that he's going to fight. Once he made that decision, he's gone after them with a vengeance. I think Tony feels now that he's riding a tiger on a wild dash through the jungle, not sure where he's going, but afraid to let go."

"So you both view this case involving the mob as a grand adventure, for one reason or another?" Chris asked with a smile.

"Something like that," Charlie answered, returning her smile. "But tell me what *you're* up to. I understand your paper is investigating organized crime in Arizona, with the idea of running a series sometime soon. What can you tell me that might relate to our case?"

"This is something that we've been concerned about ever since I became editor of the *Sun* seven years ago," Walt replied. "Things have been getting worse and worse here in Arizona. After Chris was named our chief investigative reporter six months ago, we decided that she'd conduct an in-depth investigation of organized crime here and that the paper would run a hard-hitting series of articles based on her findings. Chris has been working on it out of our office here and collecting data from every conceivable source. We plan to run our series later this fall. In fact," he said, rubbing his chin, "come to think of it, we might want our series to coincide with your trial, especially if you'll be putting in evidence that the plaintiffs in your case are working with mob figures in Arizona."

"Well, that's something that you can influence, Walt," Charlie responded. "Just give us some good evidence that we can use to tie the pieces together, and we'll make sure it's presented to the Court. Hell, you could even have your article written in advance. It'll probably get picked up by the Chicago press and read by some of our prospective jurors. That certainly wouldn't hurt," he added with a smile. "There are all kinds of possibilities here."

"There sure are," Walt said, half to himself. "Chris, why don't you give Charlie an overview of what you've developed to date. By the way, I should warn you, Charlie, that Chris has become the world's greatest authority on Angelo Bruni, our local Mafia Don. Over the past few months she's read everything ever written about the man. She probably knows more about him now than his mother does."

"That's no trick," Chris retorted. "His mother died ten years ago."

"Quit showing off, just tell Charlie what you've learned."

"Sure," Chris replied. "By way of background, Angelo Bruni was exiled from New York about twenty years ago as a result of a power struggle between the major Mafia families. They didn't kill him because he was a native-born Mafioso, plus his death would have triggered a massive gang war. So, he was allowed to retire here in Arizona, where he had some old friends, on the condition that he stay out of east coast affairs forever. He agreed;

but what choice did he have? When he arrived in Tucson he brought only two things of value; a suitcase full of money, reputed to be about four hundred thousand dollars and his lawyer, Joseph Augustino. Augustino is one of those lawyers who has only one client. He was, and still is, the consigliere of the Bruni family."

"Do you mind if I take a few notes?" Charlie interrupted, pulling a folded piece of paper from his back pocket.

"Of course not."

Before Chris could continue, Walt interrupted. "If you don't mind, I'm going to have to run. I wanted to meet you, Charlie, to get a sense of who you were and where you folks were coming from. Frankly, I'm satisfied now that we're all on the same side and that we can both benefit from exchanging information. I'll leave the rest up to you and Chris to work out. Besides, if I don't leave soon I'm going to be late for my own anniversary party, which would probably not be a good idea." Walt rose, shook hands with Charlie, and left.

"Walt's a great guy," Chris volunteered after he had left.

"He sure seems like it. But finish telling me about Bruni. The story was just getting interesting."

"Sure! Well, at first, after he came to Arizona, Bruni got involved in just a couple of real estate developments near Tucson. They were organized by Augustino and financed by a major union pension fund. Bruni has had friends in the unions for years. These were the kind of developments where retiring couples in the northeast would be conned into buying worthless desert tracts. I guess that naive people in the Rust-Belt will never learn that you can be only a 'fifteen minute drive from beautiful downtown Tucson,' as the ads would say, and be in the middle of the Mohave Desert."

Chris took a sip of her margarita, before continuing. "During that same period of time a number of Bruni's old associates and relatives moved down to Tucson from the New York area. Not all at once, but apparently as they were called by the old don. In any event, within a couple of years, and after running through a dozen or so fronting companies, Bruni had rebuilt his war chest and his organization. In the process he arranged for some local pols to make a few bucks, so he had some new political allies here. In 1979 he opened a disco on the north side of town; one of his lieutenants managed it. Tucson had never seen anything like it before; it instantly became the hottest place in town. No pun intended," she interjected with a wink.

Charlie returned her smile, leaning back. The lounge was becoming crowded now, and he glanced around to make sure no one was within earshot.

"Within a year he opened a second club on the east side of Tucson," she continued, lowering her voice. "It was just as successful. The first one catered to the convention business, while the second was aimed at yuppies. With access to that clientele, it was easy for Bruni to move into drugs and prostitution in a big way. His prostitution operation had to go underground in 1982 after a local mini-scandal, but his drug network continued to expand. He made arrangements with some of the Mexican cartels, and is now supposed to be one of the biggest drug operators in the world. He was the classic right man in the right place at the right time. When the Turkish and Middle Eastern drug networks were broken up a few years ago, Bruni filled the gap immediately with his Latin American connections. Today he controls the major drug pipeline from Columbia and Panama into the United States. With the money he's generating, doling it out carefully to a number of his cronies and their lieutenants, he's been able to buy back a major position in the mob."

"Sounds like he's a candidate for Comeback of the Year," Charlie interjected.

"Comeback of the Decade might be more accurate. One of the main reasons he's done so well is that he's totally ruthless. He demands absolute loyalty from his lieutenants and soldiers. I've compiled a list of fourteen of Bruni's people who have been murdered or who have disappeared in the past few years. In every case, they died or vanished after questioning Bruni's decisions or responding to contacts from people looking into his activities. All of them worked for him or one of his companies before their untimely deaths."

"Do you intend to publish that list in your series of articles?"

"Absolutely!" Chris nodded vigorously. "The publication of that list, the photos of the victims, coupled with my narrative of the facts surrounding each of their deaths will be one of the major articles in the series."

Charlie took a deep swig of his beer, emptying his glass. He looked at the attractive young woman sitting across from him and asked her the same question she had asked him earlier, "Aren't you worried about your safety, or your family's, if you print those articles, and particularly, that last piece?"

"I can answer that question at two levels, the intellectual and the emotional. Let me give you my intellectual answer first. I've heard from several people that Bruni adheres to the old Mafia sense of justice, based on the fact that loyalty is the greatest virtue in his eyes. If you're someone like a cop or a lawyer or a reporter working against him, just doing your job, he'll respect your loyalty to your superiors and won't attack you personally. But if you've dealt with him, or have been part of his organization, and turn against him, or cross him in any way, well, God help you."

"But if that's true," Charlie interjected, "why has my boss had so many threats against him? He's just doing his job."

"I'd guess that's because your antagonist so far hasn't been Angelo Bruni, but William O'Coogan, and probably some lower-level thugs he's enlisted. O'Coogan is just as ruthless as Bruni but doesn't share the old don's peculiar values. At least that's my guess." Chris took a sip of her drink. "Plus O'Coogan isn't really part of the Bruni family; he's more of an independent contractor working with

Bruni. I'll bet that Bruni doesn't know much at all about O'Coogan's libel suit against your clients."

She lit another cigarette. "So that's my intellectual response," Chris continued, "I'm not sure that I'm really in that much personal danger if I print my series on the mob. After all, I'm just doing my job."

"You said you had an emotional response to my question, too. What is it?"

"Actually, I find it exciting, like you do; I don't have any family to worry about, so what the hell."

Charlie considered changing the subject to something of a more personal nature. He was finding Chris Anderson to be a fascinating woman. He took a sip of the new Bud that had been brought but thought they should finish discussing their business first. "How does our plaintiff, William O'Coogan, fit into Bruni's operations? Do you know?" he asked.

"I understand that he's set up some system of laundering Bruni's narcotics income, and distributing it throughout the world, as directed. But I've never heard any details beyond that," she answered.

"What about Battaglia; Leonard Battaglia?"

"His family is from Naples, not Sicily, so he's not likely to ever be in Bruni's inner family, but he's considered a young man on the rise. He's doing some work for O'Coogan right now, but he's really part of Bruni's organization and he's done a couple of 'special projects' for the mob in the past that have placed him in good stead. I can't tell you anything beyond that, except that he's known to have a real mean streak."

"We can certainly verify that," Charlie responded. "Let me tell you what we know about O'Coogan and Battaglia. We're confident that they launder the money Bruni raises from his drug operations, and channel that money to mob figures all over the country as ostensibly legitimate income. That's one thing that we're in the process of trying to prove. In fact, we think we've uncovered one or more companies that operate pipelines of income into the Chicago area. We may run across others too."

"What corporations are you looking at?"

"Nonno's Health Care, Inc. and Lydian Associates. Plus, we've identified some other corporations O'Coogan controls in Illinois that might be conduits as well." By now Charlie had decided that there was no need to hold back any information. He added, "Are you aware of any other companies that Bruni controls here that might have a bearing on our case?"

Chris had been taking notes, apparently at least one of the corporate names Charlie had mentioned were new to her. After a moment she looked up and replied, "Well, one of Bruni's companies that has been awfully active around here the last few months is one that you mentioned, Nonno's Health Care. They administer the union dental programs that some employers in this area have agreed to sign on to. A couple of Bruni's lieutenants run it. In fact, Bruni's longtime body guard, a guy named Rocco Napoli, is listed as its president. What a joke! If he knows anything about health or dental insurance then I'm the Queen of Sheeba. But beyond that, I don't know a thing."

"It sounds like there might be a direct tie-in with O'Coogan's Dental Academy," Charlie responded. "You don't have a list of the company's other officers and directors, do you?"

"No, but you shouldn't have any trouble getting that information from the Secretary of State's office downtown. They'll be open tomorrow."

Charlie leaned forward, looking at his attractive companion for a moment. "Chris, I don't have any plans for the evening. I'd love to buy you dinner."

"I'd like that," she replied. "I don't have any plans either." She leaned across the table as she spoke and put her hand lightly on Charlie's. It was a casual gesture, but it told him a great deal. He sensed that it was going to be a very interesting evening.

Charlie was wakened the next morning by a gentle kiss. He opened his eyes, there was Chris sitting next to him on the edge of the bed, buttoning up her blouse.

"Yo, sleepyhead," she whispered. "It's eight o'clock. I've got to get going. I want to stop at my apartment and change before I go to the office." She leaned forward and kissed Charlie again gently. "I had a wonderful evening… and night. Thanks for everything."

"Thank *you*; I had a great time too." Charlie reached out and lightly touched Chris' cheek. "I'll be in touch soon."

“I hope so.” Chris smiled again, stood up, and left the room without another word.

Charlie laid in bed for a minute or two, smiling and staring at the ceiling. He was savoring the lingering suggestion of Chris’ perfume and his memories of the previous night. Finally, he decided that he’d better get up and get going.

He was washed, shaved, and packed within a half hour, then was downstairs in the Camelback’s coffee shop ordering breakfast. Two eggs over easy with white toast and orange juice. And coffee; several cups of coffee.

He thumbed through the *Phoenix Sun* while he ate. Most of the articles he just skimmed over; City Council disputes, an abandoned building fire on the east side of town, and the usual body-bag reporting. The only stories that held any interest for him were on the third page; a train wreck in India killing several dozen people; a California wild-fire that threatened three towns and the latest poll showing Senator Joshua Nightingale taking the lead in the race for the Democratic presidential nomination.

As he tried to read, though, Charlie’s thoughts kept drifting back to Chris. There was no question about it; she was the most exciting, the most sensuous woman he’d ever met. He knew he’d be seeing her again.

He checked out, picked up the rental car he’d reserved and drove into downtown Tucson. He found the secretary of state’s office without any difficulty. Once inside, he asked a woman at the counter if he could take a look at the corporate records of Nonno's Health Care, Inc. the company Chris had mentioned. After a short wait, he had a microfiche card and was directed toward the bank of viewing machines on a nearby counter.

It took him a few minutes to figure out how to use the old-fashioned machine, and how to find records of any particular company on the data card he had been given, but he finally managed it. The most recent annual report of Nonno's Health Care, Inc. listed Rocco Napoli as the corporation's president, just as Chris had said, with Joseph Augustino as the secretary and registered agent. That wasn't surprising since he was Angelo Bruni's attorney, and more importantly, consigliere of the Bruni Family. Two names that Charlie didn't recognize, were listed as the other company officers and directors. What did this prove? Nothing.

Charlie scrolled back through the corporation's annual reports and various other records in the secretary of state's file, but nothing of value appeared. Finally, he was all the way back to the original Articles of Incorporation, which had been filed over two years ago. Then he saw it. The Articles of Incorporation were signed by the company's two initial incorporators: Joseph Augustino, whose signature Charlie had expected to see, and someone whose name Charlie hadn't expected to see; *Leonard Battaglia.*

There was no doubt about Battaglia's signature, Charlie recognized it from the Dental Academy records he'd reviewed earlier. He leaned back and smiled.

Charlie had certified copies made of all the corporation's records, closed them in his briefcase and left. Tony would be very pleased. They finally had found compelling evidence linking O'Coogan's Dental Academy with the Angelo Bruni Mafia organization. Lenny Battaglia was the link they'd been searching for.

Chapter 15

September 23

The phone on Tony's desk buzzed, breaking his concentration as he pored over the corporate records that Charlie had brought back from Arizona.

"Tony Jeffries," he announced briskly.

"Jeffries, this is Jack Malone. I'm afraid I've got some bad news for you."

"Oh, what is it?" Tony's mind was racing, trying to place the name. Suddenly, he recalled; Malone was the weaselly local attorney for Nonno's Health Care, Inc..

"There was a terrible fire last night out in the 5400 block of Lawrence Avenue. The building was burned to the ground. All my clients' records were destroyed. I'm afraid that we're not going to be able to respond to your subpoena for my client's corporate records."

"Son of a bitch!"

"That's the same way my client feels about it," Malone

replied flatly. "Terrible loss. By the way, I also represent some other clients who had offices in that building whose records you recently subpoenaed, five of them I believe. Same thing applies to them. All their records have been destroyed."

Anger surged through Tony. He stood up, squeezing the phone in his right hand, and clenching his left into a fist. "I don't suppose any of your clients maintained any duplicate records anywhere else."

"No. They probably should have, but they didn't. But that's the way a lot of these small businesses operate. Sorry."

"Your office was in that building, as I recall," Tony snapped. "Did you lose all your files and records too?"

"Surprisingly enough, no. As luck would have it, I moved my office down the street just a couple of days ago. It was very fortuitous."

"Fortuitous, bullshit! You tell your clients they're not going to get away with this!"

"Why, counselor, I don't know what you mean," Malone unctuously replied. "My clients have suffered a terrible loss."

"You'll be hearing from us!" Tony shouted as he slammed the phone into its cradle. He sat down, trying to control his anger as he decided what to do. He was as mad at himself, he should have anticipated this, done something to prevent it. He picked up his phone and punched in Charlie's intercom number. "Charlie, we've got a new problem in the Dental Academy case. Are you free now?"

Within a few minutes, Charlie appeared in Tony's office and when he heard the news, he shared Tony's outrage.

"I'll tell you one thing that we should do," he offered. "Confirm that the building was really destroyed with nothing salvageable. Why not call Wysocki, have him check it out? He lives near there."

"Good idea. Let's see if we can get him right now." Tony punched in a number and the speaker button on his phone. Luckily, Wysocki was home and they were able to quickly fill him in on what had happened. Tony asked him to drive by the site of the fire on Lawrence Avenue as soon as possible, and let them know how it looked.

"I'll get right on it," Wysocki promised. "I'll take Polaroid photos of whatever I find and bring them to you by late afternoon. I'll bring the official police and fire reports too."

"There has to be some other way to find out who's been on the payroll of those companies," Tony said after he hung up, trying to cut through his anger and sort out their alternatives. "There must be some other records somewhere that we can get our hands on."

"1 doubt it, Tony. Even if they kept duplicates somewhere else, they'd get rid of them now. They'd say everything was destroyed in the fire. These guys may be bastards, but they're not stupid."

Tony got up and began pacing around the office, mulling over what Charlie had just said. "They'd pay everyone with checks," he said half to himself. "They'd have to, because the whole purpose of the operation is to legitimize cash flow to guys in the mob. Most banks keep photos of checks written on their accounts." His mind was racing now. "So, if we could find out which banks those companies use, we could subpoena the banks' records, and get the same information through the back door."

"Great idea! But how do we find that out?" Charlie responded. "You don't think they'd use the same bank the Dental Academy uses, do you? We know it from the discovery. It's the Adams National Bank."

"No. You're right. They wouldn't be using the Adams. The Dental Academy's bank accounts were originally set up by Rolf Sorenson, long before O'Coogan and Battaglia appeared on the scene and as far as we can tell that hasn't been changed. O'Coogan has got to have a friendly bank somewhere else that he'd be using for Nonno's and the other companies involved in his laundering operation. But we can't just assume that. Let's have a subpoena served on the Adams National Bank for any accounts in the name of those six companies to see if we catch anything. I'll be surprised if we do, but it's worth trying."

Tony stopped pacing, paused, then added, "I'll tell you something else to check. Didn't you tell me that Nonno's Health Care, Inc. paid the latest real estate taxes on the building the Dental Academy leases?"

"I sure did," Charlie answered. "That's how we first learned about Nonno's; through the county treasurer's records."

"That's what I thought, Charlie, the county treasurer keeps photocopies of all checks that are used to pay real estate taxes. Why don't you run over there and get a copy of the latest tax payment check; let's see what bank it was written on. If you slip Max behind the counter twenty bucks, he'll get you a copy while you wait."

"I'll do that right now," Charlie said rising to leave. He suddenly stopped, then added, "We might have another lead, come to think about it. Do you remember when the case began heating up, and Jake suggested that I have my secretary or someone else send a small check to the Academy with a note thanking them for the petty cash advance?"

"Sure I do. Did you do it?"

"Yes, I asked Betty to do that, but I never followed through to find out if her check was cashed. She lives here in the city, up in Rogers Park. I'll send her home in a cab right now to find that check, and bring it back. Let's see where it was cashed."

"Good, let's get going on both those items. In the meantime, I'll have Judy prepare two subpoenas for copies of all checks written on the accounts of any of those six companies; both sides of all checks. One subpoena will be directed to the Adams and the other recipient will be left blank for the time being. We'll do the same to any other banks whose names come up. I want to be able to serve those first two today, with the responses due in no more than two business days."

With their plans agreed on, Charlie left. He stopped on his floor to speak with Betty for a few moments, gave her two twenties for cab fare, then took the elevator down to head over to the county treasurer's office.

While Judy was preparing the two subpoenas, Tony's phone buzzed. It was Wysocki, calling from West Lawrence Avenue. It was true, he reported, the entire building at 5401 had burned to the ground. There were still a few firemen on the scene who confirmed that nothing had been salvaged. They also told him that the fire had broken out in three places simultaneously with arson strongly suspected.

Charlie was back from the County Building in less than an hour. He walked into Tony's office with a wide grin on his face. "This is it!" he said, presenting Xeroxed copies of the front and back of a check. "This is the check that Nonno's Health Care, Inc. issued to pay the real-estate taxes on the Dental Academy's building on Lake Street. It was written on the Logan Square State Bank."

"Great!" Tony quickly grabbed the copy and gave it a once-over. The check was signed by William T. O'Coogan.

While Tony was examining it, Betty rushed into the room, back from her apartment in Rogers Park with the $23.00 check she had mailed to the Dental Academy in August. She handed it to her boss along with some change. Charlie looked at both sides of the check, smiled, and handed it to Tony without saying a word. It had been cashed at the Logan Square State Bank and was endorsed by Leonard Battaglia.

"This confirms it!" Tony exulted. "We've got another bank!" He called Judy back into his office and told her to direct the second subpoena to the Logan Square State

Bank and arrange to have both subpoenas issued and served that day.

"Betty, you're a sweetheart," Charlie told his secretary. "I owe you a lunch for that."

"Only a lunch? I'd think it'd be worth at least a dinner," she replied with a wink.

Charlie smiled. "Talk to you later about that."

"Charlie, do you know what else that second check tells us?" Tony asked.

"Sure. It tells us that Lenny Battaglia is a crook through and through; he was stealing from his own boss."

"Exactly! He didn't deposit or cash Betty's check at the Dental Academy's bank, Adams National. Instead, he cashed it at Logan Square and just pocketed the money. He probably figured that since the twenty-three bucks didn't appear anywhere on the Academy's books, no one would ever know the difference. Logan Square cashed it for him as president of the Academy because he's such a good customer and they're used to making accommodations for him. Besides, it's such a small amount."

"I'll bet it isn't the first time that brother Lenny filched money from the Academy," Charlie commented with a smile. "It would be interesting if we could develop that."

"It sure would be; but I doubt we've got enough time to start any new lines of investigation. We'll be damn lucky to finish what we already have going before the close of discovery."

The subpoenas required both banks to produce all the specified records in their possession by the close of business the following Wednesday, September 25th. Both banks complied, although in dramatically different fashions.

The Adams National Bank sent a one-page letter by messenger to Tony stating that they had no accounts in the name of any of the six listed corporations, and therefore had nothing to produce.

The Logan Square Bank, on the other hand, had a vice president call Tony about noon that day. He said that they were in the process of complying with the subpoena but insisted that they be compensated for their Xeroxing costs, since there were so many documents involved. Tony agreed that his firm would reimburse the bank for its costs; a messenger would deliver a Wilson, Thompson & Gilchrist check for the agreed upon amount of $240 to the bank that afternoon and would pick up the bank's package of account records and check copies in exchange.

When the messenger delivered the package a little after five that afternoon, Tony and Charlie were eagerly waiting in the conference room A along with Jake Wysocki whom they'd asked to join them, knowing he might recognize some names they wouldn't. They had with them the portfolio that Charlie assembled earlier, with data on all the known mob figures in the Chicago area.

Tony tore open the package like it was a kid's first present on Christmas morning. Inside were six bundles of xeroxed checks, one for each corporation, each wrapped in copies of the monthly statements for that account. This was what they had been searching for. Tony quickly located the bundle for Nonno's Health Care, Inc., put aside the monthly statements, and began flipping through the individual checks. Charlie and Jake watched over his shoulders.

The first check was payable to Northern Illinois Gas Company for $112.00; the second, to Illinois Bell for $78.24, the third to Commonwealth Edison for $98.40. A sudden fear seized Tony: *We're wrong; we don't have anything*. He flipped over the next check; it was payable to Angelo Rosanova for $10,000. Rosanova was a major old-line mob boss in Chicago. "Look at this," Tony whispered, as a sense of triumph swept over him.

"That's it! That's exactly what we've been looking for," Charlie responded. Old Jake just smiled and nodded.

Tony put Nonno's checks on the table and began spreading them out. Almost all of the rest of them were payable to known mob figures. The ones in round numbers, like the check to Rosanova, had the notation "loan repayment" in the lower-left corner. Most of the rest were in odd amounts, with the notation "net wages," with similar checks being issued every two weeks. While Tony was thus occupied, Charlie and Jake opened up two other packets of checks and began spreading them out. The patterns were the same, most of the checks were payable to major mob figures and their lieutenants in the Chicago area; only a few to ostensibly legitimate suppliers like AT&T.

"Let's organize these on the basis of the recipients," Tony directed. "That way we'll be able to see how much each person received all together. It looks like most of these guys were paid as full-time employees by each of these companies.

Tony was flipping through a series of checks when he stopped suddenly. "Look at this," he said. "A check for $250,000 from Lydian Associates to the Land of Liberty Foundation of New York. What the hell is that?" Charlie and Jake just shrugged. Tony thought for a moment, "Charlie, why don't you have Larry go down to the library and run Land of Liberty Foundation of New York through Lexis. Let's see what it's all about."

"Fine," Charlie said. He put down his coffee and left. Tony and Jake continued to sort checks. Within fifteen minutes, Charlie had returned.

"That damn foundation doesn't show up anywhere!" he said. "It's not listed by the IRS as a tax-exempt foundation. Lexis comes up a complete blank."

"That's really surprising," Tony responded. "We'll have to figure that out after we sort out all the checks. Why don't you grab a packet and give us a hand."

They kept on examining and organizing the checks well into the evening, there was little talk. At eight Tony sent out for a pizza. They were all fascinated by the enormity of what they had uncovered. After a while Tony brought in an adding machine and began running tapes which he paper-clipped to each stack of check copies. They finished around ten, exhausted.

Tony walked around the table to one of the larger stacks and picked it up, “Are you gentlemen aware that in the past four years, Angelo Rosanova has received from these six companies, presumably as loan repayments, the grand total of $843,000?”

“That’s incredible,” Charlie said softly.

“Or that Al Pontico, Lenny Battaglia’s uncle, received an even $600,000?” Tony continued picking up another stack of checks.

“With that kind of money you’d think he’d buy some decent clothes,” Wysocki interjected. “The guy dresses like a bum, always has.”

Tony leaned forward and put both his hands on the table, surveying the stacks of checks that covered it. “In fact,” he went on, “there are about a dozen men here who each received more than a million dollars through this network over the past four years. Plus dozens who received lesser amounts. This is one hell of a distribution system!”

Charlie thumbed through the many smaller stacks that were clustered at the end of the table and picked one up. “Here’s something interesting,” he said. “State Senator Richard Van Devitt of downstate Benton has been on the payroll of Lydian Associates for the past year, drawing two thousand bucks a month. That should interest a lot of people.”

“It sure should,” Tony responded. “Especially since he’s chairman of the state Liquor Control Commission. Gentlemen, we’ve got a gold mine of information here, we haven't even begun to analyze it. Think what the feds can do with this. For one thing, they'll be able to tell where every mob figure in the Midwest maintains his personal bank account. I'm going to let Ellington at the Bureau know that we have this data. Let's see if he's interested in trading us additional evidence that we can use in trial." Tony was exhilarated by what they had uncovered.

"Have you noticed all the payments to Land of Liberty?" Charlie asked. "A quarter of a million almost every month. We should look into that. It looks like they were all cashed through Chase in New York."

"Good point, Charlie. Let's get a subpoena issued to Chase. Talk to Judy tomorrow about that. Let's find out who cashed all those checks, what that Foundation is all about, and what it does with its money."

Tony stood quietly for a moment, looking at the stacks of checks that covered the table. They had broken the case wide open.

"We're taking O'Coogan's deposition on Friday!" Charlie exclaimed, "You'll really be able to hammer him with all this material. I'm looking forward to that!"

"No, Charlie, I don't plan to do that. I want to hold this evidence for the trial and hit him with it then. He might not realize the scope of what we know now, and I don't want to educate him in the deposition. I'll itemize all these checks in our pre-trial list of exhibits as simply 'several checks to various parties'. And I'll tell you this," he added with a smile, "the trial of this case is looking more and more interesting."

Chapter 16

September 27

Tony planned to take William O'Coogan's deposition late in the discovery process, after the rest of the evidence had been developed and could be used to question him. That time was now. The deposition was set for the morning of the last Friday in September.

O'Coogan appeared promptly at ten along with David Epstein who explained that "Mr. Harrington" was on trial and wouldn't be attending. Tony and Charlie were waiting for them in Wilson Thompson & Gilchrist's conference room A, together with Joan Saunders of Lake Shore Reporting Service. Charlie had an array of documents surrounding him at the table, just as in the earlier depositions.

Bill O'Coogan was six foot two, a handsome Irishman, impeccably dressed in a dark-blue blazer with gold buttons and cufflinks, nicely paired with his camel slacks. He had a deep, even tan, carefully groomed white hair and was accompanied by a hint of musk after-shave. Tony guessed that he'd probably turned gray prematurely, as Irishmen often do, and also that his blue silk tie cost as much as the suits of some of the firm's younger lawyers.

After the preliminary introductions, Joan Saunders, swore in the witness.

"Would you state your full name for the record please," Tony began.

"William Thomas O'Coogan."

"You are the individual plaintiff in this case, is that correct?"

"You'd better believe it." O'Coogan took a thin, tapered cigar from his inside coat pocket, unwrapping it as he answered.

"I take it that your answer to that question is 'yes'."

"That's correct."

"What's your relationship with the plaintiff corporation, the Federal Dental Academy?"

O'Coogan lit his cigar with a gold Dunhill lighter. He slipped the lighter into his right front blazer pocket, gave the cigar several puffs, then looked at Tony through the smoke.

"I own it."

"Are you also an officer of the company?"

"I'm the president. I'm the president of all the companies that I own or have an interest in. I never want there to be any question about who's in charge." O'Coogan turned and gave Epstein a wink. He looked like he was enjoying this.

"You're also a director of the Federal Dental Academy, I take it?"

"Of course. It would be fairly stupid not to be, since I own the place, wouldn't it, counselor?"

"I'm asking the questions here, Mr. O'Coogan," Tony responded dryly as he scanned his notes.

He then moved into a series of questions exploring the man's background, education and early business experience. O'Coogan's consistent demeanor was that of one in command. He showed a clear disdain for Tony, who as far as he was concerned, functioned at a much lower level than he did, both socially and economically. Tony was reminded of a quote recently attributed to O'Coogan in a local gossip column. "Lawyers, even the successful ones, can be bought or sold at the whim of the real power brokers. They are bystanders, not participants, in the big games."

The contempt was clear.

Through his questions Tony elicited that O'Coogan had been born in Chicago in 1935, was the son of Francis X O'Coogan, an electrical contractor who weathered the depression by often taking his compensation in forms other than cash; he sometimes received parcels of real estate or pieces of the companies he worked with. Although O'Coogan wouldn't admit it, Tony knew that his father was also paid by his well-placed private clients with lucrative non-bid contracts on state and city projects. That became a significant part of his business in the 1940's.

By 1950 the senior O'Coogan was a very successful, very wealthy man. Many of his real estate and business receipts from the early years had ripened and been sold for hundreds of times their initial value. His political connections in the Democratic Party also matured to the point that the Francis X. O'Coogan Electrical Contracting Company was involved in every major construction project in Chicago and surrounding Cook County, many on no-bid contracts. He bought a magnificent twenty-room mansion on Sheridan Road in Evanston and sent his three children to the finest schools he could. His only son, Bill, went to Princeton after graduation from St. George's High School. O'Coogan's political contacts undoubtedly helped a bit with the Ivy League connection.

"When did you begin working for your father's company on a full-time basis?" Tony inquired.

"In 1961, when I got out of the Army."

"What was your first position after you joined the company?"

"Missionary, as I recall," O'Coogan replied with a smirk.

Tony put his pen down, leaned back in his chair, and looked at him. "Mr. O'Coogan, I'd like to remind you that you're under oath, this is a serious matter and your testimony here is being transcribed verbatim by a court reporter. With those things in mind, are you testifying that the Francis X. O'Coogan Electrical Contracting Company was involved in the missionary business in 1961?"

"No, no, of course not," O'Coogan laughed. "I was just trying to inject a little levity into these dreary proceedings. But, I forgot; I'm dealing with lawyers. Lawyers are a depressingly dull group. No sense of humor at all. With a few exceptions, of course," he added turning to Epstein with a slight nod. "What was your question again, counselor?" O'Coogan emphasized the word "counselor" just enough to make it sound like an insult.

"Would you read the last question back please, Ms. Saunders?" Tony asked, his eyes never leaving O'Coogan's. The court reporter did.

"The first position I had with the company was vice president in charge of labor relations," O'Coogan answered. "My job was to make sure that we never had any union problems, either with our own employees or with other tradesmen on the job sites. I got to know the union reps well. We never had any trouble."

That answer told Tony a lot. William O'Coogan, the owner of the largest electrical contracting firm in the city, never actually worked as an electrician. He started out on the dark side of the business, as a fixer, an arranger, and stayed there.

O'Coogan said he'd taken over the management of the business in 1975, when his father suffered a minor stroke. Frank O'Coogan died three years later, and his will established a trust providing for his widow and three children. His son, Bill, not only would inherit the company outright, but also was named sole trustee for his mother and two younger sisters.

As O'Coogan spoke, Charlie slipped Tony copies of some court documents. Under prodding, O'Coogan admitted that after his mother died, in 1979, his two sisters sued him for breaching his fiduciary duties as trustee. They contended that he was using their trust assets for his own benefit. The suit was dismissed, O'Coogan said, because of the broad powers their father had given him as trustee.

"That suit was dismissed by Judge D'Amato of the Circuit Court of Cook County in 1981, wasn't it?" Tony asked, glancing down at a copy of a court order.

"Yes, I believe so. A fine jurist." O'Coogan relit his cigar, and slipped his gold lighter back into his coat pocket.

"You served as finance chairman of Judge D'Amato's campaign committee when he ran for re-election in 1980, didn't you?"

"I might have, counselor," O'Coogan said and shrugged. "But then, I serve on so many civic committees that it's hard to keep track of them all."

"I'm sure," Tony said, putting one stack of documents aside and picking up another. *He bought the goddamn judge*, Tony thought. *The bastard has screwed everyone he's ever dealt with, including his own sisters!*

Since that lawsuit was resolved, O'Coogan added, both the company and he personally had done well and had diversified their investments.

"Well, I guess that brings us to your investment in the Federal Dental Academy, doesn't it?" Tony asked with the air of a boxer who has finished sparring with his opponent and is about to step up the pace.

"I thought we'd get around to that sooner or later, counselor," O'Coogan replied with a courtly nod and a smile.

"Why don't you tell us, Mr. O'Coogan, how you came to be an investor in the Federal Dental Academy."

"Certainly," O'Coogan said, pausing to take a deep drag on his cigar. Tony pushed his chair back slightly; he didn't care for the acrid smoke. "I'm always looking for new investments. It's important to diversify. During the last few years I've been looking at the health-care industry in particular. I don't know who mentioned the Federal Dental Academy to me originally, but it was probably someone at Buchanan Finance. They handle a lot of my finances. I initially loaned the school sixty thousand bucks through Buchanan. It was strictly a passive investment with some good upward potential." He studied the ash on his cigar, before carefully tapping it into the ashtray in front of him on the table.

"After a few months, however, I became aware that the school wasn't keeping up its payments," he continued. "They had to roll over their note two or three times to cover the interest and penalties. I got a little concerned. It looked to me as though the school didn't have a good handle on its finances. So, I finally told the fellows at Buchanan that I wasn't going to extend the school any more credit unless they put someone in charge of the school's finances who we had confidence in. They agreed, offering one of their accountants, Lenny Battaglia, to fill that role. It was a nice gesture on their part. Battaglia had been monitoring the Dental Academy from his desk at Buchanan, so he could hit the deck running. Besides, I had met Mr. Battaglia earlier and had confidence in him. That was the deal. We extended their credit and Battaglia went over to the Dental Academy to handle their finances."

"What happened after that?"

"Part of Battaglia's job was to let me know if he saw anything irregular going on as far as the Academy's finances were concerned, or if their finances were in such a state that he had concerns about their ability to survive. Within two weeks he reported that a number of things there bothered him. I let it go initially, but a couple of weeks later he called again; sounded really concerned. So I set up a meeting with the dentist who owned and ran the school."

"Dr. Jack Roberts?"

"Yes, that's him. We had a meeting at the Academy. Roberts was there, along with Battaglia and me. There was also some other administrator there at Roberts' request."

"It was Rolf Sorenson wasn't it?" Tony felt a sudden surge of anger as he asked the question. *Don't tell me that you've forgotten Rolf Sorenson,* Tony said to himself. *You had him killed, you son-of-a-bitch!*

"Yes, Sorenson. Quiet fellow. Anyway, I explained to them that as a lender, I was becoming very concerned about my investment. By then they were in to me for close to a hundred and twenty thousand, as I recall."

"How long was this after you made them the initial

loan through Buchanan?"

"Seven or eight months."

"So your initial loan of sixty thousand dollars to the Dental Academy had grown into a one-hundred-and-twenty-thousand-dollar debt in only seven or eight months? You must have been charging one hell of an interest rate."

"Objection" David Epstein interrupted. "That's not a question. It's an improper comment by counsel. I'll move that it be stricken from the record."

"Your objection is noted for the record, counsel. Let me rephrase that," Tony responded. "Mr. O'Coogan, how did the outstanding balance of your loan to the Dental Academy double in only seven or eight months?"

"That's what happens when you don't make payments on a loan, counselor. You've got late fees, penalties, interest, all compounding. You'd be surprised how it runs up. But, I've got to say this; the men who were running the Dental Academy at the time, Dr. Roberts and this fellow Sorenson, were terrible, naïve businessmen. They didn't even realize that when you borrow money from a finance company like Buchanan, there's a third-party lender that's usually involved. When I had to explain that to them, and show them the assignments of their notes from Buchanan to me, I felt like Christ talking to Doubting Thomas. Here, I felt like saying, put your hands into the wound, if that's what it'll take for you to understand what's going on. Anyway, after talking to them for a few minutes I decided that it was hopeless; the only way I was going to salvage anything was to get them out of there. I knew

I had to foreclose on my notes, and try to run the place myself with Battaglia's help. I told them that."

"What happened next?"

"Not much. Roberts groused a little bit, just got up and walked out. Sorenson followed him. I never saw either one of them again. As far as I was concerned, Roberts abandoned his stock in the Academy in satisfaction of my note."

Tony was fascinated with O'Coogan's story. It sounded plausible; a jury might well believe it, especially if neither Roberts nor Sorenson was present in court to testify to the contrary. O'Coogan's comparing himself to Christ might turn off a few people, but on the whole his story hung together pretty well - so far.

"Mr. O'Coogan, aren't you leaving something out?" Tony asked. "Didn't a fairly dramatic event occur in your meeting just before Roberts and Sorenson walked out?"

"Why, no, not that I recall."

"Let me try to refresh your recollection, Mr. O'Coogan. Didn't you pull out a gun and lay it on the table between you and Dr. Roberts when he began complaining about your foreclosure?"

"No, that's absurd!"

"But you do own a handgun, don't you? Actually, you have three handguns registered in your name, as I understand it." Tony was looking at certified copies of three gun registrations that Charlie had slipped him.

"Yes, that's true," O'Coogan replied, eyeing the documents Tony had in front of him.

"You carry a gun when you're out in public from time to time, don't you?" Before O'Coogan could answer, Tony turned and crisply said, "Charlie, give me those affidavits, please."

O'Coogan hesitated while Charlie thumbed through one of his files, then smiled broadly and said, "Of course I do, counselor. I'm authorized to. I'm a special deputy sheriff."

Special deputy sheriff with no particular assignments, Tony thought, looking down briefly with a slight shake of his head. *That's one of the perks that big political donors receive in Cook County. What a system!*

"Does that mean that you can carry a gun whenever you want to?"

"Only when I'm also carrying my deputy's badge."

"May I see your deputy's badge, please."

"Sure, counselor, right here." O'Coogan pulled a badge out of his left front coat pocket, laying it on the table between them. As Tony leaned forward to look at it, O'Coogan reclined in his chair with a smug smile. As he did, the bulge under his left lapel was unmistakable.

"You're carrying a gun right now, aren't you, Mr. O'Coogan?"

"Why, no..." O'Coogan answered defensively. "Why would I do that?" Epstein was looking closely at his client.

"Well, you're carrying your deputy's badge; why would you be carrying your badge if you weren't also carrying your gun? What would be the point? Besides, I can see it under your coat. You're carrying a gun right now, aren't you, Mr. O'Coogan?"

O'Coogan was silent; he looked flustered for the first time. Suddenly, Epstein spoke up. "I'd like to confer with my client, if you don't mind." Without waiting for a response, he stood up, lightly pulling O'Coogan to his feet with him, and led him out of the room. Charlie and Tony looked at each other for a long moment and shrugged. Joan Saunders took the opportunity to pull a paperback novel out of her purse and began reading it.

She'd read less than a page when the door opened and O'Coogan and Epstein reentered the room and took their seats. "Mr. Jeffries," Epstein spoke up, "it appears that my client misunderstood your last question. Would you repeat it please?"

"Certainly. I believe I asked Mr. O'Coogan whether he's carrying a gun right now?"

"Yes," O'Coogan answered quietly through clenched jaws. Epstein, sitting at his left, kept his eyes intently on his client as he spoke.

"May we see it please?" Tony asked.

"All right." O'Coogan reached under his coat with his right hand, pulled out a silver gray revolver, and laid it on the table facing Tony. Tony could see the bullets in the chamber. He felt extremely uncomfortable.

Tony turned to the court reporter. "Let the record reflect that the witness, Mr. O'Coogan, has just pulled a silver .38 caliber pistol from his shoulder holster and laid it on the table." Turning back to Epstein, he added, "Is that a correct characterization of what's just happened, Mr. Epstein?"

"Yes, it is," Epstein answered after a pause, aware that his client had turned and was staring steadily at him.

"Would you turn the gun to face the wall, please?" Tony asked. O'Coogan turned the pistol. "Did you have this gun on you when you met with Roberts and Sorenson the day you took over the Dental Academy?"

O'Coogan paused, nodded, then answered, "Yes." David Epstein never took his eyes off him. The flush on his face and his tightly drawn lips showed Epstein's rising anger.

"At any time during your meeting at the Dental Academy that day did you take your gun out of its holster?"

O'Coogan fidgeted with his badge, hesitating.

Epstein spoke up icily. "Would you repeat the question, counsel? I don't believe my client heard it."

Tony repeated the question.

"Yes, come to think of it, I believe I took out my gun once to show it to them. It's a nice piece and I like to show it off to my friends."

"And you laid it on the table between you, is that correct?"

"Yes, I guess I did."

Tony leaned back, looked down at his notes and took a deep breath. He'd finally gotten the testimony that O'Coogan had pulled out his gun at that meeting. Roberts wouldn't testify about that and Sorenson couldn't, but he had the testimony now through O'Coogan's own admissions. All because the guy had an honest lawyer. David Epstein wasn't going to allow a client of his to commit perjury. Tony didn't know what this was going to do to Epstein's relationship with his boss, Jack Harrington, but he knew it was one of the gutsiest displays of ethics he had ever seen.

Much later that evening, David Epstein sat alone in his office overlooking the city, half way through a bottle of Jim Beam Bonded. He'd received the bottle from a friend as a gift for passing the bar exam last year and had been saving it for something special. He decided to drink it tonight. All the lights were out in Jack Harrington's suite, except for a banker's lamp on Epstein's desk. It was hot and stuffy. The building's air conditioning had been turned off at six.

How could I have been so stupid? Epstein thought. It was clear now what kind of a man William O'Coogan was. *He's a lying thug who took over the Dental Academy through raw intimidation. He is almost certainly connected with organized crime. All those stories are probably true.*

Epstein laughed out loud as he recalled his indignation in San Francisco when Tony suggested that O'Coogan had pulled a gun when he took over the Dental Academy. Jeffries was right, and poor old Rolf Sorenson was somehow intimidated into denying that the event ever occurred. Sorenson died right after that. Mysteriously, before he could change his story. There was no doubt in Epstein's mind now that, directly or indirectly, his client, William

O'Coogan, had coerced Sorenson and ultimately had him killed.

David Epstein had always thought of himself as being scrupulously honest. He deliberately chose not to work in one of the large law firms that pander to big business. Instead, he took a job in a small firm that specialized in plaintiffs' class action and antitrust work because that was the best way to use his skills to advance the common good. Now he realized that he'd been working for a client who was a gangster, someone who would have casually committed perjury if Epstein hadn't prevented him from doing so. That one act of O'Coogan's forced him to face the reality of who William O'Coogan really was. David felt used. He felt dirty. He owed many people an apology; an apology that he knew he could never give. How could he escape from this moral morass that was swallowing him?

On Epstein's desk was a stack of papers that he had carefully assembled earlier that week in response to the defendants' request for the production of documents in the Federal Dental Academy case. With them was a short cover letter and a large stamped envelope that his secretary had prepared, addressed to Charlie Dickenson at Wilson, Thompson & Gilchrist.

David Epstein opened his top-right desk drawer, thumbed through some papers, and pulled out a stapled multi-page document. He looked at it for a moment, then inserted it in the middle of the stack of documents that were being produced, re-typed the cover letter with one small change and sealed it all in the large envelope that had been prepared.

David wrote out, in long-hand, a simple letter of resignation. He walked down the darkened hall and placed it on Jack Harrington's desk. He returned to his office, threw the whiskey bottle into the wastebasket, picked up his briefcase and the large envelope of documents, turned off the desk lamp, and left. When he reached the building's lobby he dropped the large envelope into the mail-box. He would fly to his family's home in Cleveland the next day and never return to Chicago.

Chapter 17

September 30

~~~

By the end of September, the defense team had entered that stage of frenzied activity that precedes every major trial. Charlie was working on the trial book they would be using, Carol James was preparing a reply memo in support of the defendants' motion for summary judgment on the antitrust counts, Larry Crowe was working on Lexis to locate specific cases and citations that Carol needed while Tony was planning the examination and cross-examination of all the major witnesses.

Every seasoned litigator has his own form of a trial book, pulling together everything the attorney anticipates needing at hand during a given trial. The format that Tony developed over the years was a three-inch loose-leaf binder with tabs to quickly locate the complaint, the answer, prior court rulings, copies of each side's expected trial exhibits, a detailed outline of the defendants' case, a projected trial schedule, anticipated court orders on trial motions and examination questions for all the expected witnesses produced by either side. It was Charlie's responsibility to pull this data together and assemble the book for the Dental Academy trial, in multiple copies, one for each member of the team. The book was loose-leaf so that any relevant document could be immediately taken out and handed to the court and opposing counsel, if and when appropriate.

Tony also asked Charlie to prepare and include in the trial book three short memos of law on the admissibility of certain defense evidence that he anticipated being challenged during the trial. If Harrington objected to any of that evidence Tony wanted to be able to immediately produce a memo of law right on point. Anticipation, Tony often said, is one of the keys to winning trials.

Tony stopped at Charlie's office a little before four on his way to the monthly partners' meeting held in "the basement," as the seventy-third floor had been dubbed at Wilson, Thompson & Gilchrist. Charlie's office was smaller than Tony's, faced west, and overlooked the city.

Charlie had papers spread all over his desk when Tony walked in. He was staring at a document he was holding, and looked confused.

"Tony, what the hell do you make of this? I was going through the last set of documents that the plaintiffs produced, the ones that came in the mail today from Harrington's office, and I can't figure this one out at all. They were supposed to furnish us copies of all the exhibits they intend to introduce at trial. This was part of the hundred and eighteen pages that they sent us." He handed a stapled multi-page document to Tony.

Tony took a look at it. It was a typed legal memorandum entitled "Analysis of Plaintiff's Antitrust Case." Skimming over it quickly, he could see that its first section dealt with the strengths of the plaintiff's antitrust case against the American Dental Society, and the second section analyzed their weaknesses. It appeared to be very well prepared, and the latter portion of the brief cited some cases that Tony had never seen.

"This is dynamite!" Tony exclaimed. "It lays out all the weaknesses in their antitrust case, point by point. The second part of this memo is a roadmap of the way to attack their position."

"I know. But why would they send it to us? It was stuck right in the middle of their trial exhibits. It must have been a mistake."

"Let me look at the cover letter," Tony asked. "If that document was sent inadvertently we're obligated to return it to Harrington and not review it any further." He skimmed the letter that Charlie handed him, then said, "No, this doesn't look like it was sent to us by mistake. It refers to the hundred and eighteen pages that are enclosed, and that's the number of pages in this production, including this memo. It doesn't look inadvertent, dumb perhaps, but not inadvertent. We don't have to return it."

"Maybe," Charlie responded slowly. "Or maybe it's a red herring, designed to throw us off. Carol should be able to tell that in just a few minutes. All she'll have to do is check out these new cases they've cited to tell whether it's legitimate or not. If it's for real, Carol might be able to use some of this material in the brief in support of our motion for summary judgment. If it's legit, it's a great break for us, the kind that doesn't come along very often."

"That's for sure. Let's take advantage of it and stuff it down their throats. Give a copy to Carol and tell her how they screwed up in producing it. I've got to run now, though, I've got a partners' meeting to attend. Talk to you later."

Tony left Charlie's office and walked around to the east side of the seventy-third floor, where conference room G was located. The meeting had already begun and the firm's chief financial officer, Luke Smith, was giving the partners an update on its financial picture. Apparently, September was going to be a very good month; both billings and collections were ahead of budget.

Conference room G was the firm's largest meeting room, with twenty-four comfortable seats around a long, highly polished wooden table. A large portrait of the legendary Nathan B. Wilson, who ran the firm for forty years, hung at the far end of the room. It was as though he was still presiding over the business conducted there.

Since the firm had grown so much in recent years, it now had almost fifty partners, anyone who arrived late for these monthly meetings had to take one of the folding chairs set up around the room's back and sides. Tony slipped into one near the door.

The meeting was chaired, like every firm meeting for the past decade, by Barton Thompson, chairman of the management committee. He sat at the head of the long table under the portrait of his late predecessor, flanked by Henry Gilchrist and the other most senior partners. Thompson had been Nathan Wilson's protégé for nearly his entire career. When Wilson died suddenly of a stroke, he assumed leadership as a matter of course and had run the firm ever since. In fact, management of its affairs was now his primary responsibility. He had long since passed his clients on to younger partners.

It took only about thirty minutes to run through the routine business and committee reports. As chairman of the Hiring Committee, Tony reported that the summer-internship program had been very successful; fifteen interns had accepted positions as full-time associates after their graduation from law school. That would fill all the firm's hiring requirements for next year.

Barton Thompson then asked if anyone had any new business to discuss. The question, routinely asked at the close of every partnership meeting, was rarely answered in the affirmative. Traditionally, if any new business was presented to the firm, it would be presented by the Management Committee. Today, however, was different.

"Barton," Sid Johnson spoke up, "I would like to move that we invite Bill Fremont with his group of five attorneys at Cronin and Ross to join the firm on terms that would be mutually agreeable."

"I'll second that motion," Walt Jablonski interjected

before Thompson could respond. *They're going to force the issue,* Tony was sitting forward in his chair, ready to support Sid's motion. Sid glanced at him and nodded; Tony nodded back.

"Gentlemen," Thompson replied, ignoring the two women partners present, "that matter has been carefully considered by your management committee, and we have decided that it would not be in the firm's best interest to bring in an outside group at this time. I'm sorry, but it's a closed issue."

"Just a minute, Barton," Sid persisted. "There are many of us who think it would be a great idea. Fremont is well-respected on the street. He has some good clients who'd follow him if he were to change firms, and I think it's something we should discuss with the entire partnership here." Sid was getting into dangerous territory now, clearly challenging Thompson and the management committee.

Barton Thompson couldn't control the debate that followed. Sid and his allies had done their homework, and had many of the younger and mid-range partners lined up in support of their position. In fact, Tony observed, the younger partners were much more aggressive and outspoken than he had ever seen them before at a firm meeting.

"Who are Fremont's clients anyway?" someone asked.

"He has three major clients that he'd have to bring with him to make the economics work out," Sid responded. "Metron Construction Company; Streeterville Bank and Trust; and the O'Coogan Contracting Company. I've checked them all out, and there's no conflict of interest. None of them are engaged in litigation with the firm."

"Wait a minute," Tony heard himself saying. "Can you repeat the name of the last company?"

"The F.X. O'Coogan Electrical Contracting Company. Fremont handles all their corporate work."

Tony felt as though he'd just been kicked in the groin. "I'm sorry to say that I've got a problem with that company," he said, glancing at Johnson. "I'm involved in some heavy litigation with its owner."

"That doesn't show up in our conflict-of-interest file," Sid answered, showing concern as well as surprise.

"The company wouldn't show up, our conflicts-of-interest file only lists the principal parties we're engaged with. Secondary parties are listed in the file, not in the title. It's the owner, O'Coogan, that I have a problem with. A really serious problem." Tony knew that they'd have an impossible situation on their hands if O'Coogan's company were to become a client of the firm. He realized now, too late, that he'd made a mistake in not checking out Fremont's clients before making a commitment to Johnson.

"Sid, couldn't we bring in Fremont with the understanding that his O'Coogan business would stay with his present firm?" Tony asked. "Just that one client?" He was groping for a solution to the problem that he had helped create.

"No, absolutely not," Sid responded quickly. "The

work that Fremont does for the O'Coogan Electrical Contracting Company is his most profitable business. There's no way he's going to leave it behind."

"Well, Jeffries, what's your opinion on this question? Do you want to bring in Fremont as a partner? With his clients?" Barton Thompson pressed, seizing the weakness he had found in Johnson's support. "Or does it appear that your conflict-of-interest is insurmountable?"

"Well, I'm in favor of the concept," Tony answered defensively. "But I've got a real problem with William O'Coogan, the owner of that one client. I'm afraid that I can't support the proposal as it stands."

"It certainly looks like an insurmountable conflict." Henry Gilchrist spoke up, sitting next to the Chair.

"It's about time one of our younger partners showed some good judgment," Thompson said, nodding to Tony. "Let's see who else has the best interest of the firm in mind. It's time to vote on this issue."

Tony's defection broke the back of the dissident partners' stand. If Tony Jeffries wasn't supporting Sid Johnson in his confrontation with the management committee, why should the other partners stick their necks out? The vote was taken, with each partner casting votes equal to their ownership interest in the firm. The Johnson resolution lost, 70 percent to 30 percent.

That was the last item of business for the day. As the partners began rising to leave, Barton Thompson spoke up, loud enough for everyone to hear. "Johnson! I'd like to see you in my office immediately following this meeting." From the icy tone in his voice, it was clear that Sid had a serious problem on his hands.

Tony waited for Sid as everyone filed from the room. He needed to better explain to him why he'd voted as he did. But as Sid walked by him on the way out, he whispered without stopping, "You son-of-a-bitch! I was counting on you! I'm not going to forget this." Before Tony could respond, Sid was caught up in the exiting crowd and was gone.

A man and a woman, both about fifty, were enjoying dinner at the corner table of the Plaza Club, atop the Prudential Building. The lights of the city twinkled below them. They dined with the ease of old friends who were quite comfortable with each other.

"Sid," the woman said as she sipped her after-dinner brandy, "one of the young attorneys in your firm appeared before me this morning - a woman. It was a contested motion. She handled herself very well, very professionally. Her name was James, I believe. I think you've got a keeper there."

"Why, thank you, Pat. Yes, we've got a young associate named James, Carol James. Thanks for your comment. I'll pass that on to the management committee."

Patricia Katsoris and Sid Johnson had been classmates at Harvard many years earlier. They were part of the same study group, supporting each other through the rigors of law school. From that crucible came a lasting friendship that both of them had nurtured over the years. Now they were at the twin peaks of their profession, she as a federal judge, he as a partner in one of the city's most prestigious law firms. They still found ways to support each other.

"By the way, Pat, I've been making some progress on your appointment to the Court of Appeals. The senator's on board."

"That's good news, Sid. What competition do I have left? Do you know?"

"The only one you have to worry about is Rollings from Milwaukee. He's got some friends too. *Good* friends."

"Well, I appreciate everything you're doing. But I'd sure like to get that appointment confirmed this winter. If some Democrat comes out of the woodwork and beats Bush next year, I can forget about the court of appeals for the next four years, maybe eight. Then it'll probably be too late for me." Patricia Katsoris sat back and lit a cigarette as the waiter refilled their brandy snifters.

"One thing has come up, Pat, that I should probably mention to you." Sid took a sip of his brandy. "I don't like it, but I feel I should mention it to you, as an old friend. It has to do with that case involving Bill O'Coogan that's going to be tried before you next month."

"Yes, I know the case. What about it?"

"Well, Bill O'Coogan's been a heavy contributor to both parties for a long time. He's paid a lot of dues. Some people are worried that he's not going to get a fair shake in the trial. There are some people who even think he should be given the benefit of the doubt on any issues that deal with his character."

Pat Katsoris took a deep drag on her cigarette, then slowly exhaled. She did not like the way this conversation was going. "The people who have these concerns," she asked looking into her brandy, "are they people who have some influence on the court of appeals appointment?"

"Yes, I'm afraid so." Sid swirled the brandy in his glass. "I know it's a jury trial, Pat. But even so, there are things you can do in dealing with motions that will influence the outcome. I hate to say it, but it might be worth your while to lean O'Coogan's way on some close calls, and keep the verdict down if it goes his way just to show that you're being fair to him, without destroying the ADS."

"I don't like it, Sid," Pat Katsoris said. She ground her cigarette out in the crystal ashtray. "Not a bit."

"I don't either, Pat. But it's part of the reality that we have to deal with. What makes this conversation particularly awkward for me is that the defendant in that case, the ADS, happens to be a client of our firm, which, by the way, I've decided to leave before too long. But one has to be a pragmatist in all things. I think that's why they approached me; they know we're friends and that I'm one of the few people around who could raise this with you. What it might come down to is that if you want to get to the court of appeals, and possibly beyond that, you've got to do Bill O'Coogan a favor in this trial. Let O'Coogan have a moral victory, not necessarily a financial windfall. Think about it."

"I'll think about it. But I still don't like it."

During the remainder of that week Tony held a series of meetings to flesh out the trial testimony he would be presenting. Ellington of the FBI was now quite willing to trade information and evidence. The Bureau was extremely interested in the checks and financial records Tony had subpoenaed from the Logan Square State Bank. In exchange, Ellington provided a considerable amount of new evidence involving Angelo Bruni's financial operations, and gave Tony access to the transcripts of several court authorized wiretaps. Tony planned to introduce in the trial all the evidence of Bruni's long history of crime, conclusively proving that referring to O'Coogan, orally or in writing, as a member of organized crime was far from defamatory.

Tony also met with Bill McNulty, chairman of the Chicago Crime Commission, to prepare him for his role as an expert witness. McNulty was given the names of all the men who received money through O'Coogan's laundering pipeline, he cross-checked them with the Crime Commission's files, and was prepared to testify as to which of those payees were known members of organized crime along with their particular involvement. Tony also obtained, to present in trial, certified copies of the criminal records of each of those men.

Charlie spent much of Thursday with two economists who were going to be their expert witnesses in defending the antitrust counts. The economists were going to testify that the American Dental Society's action in recommending denial of the Academy's application for accreditation wasn't anti-competitive. The Federal Dental Academy hadn't suffered any measurable losses as a result of the defendants' activity, a requirement for a finding of an antitrust violation. Carol James, always dressed in business-like but distinctly feminine suits, attended those meetings too, taking copious notes and adding the occasional well-considered comments. Their testimony had been reduced to affidavits supporting the defendants' motion for summary judgment which had been filed. They were being prepared now to corroborate that testimony in court, if necessary.

Late Thursday afternoon, Charlie offered to fly down to Tucson the next day and review their new evidence with the *Phoenix* Sun journalists. It was entirely possible, he suggested, that the financial records they had subpoenaed would tie in with some other evidence Chris and Walt had developed. Tony agreed. It was nice of Charlie to offer to fly to Arizona on such short notice he thought with a smile, knowing that potential news leads weren't all that was luring his colleague to Tucson.

Tuesday afternoon Judy had the subpoena to Chase Manhattan Bank ready to be served. She had typed it earlier in the day, had it properly issued by the clerk of the United States District Court in Chicago, and was now going to send it to New York for formal issuance by the New York District Court and service on the bank. Chase would be required to produce copies of all checks (both sides), deposit receipts and banking resolutions of the Land of Liberty Foundation of New York.

Time was running out. They had only a few days left to access Chase's records before the discovery cut-off ordered by Judge Katsoris. This was their last chance to learn what the Land of Liberty Foundation had to do with Angelo Bruni's operations.

After Tony's review and approval, Judy slid the subpoena and supporting documents in a Fed Ex envelope, attached a delivery label, and sealed it. Since the Fed Ex office was located on the first floor of their building, Judy decided to take the envelope there herself. The boys from the mailroom had already made their last sweep through the office, picking up outgoing mail.

Sid Johnson was already in the elevator corridor, waiting to go down when Judy got there. They made some small talk, but Judy could see that Sid was distracted. He seemed upset about something.

"Are you going down just to drop off that Fed Ex package?" he asked offhandedly.

"Yes. It's an important subpoena for Tony. It's got to be served in New York tomorrow."

"I'd be happy to take it down for you. I walk right by their office."

"Gee, that's great. Thanks, Sid." Judy handed him the package as the elevators door opened.

"No problem at all." Sid stepped into the elevator, smiling at Judy as the door shut.

Ninety seconds later, the door opened at ground level. Sid stepped out, walked down the corridor past the Fed Ex office, and left the building on the Chestnut Street side. On the curb was a half-filled trash container. He took the package and buried it under some newspapers.

"You can rot in hell, Tony Jeffries."

"Welcome back Charlie. It's good to see you," Tony said as Charlie walked into the office Monday afternoon. "Looks like you got a little tan while you were down there…"

"That's not all I got." Charlie said laughing.

"Doesn't surprise me. Guess you hooked up with your girlfriend again…"

"Well, you know what they say about all work and no play! Besides, I've got some good new data connecting O'Coogan with Bruni."

"Good. Well a man's gotta do what a man's gotta do I guess," Tony said, chuckling. "I'm glad I caught you because we're under the gun again. Charlie we've got to get this list of our proposed trial exhibits over to Judge

Katsoris' office in the Federal Building tonight by five."

"Five? It's after four now!"

"I know. I'm in the middle of a break in a deposition, all our messengers are out and Larry's home sick. This is imperative Charlie! Why don't you run this over there for me?"

"You know, Tony, my car is still in Evanston, I came here straight from O'Hare. I'll have to take a cab."

"That'll take at least a half an hour Charlie, maybe more. This is rush hour in the Loop and with that convention in town the competition for a cab is going to be intense. We don't have time." Tony handed him his key chain. "Take my car. It's in the lower parking facility on the north side. You've seen me park there a million times. While you're delivering this to the Judge, you can park the car in that building right across from the Federal Building."

"Yeah, yeah…okay," Charlie grudgingly replied, grabbing the keys and the envelope addressed to the judge, turning and striding towards the elevators. He exited through the lobby and took the elevator down to the third lower level. When the door opened he immediately saw Tony's gray Lincoln Town Car wedged in the corner between a huge blue van and the wall. That didn't surprise him. Tony had never learned to park in the city.

He looked at his watch – already 4:15 – not much time… He ran over to Tony's car and squeezed his way, slowly, between the Lincoln and the van. "Jesus, Tony!" he said to himself. "Talk about sandwiching yourself in!"

At one point he just couldn't move but he sucked in his gut and inched himself the rest of the way through. He made it to the car door. He reached down, lifted the handle and the door popped open. That didn't surprise him. Tony never locked his car. He squeezed into the front seat and put the keys into the ignition. He suddenly heard a ticking sound, right under him. That did surprise him.

Immediately Charlie opened the door and tried to step out of the car. He was still sandwiched in between the van and Tony's car, and did his best to push his way free. The ticking seemed to get louder. He knew he had only a few seconds. He got stuck again in the narrow space between the rear wheels of the two vehicles. His heart was pounding. He pushed and pushed, and almost made it before the explosion.

When he opened his eyes again he was in a hospital bed with a pounding headache. Tony was standing over him. Tubes were in both his arms.

"Charlie? How do you feel?"

"I'm alive, I guess that's the best to be expected."

"Yeah, they said you were thrown a few feet but there are no serious injuries. The bomb malfunctioned and went off only partially. Thank God."

"What about those papers!" Charlie winced as he asked. "Did the Judge get them in time?"

"After the bomb blast I called her office and, under the circumstances, she gave us an extension to submit our list of trial exhibits. That's been taken care of."

Charlie just looked at him.

"My God, a bomb in one of our cars!" Tony mumbled, staring at Charlie. "What's going to happen next?" The two men looked at each other for a long moment. "Well, clearly you need some time to recuperate. I'll tell Carol she'll have to step up and pick up your work. Then when you're back, we'll re-strategize how to proceed."

"No," Charlie said firmly.

"No?"

"No, Tony. I've had enough. This is the end. I'm out of this case. Period. Shouldn't be a big surprise."

"But Charlie, are you going to let the mob bully you into quitting?"

"I don't care! Jesus, Tony here I am lying in a hospital bed. I almost died out there! First Sorenson gets killed; now you wanna kill me too?"

"Charlie!"

"Sorry about that Tony, that was out of line. But I've just had enough, okay! I want out now…"

"I need you Charlie. If we quit, they win!"

"If I don't quit, I die Tony. Maybe you too. Simple as that in my mind. Not worth it. Look Tony, I signed on to be a litigator, not a Navy Seal."

"Who's gonna help me with the trial?"

"Carol."

"She's a first year associate! She can't handle this! I'm not sure she'll even want to be in that spotlight."

"She's an ace, Tony. She can handle this as well

as anyone else there can and she'll take it, believe me. Besides, she's all you've got, 'cause it's not going to be me sitting next to you at that counsel table during the trial."

"Alright. Alright. Like I said, we'll give you time to recuperate – a few weeks even. Your next case will have nothing to do with the mob so there will be less stress involved…I promise."

"NO!"

"You mean your quitting the firm? Over this?"

"Tony, I don't want to quit the firm; I just can't deal with your last-man-standing style of litigation. You've taught me a lot, which I appreciate. But I've just had enough. You get me transferred to another group, one with less bloodshed, and I'll stay. If you can't, or won't, I'm out of here. I mean that."

Tony took a deep breath, looked out the window for a minute, "You've been through a hell of a lot in this case, Charlie, more than your share. Okay, I'll get you transferred. There are plenty of other partners who'd love to have you working for them."

"Thanks, Tony," Charlie replied quickly. They shook hands, then Tony turned, hesitated, and left the room.

He walked slowly toward the elevators. He had lost his right-hand man and an excellent associate. He knew what Charlie had been through, and found it hard to blame him. But this still hit him hard. He didn't really expect Charlie to be one of the casualties. Tony took a cab back to the Hancock, and an elevator up to seventy-six feeling very alone.

He hoped he and Carol could muddle through this successfully. Even more, he hoped that Charlie had exaggerated the dangers of going forward.

"Carol, how about a drink over at Ditka's?" Tony said as he poked his head into his associate's small office. It was after six and already getting dark outside.

She looked up, a bit surprised, then responded, "I'd love to, thanks. I've been up to my ears in this damn dental case all day and could use one. Give me a second and I'll be right with you."

"Great!. And maybe a bar bite too, if you'd like. I noticed that you worked through lunch."

"Thanks, I just might take you up on that." She stuffed some papers into her shoulder bag, grabbed her coat and said, "I'm ready, thanks for the invitation."

"Well, we haven't had a chance to talk much lately," Tony replied as they walked through the lobby to the elevators. "And I thought we ought to catch up. Besides, there's some business I'd like to run by you. I'm going to have to leave before too long in order to catch the seven-thirty-five train. Karen and I are meeting friends at a neighborhood restaurant in Wilmette, but we should have a few minutes to talk before I have to run.

They boarded an elevator, took it all the way down, and left the building headed for Ditka's a half block west on Chestnut. It was a cool but pleasant evening and Michigan Avenue's colorful array of lights was a bright change from the comparatively sterile environment of their office, now a thousand feet above.

They grabbed two stools at the end of Ditka's bar, both ordered Chardonnay and Carol asked for an order of chips and artichoke dip.

Carol was only a year out of the University of Chicago Law School, but she was a fast learner and had impressed Tony with her maturity as well as her ability to successfully take on different projects. He wondered, though, if she was ready to step into the spotlight.

"Carol, this Dental Academy case has gotten pretty nasty," Tony commented as the bartender served their drinks. "I'm sure it's not what you anticipated when you decided to become a corporate litigator. How do you feel about that? Does it bother you that you're involved in a case with some potential danger?"

"No, not at all! I love it. Frankly, it's much more exciting than I anticipated!" Her face brightening at the subject. "Thanks for including me on the Dental Academy team."

Two men in business suits took the bar stool next to Tony. The place was filling up.

"You're welcome, I think," Tony responded quietly with a gallows smile. "But we know now we're up against organized crime, the mob. It's getting rough, and, to be honest, possibly dangerous. You know what happened to Charlie. He was almost killed."

"I know. That was terrible."

"What I'm leading up to, Carol, is that Charlie's off the case permanently, at his request. I'd like you to step up and be my number-one back-up in the case, including at the trial. It'll raise your visibility, and probably your vulnerability too. And I'm not sure you're ready for that, or even if you want to bring that spotlight down on yourself. There may be some real danger involved. If you're not ready for this, or you're concerned about your safety, I could easily bring in a more senior litigator to take Charlie's place, and there wouldn't be any hard feelings. What do you think?"

Carol didn't pause a moment. "I'd love that, Tony, and I'm flattered as hell that you think I could handle the job. This is the most exciting case in the office, and maybe the most exciting one I'll ever be involved in. I don't have a family to worry about like you do. I've thought about those dangers, but I'm not afraid. So, if that's an offer, Tony, I'll accept it in a heartbeat," she responded flashing a broad smile.

Tony breathed a sigh of relief and leaned back. That was exactly what he wanted to hear. "Okay, Carol. You've got the job. You better hang on for what might be a rough ride."

Carol nodded and raised her glass in acknowledgement of her new role. As she did, the bartender served them their chips and dip.

"By the way, that's too bad about what happened to Sid Johnson," she said as she put her glass down.

"What do you mean?"

"Well, after he left here," she answered, "he jointed the Cavanaugh firm."

"Yes, I know that." Tony picked up a taco chip, scooped up some artichoke sauce and popped it in his mouth. It was delicious.

"But did you hear that within a week of joining Cavanaugh, their CFO was arrested for fraud, among other things. Seems that he hadn't been making the firm's required payments into its pension plan; kept the dough himself. And now the firm's on the hook to make up the deficiency in the pension plan."

"No, I hadn't heard that," Tony reacted, shocked.

"Yes, it seems the whole firm and all its assets have been taken over by the feds. Their pension plan was short millions. All the partners have lost their equity, including Sid. And I heard that there may be personal claims against them all; big bucks. It just came out this morning."

"Wow, most of the partners are going to have big financial problems. Some of those guys may be ruined."

"Yeah, well, I never cared for Sid, myself," Carol shrugged.

"Love to talk more," Tony said, glancing at his watch, "but I've got to run to catch my train. "Here," he continued as he laid two twenties on the bar and stood up, "this should cover the tab. See you in the morning, Carol."

"Right. Thanks for the drink and chips. Good night, Tony."

Tony spent the next couple of days preparing his cross-examination of William O'Coogan. He found it hard to stop thinking about the bomb and Charlie, but he knew he had to focus on the case at hand, blocking out any distractions. He constructed several trial traps for O'Coogan, using the evidence he now had. Each trap consisted of a series of questions designed to lead O'Coogan into a blind alley, where he would have to answer the final question with either a damaging admission or an obvious lie. Tony enjoyed cross-examining adverse witnesses, particularly when, as in this case, he had good material to work with. He anticipated that the documents he'd be receiving from the Chase Manhattan would give him even more ammunition.

It was quiet around the house that weekend, making it easier for Tony to concentrate on the case. Mark was on a Boy Scout camp out, and Roger and Billy were at neighbors for an all-day session of Dungeons and Dragons. Debbie went shopping with Karen most of Saturday; and Sunday she spent at the Nelsons. Karen seemed perfectly willing to leave Tony alone. In fact, he noticed, she seemed preoccupied with thoughts of her own.

When Tony arrived at the office the following Monday morning, Judy told him that Mr. Gilchrist would like to see him. After thumbing through the morning mail and taking a sip or two of coffee, he walked up the circular staircase in the center of the office to the other side of the seventy-seventh floor where Henry Gilchrist's office overlooked Michigan Avenue and North Lake Shore Drive.

Dr. John Schofield of the American Dental Society was chatting with Gilchrist when he walked in.

"Good morning, Tony," Dr. Schofield said pleasantly as he rose and shook hands with him. "I was just telling Henry how pleased we all are at the ADS with the way that you and your team have handled the defense of this Dental Academy case. When that suit was first filed we were very nervous about it, but it appears now that you've really turned things around."

"Thank you, Doctor, that's very kind of you," Tony replied as both he and Schofield sat down in the two padded chairs across from Gilchrist's desk. "But it's not over yet. We still have the trial to get through, although I'm feeling rather optimistic about that."

"That's what John and I wanted to talk to you about, Anthony," Gilchrist said. "Isn't there some way that a trial can be avoided?"

"Avoided?" Tony was startled. "We're the defendant. The only way that we can avoid a trial is to settle on the plaintiff's terms. Is that what you're talking about?"

"Not in the usual sense," Gilchrist answered. "But if this trial goes ahead, there's some risk involved for both sides. The plaintiff is still seeking substantial damages under his antitrust counts. Regardless of how optimistic you may be, there's still some exposure there. Isn't that correct?"

"Yes, there is, but I don't think the risk factor is very high."

"Nonetheless, the American Dental Society does bear some risk if the antitrust issue is tried. Uninsured risk, I might add. On the other hand, from the evidence that I understand you've assembled in defending the defamation count, William O'Coogan is going to be sorely embarrassed by the facts that are likely to come out if the count goes to trial; isn't that true?"

"Definitely. And not just William O'Coogan, but a number of politicians and mob figures both here and in Arizona."

"Then it seems to me, Anthony," Gilchrist continued, "that both sides would be served by having the trial, as we say, avoided. In exchange for the plaintiff's dropping his antitrust and defamation charges against the American Dental Society, we could agree to keep confidential the damaging evidence that you've collected against him. Let them have their damn conditional or initial accreditation. Do you see what I mean?"

Tony was irritated by the suggestion. "I don't like it, Henry. We can win this case straight out. We don't have to make a deal. Plus, I think that the people in this town ought to know what kind of a man William O'Coogan is."

"I know how much you enjoy winning trials, Anthony, and I know how much you've prepared for this one. But the client's interests come first. If we, as attorneys, can resolve a matter in such a way that our client bears no risk whatsoever, then I think we're ethically obligated to do so."

"What about Barton Thompson?" Tony interjected. "He feels that we have some obligation to publicly prove the allegations that we've made against O'Coogan, now that we've raised them, or I've got a problem with the firm."

"Barton won't have any problem with a resolution along these lines. Don't worry about him, leave that to me."

Tony wasn't sure he believed Gilchrist, but felt that under the circumstances he had to defer to him.

"John and I discussed this matter a bit before you arrived," Gilchrist continued. "We're in agreement that this is the course of action we should pursue. Isn't that correct, John?"

"Yes, it is," Schofield replied. "The only question in my mind is whether the plaintiff and his counsel would agree to simply dismiss his case on this basis.

What's your judgment on that, Tony?"

They're right, of course, Tony thought. As much as he was now looking forward to trying this case, it would clearly be in the best interests of the American Dental Society if there wasn't a trial at all. That was the only way that they'd be completely free of exposure. Tony had already turned over to the FBI all the evidence he had uncovered so far. *A settlement won't interfere with any criminal prosecutions that are warranted.*

"That gets complicated," he finally responded. "It would be dangerous, though, to get into that kind of a discussion with Jack Harrington. The only way that we could convince him of O'Coogan's risk at trial would be to completely divulge our trial strategy, particularly any evidence in defense of the libel count. What would happen if we made that disclosure, and couldn't settle the case? Harrington's a good enough lawyer that, with that sort of advance notice, he could probably keep a lot of our evidence out." Tony paused, his mind racing through the alternatives. "And if he concluded that he couldn't keep most of that evidence out, he could always dismiss the libel count on the eve of trial. No, that wouldn't work, at least not by dealing through Harrington. The concept is good, but we'll have to figure out some other person to deal through."

"What about approaching O'Coogan directly?" Schofield asked.

"We couldn't go around O'Coogan's attorney. That would be unethical," Gilchrist answered quickly. "But I agree with Anthony's analysis of the outcome if we were to approach Jack Harrington. There has to be some other way to accomplish this."

Tony stood up and walked over to the window. He stared down for a long moment at the slowly incoming waves off the lake. The other two were silent, watching him. Finally he turned around. "There is another way," he said quietly. "If the libel count is tried and our evidence becomes known, there will be two people who are going to be very embarrassed and maybe indicted - William O'Coogan and Angelo Bruni. Bruni sure as hell wouldn't want all his business dealings and money laundering to be made public, besides possibly going to jail. There are a number of federal felonies involved. My guess is that he also couldn't care less about O'Coogan's antitrust suit; he might not even know about it. Henry, I'll bet that if we could somehow get your proposal to Angelo Bruni himself, let him know what we have and what will come out in trial, he'd accept it instantly. He'd force O'Coogan to drop his whole suit."

Gilchrist and Schofield were speechless. Things had taken a far more sinister turn than either of them had anticipated. It was Gilchrist who finally spoke up. "How in the world would you do that, Anthony? You can't just telephone a Mafia Don, even if you had his private number, and say 'Don, there's something we should talk about.'"

"We've learned from the FBI that the consigliere of the Bruni Family is a Tucson lawyer named Joseph Augustino. No family; a lawyer with only one client. We haven't taken his deposition or even personally met him," Tony slowly thought through his concept as he spoke. "He's Bruni's closest advisor. The contact would have to be through him. But since he's not likely to talk to us voluntarily, we'd have to force him to meet us." Tony continued pacing around. Suddenly he stopped. "I'll subpoena him for his deposition. During the course of the deposition, I'll make it clear what we know and what's likely to come out in our trial. He won't admit anything, of course, but that will get the message to Bruni."

"Dangerous business, Anthony," Henry Gilchrist said. "Very dangerous business. We're dealing with likely killers here. I don't want anyone taking any more unnecessary risks."

"Neither do I," Tony responded honestly. "But I think it's the only way to accomplish what's clearly in the best interests of the American Dental Society, which is to try to have this suit dismissed by the plaintiffs before trial. I'm willing to do it. In fact, I'll have the subpoena issued today and will schedule the deposition in Augustino's own office this Friday, October 11th. The judge has set that as the final day to conduct discovery prior to trial."

The three men exchanged a few final comments then Tony left and returned to his office. When he got there he shut the door and sat down. He had to. He had a knot of fear growing like a hungry rat in the pit of his stomach.

Karen Jeffries laid her beige suit into her hanging bag on the bed on top of the other clothes, carefully arranging the sleeves so that they wouldn't wrinkle when she folded it shut. Next she took three of her favorite blouses out of the closet, slipped them into plastic covers and laid them on top of the suit. Her bag was almost full now. It didn't hold everything she wanted to take, but held enough to last her for a week or two while she sorted things out.

She looked through the closet again. There was no point in taking any of her party dresses or summer clothes. She glanced down at the row of shoes on the closet floor. They were all paired up like little couples;

innocent, naive little couples. She picked up one pair, the tan flats, walked over to the bed, and stuck them into the side of her clothes bag.

She didn't know how she was going to explain it to the kids. She'd run through it a hundred times in her mind, first with one child, then with another, finally all of them together, but it never came out right. Still she knew that somehow they'd understand. They couldn't go on living like this. She knew they felt the same pressure she did. Their lives were all being twisted and distorted by this insane case of Tony's. *It's not fair for little kids to have to worry about whether killers are stalking their home late at night, or wonder whether a car slowly cruising by is driven by a policeman or someone else waiting to seize them.*

Karen had begged Tony to end it somehow; end their terror; but he didn't seem to be able to. Maybe he didn't want it to end. That thought had chilled Karen to her soul. Maybe Tony was so wrapped up in this case that he didn't want the excitement to stop, didn't care how it affected everyone else. She hoped that wasn't true, but the possibility kept bubbling to the surface, and it frightened her most of all.

Tony would be working late tonight, and all four of the children would be home this evening. She would announce her decision then, have them pack, and get them all moved to the Nelson's house before Tony got home. Cindy Nelson was a dear to open her doors to them. It wasn't really far enough away to suit Karen, but the kids wouldn't have to change schools, and it would at least get them out of this target that their home had become. Whether they would eventually move on a more permanent basis, and where that might be, Karen didn't know.

As Karen finished packing, she kept glancing out the window. At a little after three, Esther Jacoby dropped off Billy and Debbie from their preschool. Karen felt a surge of relief, as she did every day when they got home. Through the open bedroom window she heard them shout goodbye to the Jacoby children as Esther's car pulled away.

They kept talking as they walked toward the house. "I think it'll be neat if Tommy Jacoby is in the FBI when he grows up," Debbie said. "They chase crooks."

"Yeah, but they've got guns," Billy answered. "I want to be a lawyer like Dad. He chases crooks, and doesn't even carry a gun. That's really brave." *They're proud of what Tony's doing*, Karen thought. *Not angry or afraid - proud. I should be, too.*

"Daddy's very brave," Debbie said as they opened the front door and walked in. Karen heard the door slam. She turned and looked at the picture of her and Tony on their dresser, taken at their tenth-anniversary party, the year Tony became a partner in the firm. He gave her diamond earrings that night, the kind they could never afford when they were younger. Karen instinctively raised her right hand to her ear. She was wearing those same earrings. A hundred memories and dreams came swirling back to her.

Suddenly Debbie dashed into the room.

"Mommy, you know what?" she shouted.

"No, dear. What?"

"I'm going to ask Daddy to come to my class to talk about being a lawyer," Debbie said with a smile. "I want everyone to see how brave he is. Do you think he'll do it?"

Karen paused, then returned her daughter's smile. "Yes," she said. "I think Dad would be very proud to talk to your class."

"Great!" Suddenly Debbie saw the open suitcase on her mother's bed. "Are you going somewhere, Mommy?" she asked.

"No," Karen said as she took her three blouses out of the bag and hung them back up in the closet. "I was just rearranging things. I'm not going anywhere at all."

Chapter 18

October 11

"This way, please." The well-dressed young Hispanic woman led Tony down a short corridor, pushed open a leather-covered door at the end, and escorted him into Joseph Augustino's dimly lit inner office. Tony stopped for a moment, it was almost completely dark.

"Come in, Mr. Jeffries." Augustino was seated behind a large mahogany desk; he neither rose nor extended his hand as Tony walked in, his eyes slowly adjusting to the darkness.

"Have a seat."

Joseph Augustino was in his mid-sixties. Wisps of gray accented his thick black hair at the temples and his heavy black eyebrows. He had a deep tan, and appeared to have kept himself in shape. He was impeccably dressed in a charcoal gray pinstriped suit, a dark striped tie, and a monogrammed white shirt with heavy gold cuff links.

The room was darker than any office Tony had seen before. The only illumination came from one recessed ceiling lamp over Augustino's desk. The walls, as far as Tony could see, were paneled, the carpeting a deep maroon, and the windows covered with heavy drapes. It was impossible to tell whether it was day or night outside.

As Tony took the lone padded leather chair facing Augustino's desk, he noticed for the first time that there were two other people in the room, a dark-haired woman in her forties and a burly man seated a few feet just beyond the circle of dim light that surrounded Augustino's desk.

"This is the court reporter you ordered," Augustino said in a deep gravelly voice as he gestured toward the woman. "She just got here." Tony nodded to her and they exchanged cards.

"And this is my associate, Rocco Napoli," he said, nodding to the man seated in the shadows. Napoli kept his dark eyes set on Tony, but didn't say a word. "He's going to be sitting in." Napoli was farther back in the darkness than the woman was, it was difficult for Jeffries to discern his features.

"Is Mr. Napoli an attorney?" Tony asked.

"No, he's not. He's ...," A slight smile crossed Augustino's face, "he's my paralegal assistant."

"I'm sorry, but I'm going to object to his sitting in. If he isn't either a party to this case, an attorney, or the court reporter, he has no right to be here."

"Mr. Jeffries, this is *my* office. I'll have anybody

sitting in that I choose." Augustino leaned forward and spoke slowly, every word given ominous significance.

"As I recall, Mr. Napoli is the president of Nonno's Health Care, Inc.," Tony responded, trying to retain his confidence. "He may be called as an adverse witness in the trial of this case. We've had an order entered in other depositions for exclusion of prospective witnesses, so he has to leave." Tony was trying to be firm without seeming antagonistic or showing his nerves. It was important that Augustino regard him as simply a lawyer trying to do his job in a competent fashion. "Do you want me to call the judge to confirm?" Tony asked.

Augustino leaned back in his chair, looking at Tony. His argument was legally correct, and Augustino had no desire to get involved with a federal judge for any reason. Certainly not on a discovery motion in a civil suit such as this.

"Rocco, wait outside," he said finally. "And leave the door open."

Napoli stood up without a word, walked to the door, opened it, stepped out into the hallway, turned around, folded his thick arms, and stared directly into Augustino's office. The distant hallway light behind him made his presence even more intimidating than it had been before. He was now a faceless shadowy demon. Augustino and he had complied with Tony's demand, but Napoli could still see and hear everything that took place during the deposition. Tony had gained nothing.

"All right, let's get on with it," Tony said with a touch

of resignation. The court reporter set up her equipment and swore in Augustino.

No one from Jack Harrington's office was attending the deposition. Tony had learned the previous evening that David Epstein had quit, Harrington was on trial on another case, and no one else from his office was available. That was fine with Tony. He could now be more open and less cryptic in his questioning of Augustino.

"Would you state your full name, please?"

"Joseph Angelo Augustino."

"Where and when were you born, Mr. Augustino?"

"Messina, Sicily, August 10th, 1934."

"When did you first come to this country?"

"My family moved from Sicily to New York in May of 1938."

Tony asked some questions about Augustino's general background and education, establishing that the witness was an attorney, had never married, had no children, and was licensed to practice law in both New York State and Arizona. He had moved his practice from Manhattan to Tucson in 1975.

"Do you know a Mr. Angelo Bruni?"

"Yes."

"How long have you known Mr. Bruni?"

"All my life. The Bruni's lived near us in Messina. Our families came to New York together on the same boat in 1938."

"Is Mr. Bruni your client now?"

"Yes, he is. How is this relevant, counsel?"

"Mr. Augustino," Tony answered. "I'm trying to defend a very difficult libel and slander suit that was filed by William O'Coogan in federal court in Chicago. I attached a copy of the complaint to the subpoena that we had served on you. I'm sure you've read it. I believe we indicated in the subpoena that we would ask you questions about your knowledge of issues raised in the complaint."

Augustino nodded, but said nothing.

Tony continued, "One of the issues raised in Mr. O'Coogan's complaint is whether he or the Federal Dental Academy is connected with organized crime. In defending that count, we're being forced to dig into Mr. O'Coogan's business and personal background. Some of these questions deal with that issue."

Tony expected Augustino to say something in response, but again he said nothing. He only leaned back in his thickly padded chair, his eyes fixed on Tony.

After an uncomfortable silence, Tony resumed his questioning.

"Do you know William O'Coogan, the plaintiff in this suit?"

"I believe I met him once or twice."

"Do you recall when you first met Mr. O'Coogan?"

"I'm not sure."

"Could it have been at the Rancho Mirage Golf Club in Palm Springs on the afternoon of May 14, 1985?" Tony was now using information that the FBI had supplied him.

Augustino paused a moment before answering. "I don't recall."

"Would it refresh your recollection, Mr. Augustino, if I told you that you played golf that day in Palm Springs in a foursome consisting of yourself, Angelo Bruni, Rocco Napoli and Bill O'Coogan?"

"No, that doesn't refresh my recollection at all."

"Would it refresh your recollection, Mr. Augustino, if I told you that after golf you had dinner at the golf course's club house and that you had Steak Diane, served rare?"

For a brief moment Augustino looked startled by the question, and the data it suggested that Tony had, but he quickly regained his composure. He looked directly at Tony and softly said, "No, counselor, that doesn't refresh my recollection."

"Well, would it refresh your recollection if I also told you that at dinner that evening, May 14, 1985, at the Rancho Mirage Golf Club with those same three gentlemen you were joined by two other men from Chicago?"

"No, that doesn't refresh my recollection."

"And that you discussed that evening the concept of moving drug money from dealers throughout the United States to a single off-shore location set up by Mr. O'Coogan, who would then distribute it throughout the world through a series of corporate fronts that he would set up. Does that refresh your recollection, Mr. Augustino?"

Augustino's dark eyes narrowed as he glared at Tony. After a long silence, he slowly said, "No, Mr. Jeffries; that doesn't refresh my recollection either." His response was firm and even-handed, but Tony knew what he was wondering, "*What the hell do these guys know, and who the hell gave it to them? Do we have a rat?*"

"One of those fronts would be a dental school that Mr. O'Coogan would establish or take over in Chicago, does that refresh your recollection of the events of that day?"

"No, that still doesn't refresh my recollection, counselor." Augustino's narrowed, dark eyes never left Tony's.

Tony heard a slight sound and sensed that Rocco Napoli had reentered the room and was standing in the darkness behind him and slightly off to the left. He decided to ignore him. He had gone this far; he might just as well finish what he had started. Besides, nobody was going to do anything to him with an independent court reporter sitting right there. She was, in a sense, his life insurance.

"Don't you recall, Mr. Augustino," Tony continued, referring to his notes, "remarking to several people after that meeting how impressed you were with Mr. O'Coogan, and how you believed he could be of assistance to you and Mr. Bruni?"

"No, I don't."

"Are you aware of the fact, Mr. Augustino, that in the three months following your golf meeting with Mr. O'Coogan he organized six Illinois corporations, all with offices at 5401 West Lawrence Avenue in Chicago? Are you aware of that?"

"No, I'm not."

"In the last four years alone almost three hundred million dollars has been funneled through those six companies. Much of it has been paid out as ostensibly legitimate income to a number of men in the Chicago area who are known to be involved in organized crime. Were you aware of that, Mr. Augustino?"

"No, I wasn't, counselor. Why would I be?"

"Perhaps because one of the recipients was your brother, Michael Augustino. He's secretary-treasurer of a union local in Milwaukee, and received $500,000 during the past four years, deposited in an account of his in the Cayman Islands. I believe he's served some time in prison for racketeering charges. You weren't aware of that Mr. Augustino?"

"No, I wasn't." Augustino's eyes were riveted on Tony's and his voice was quieter. Then he looked briefly behind Tony and shook his head slightly. He had told Napoli not to do something. The court reporter, in the shadows at the other side of the circle of light around Augustino's desk, had her eyes down and kept typing. Tony was thankful that she was there. He was almost done.

"Mr. Augustino, what is the Land of Liberty Foundation of New York?"

There was another long pause before the witness answered. "I have no idea."

"You've never heard of it?"

"No, I haven't."

Tony decided that he had pressed his luck about as far as he could, and that he should start extricating himself. He had delivered his message. His next several questions dealt with inconsequential matters.

"Well, that's about all that I intended to cover," Tony said lightly as he finished. "I'm sorry that you weren't able to help me. I might have been given the wrong information, but all of this will be explored and hopefully straightened out during the trial of the case in Chicago. I guess we'll have to take the deposition of your client Mr. Bruni in the next few days; he may have a better recollection of these things. You'll both be receiving subpoenas shortly." He put his yellow pad back into his briefcase as he stood up. Glancing around the dimly-lit room, he noticed that Rocco Napoli was back in the doorway, as though he had never moved. Tony asked the court reporter for an expedited copy of the transcript as soon as it was ready and said that he'd be happy to pay for the rush service.

"I hope you know, Mr. Augustino, that I'm just trying to do my job. This O'Coogan libel suit in Chicago is forcing me and others, to probe hard into some of these other matters." As he was about to leave, he noticed a small earthen statue on a wall shelf in the shadows behind Augustino's desk. Screwing up his courage, he decided to deliver one final message.

"Interesting artifact, you have there, Mr. Augustino. It reminds me of a souvenir that I picked up in Portobelo, Panama a few years ago. That wouldn't be where you found it, would it?"

"No, it isn't." Augustino answered, his dark eyes once again boring into Tony.

"Interesting town, Portobelo. I've heard that it's a much more active town than one might suspect. You should be sure to get there some time."

"I'll keep your comments in mind, counselor."

"Thanks for your time, Mr. Augustino – I'm sorry if I inconvenienced you." Augustino neither rose nor extended his hand, but kept his eyes fixed on Tony. Rocco Napoli stepped aside at the doorway to let Tony pass. Tony's mouth felt dry as he walked down the hallway toward the reception room. His shirt was soaked with sweat and he could hear his heart pounding. He was glad, very glad, to be out of that room.

As Tony entered the reception room he noticed a young blonde woman sitting on the couch, a square briefcase next to her. She looked at him for a moment as he passed.

"Mr. Jeffries?" she asked.

Tony stopped and turned in surprise. "Yes?" he replied, with equal parts question and answer.

"I'm Maryann Williams from South West Reporting Service. I'm your court reporter. They told me you hadn't arrived yet."

Oh my God. If this woman is my court reporter, who was that woman in Augustino's office?" He mumbled something about the deposition being over and left with his mind spinning.

Much later that night, the phone rang in a luxurious North Shore mansion overlooking Lake Michigan. Bill

O'Coogan was sitting on the leather couch in his paneled den, watching TV and sipping a glass of fifty-year-old port. He turned down the sound, leaned over and answered the phone.

"Hello."

"Hello, Bill. We've got a problem." The thick voice on the other end of the line was unmistakable. It was Joseph Augustino's.

"What do you mean?" He was surprised that Augustino was calling him. They kept their contacts to a minimum. Fortunately, no one else was home that evening.

"It's about that lawsuit you have going to trial next week. Our mutual friend is concerned about what might come out. He would prefer that the case not go ahead."

"Tell our mutual friend not to worry. I have things under control."

"Our friend isn't so sure about that. And he doesn't like to take any unnecessary risks."

"I know! I won't let anything happen that would cause any of us embarrassment. I have a couple of things planned to protect us. Things I'd rather not discuss right here."

"I hope you're right Bill. Our mutual friend is very concerned. As I said, he'd very much like that case to go away *soon*, one way or another."

"I understand. Assure him that I have his interests in mind. He has nothing to worry about."

With that, they both hung up.

Chapter 19

October 18 - 9:45 a.m.

Judge Katsoris' courtroom had a number of spectators the Friday morning the trial began, even though only preliminary matters were going to be dealt with that day. The case had received considerable play in the Chicago press.

Carol James sat to Tony Jeffries' right at the defense table, organizing their documents. She looked cool and confident in her light blue business suit. Dr. John Schofield, representing the ADS, was seated at the table to Tony's left. He was clearly disappointed that the trial was proceeding; their subtle attempt to settle the case had clearly failed. Tony was also surprised that their message to Angelo Bruni had not had the anticipated effect. Secretly though he was glad; he'd been looking forward to this trial, initially with trepidation, but with mounting excitement.

Jake Wysocki was in the first row of spectators' benches on the defense side of the courtroom. Behind him were several senior staff members from the American Dental Society, along with Dr. Robert Kaminsky.

Toward the rear of the court-room on the defendants' side Charlie Dickinson was sitting with an attractive young woman. Tony recognized her as Chris Anderson of the *Phoenix Sun* from a photo that Charlie had shown him once. Charlie nodded to Tony, who smiled and nodded back.

Tony had just learned that morning that their subpoena for the records of the Land of Liberty Foundation had never been served on the Chase Manhattan Bank. He was fuming, nobody could figure out what happened to the subpoena. Tony had hoped to see how the Liberty Foundation fit into O'Coogan's plans, but now had resigned himself to the fact that he they'd have to go into the trial without that data.

Across the room, Jack Harrington and an associate were seated with Bill O'Coogan at the plaintiff's table. Tony didn't know the associate, who had been brought into the case late in the game when David Epstein quit. Her unfamiliarity with the documents and witnesses might hinder the plaintiff's case, Tony thought. Seated in the audience near their table were Lenny Battaglia, sporting a white carnation in the lapel of his charcoal-gray sport coat, and Dr. Maria Henriques from the Dental Academy. Tony recognized reporters behind them from the *Tribune*, the *Sun-Times*, the *Daily Defender* and several national news syndicates. The case had been drawing national attention.

As Carol organized their papers she saw Jack Harrington approaching from the other side of the courtroom. He nodded briefly to Tony, strode up to Carol, extended his hand and said, "I don't believe we've met before. I'm Jack Harrington, Miss…"

Carol let his words hang in the air a moment before responding and extending her hand. "James. Carol James. Glad to meet you Mr. Harrington."

He held Carol's hand in a vice-like grip, and eyed her intently, then said, "You're quite young, Miss James. Should I assume that you're a licensed attorney?"

Extracting her hand from his, Carol reached into her side pocket and offered him one of her business cards. It clearly identified her as an attorney with Wilson, Thomson & Gilchrist.

"Ah yes, so you are," Harrington replied. Then turning the card over and pulling a pen from his inside pocket he continued. "In that case, Miss. James, to keep our file up to date, where do you reside? In case we need to reach you with any emergency matters during the trial."

"I don't believe that where I reside is relevant to this case, Mr. Harrington," she replied evenly, her eyes never leaving his. "If you ever need to reach me, you can always do so through our office."

"Well, my dear," Harrington responded with a sardonic smile, "I hope you enjoy the trial, but I rather suspect that you won't."

"We'll see, Mr. Harrington. We'll see."

He gave her a slight bow of mock deference, nodding slightly to Tony as he turned and strode back to the plaintiff's table.

"You handled that well," Tony said quietly. "He was just trying to intimidate you."

"I know. What a pompous ass."

Judge Katsoris' court reporter and minute clerk were seated at opposite ends of their long desk, immediately in front of and below the judge's bench. The room was chilly. The court reporter had her sweater on and several women spectators had their coats over their shoulders.

At precisely ten o'clock the door in the front of the courtroom swung open and Judge Patricia Katsoris strode to her chair on the bench. At the same time, her minute clerk stood, banged his gavel once, and announced, "All rise. The United States District Court for the Northern District of Illinois is now in session, Judge Patricia Katsoris presiding. God save the United States and this honorable court. Be seated and come to order."

Judge Katsoris settled into place and gave a nod of greeting to each of the lead counsel. She carried in a stack of documents, which she organized on the bench in front of her while the clerk formally called the case.

"Case number 91 C 5641." Her clerk intoned. Federal Dental Academy and William O'Coogan versus the American Dental Society, et al. for trial."

Harrington rose and responded first. "John Harrington representing the plaintiffs, your Honor. Ready for trial."

Tony stood, nodded to his distinguished opponent across the courtroom, and addressed the court. "Anthony Jeffries and Carol James representing the defendants, the American Dental Society, it's Commission on Dental Accreditation and their named directors and members, your Honor. Ready for the defense."

They had begun.

Tony felt a rush of excitement. He had tried a hundred cases before, and it was always the same. When the bell rang, when the gates opened, when the trial began, he and his opponent would lock arms and wits in a deadly embrace that would end only when one of them fell to the ground beaten and exhausted and the other stood alone and victorious. He was ready.

As Tony and Harrington sat down, Judge Katsoris leaned forward.

"Ladies and gentlemen," she said. "Let's deal first with the defendants' motion for Summary Judgment on the antitrust counts."

As she spoke, she picked up one of the documents spread out in front of her. "I have carefully reviewed the memoranda both supporting and opposing the motion, and I have concluded that the defendants' motion is well taken. In my judgment, in antitrust cases of this nature the rule of reason applies and the plaintiffs must demonstrate some actual injury in order to proceed. The discovery which has been conducted does not demonstrate any material damages suffered by the plaintiffs as a result of the defendants' allegedly illegal activities. In fact, the plaintiff Federal Dental Academy appears to be doing rather well, notwithstanding the defendants' refusal to accredit it."

Judge Katsoris' eyes caught Bill O'Coogan's. "Accordingly," she continued, looking directly at him, I am granting the defendants' motion. Judgment for the defendants will be entered on all four of the antitrust counts. The trial will proceed on Mr. O'Coogan's defamation count only." There was a steely hard tone in Judge Katsoris' voice as she made her ruling.

Bill O'Coogan stared at the judge in startled disbelief. His expression slowly changed to anger.

"Beautiful! Absolutely beautiful!" Carol whispered to Tony.

"It sure is," Tony quietly responded. "This means that we're going to play the rest of the game on our court." He turned toward Dr. Schofield who nodded with a taut smile.

Tony could see that everyone at the plaintiffs' table was distraught. Harrington and O'Coogan were engaged in an intense whispered discussion. Their antitrust case had been gutted by the defendants' opening salvo.

"The next order of business is the selection of a jury," Judge Katsoris continued. "Mr. Clerk, would you bring in the prospective jurors?"

The clerk left the courtroom for a moment, then returned, leading a group of twenty men and women. The first fourteen were seated in the jury box, with the remaining six in adjacent chairs. The case would be tried before a jury of six, with two alternates. Four prospective jurors at a time would be questioned. Either side could challenge one "for cause" if a bias became evident. In addition, each side had six "peremptory" challenges that they could use to excuse anyone they wished. Tactically, both sides would attempt to use the inquiry and challenge process to shape a jury most likely to sympathize with their client's position in the trial.

As the first panel of four in the jury box identified themselves, the Judge's clerk handed Tony and Jack Harrington small stacks of biographical sheets for each of the twenty prospective jurors. Judge Katsoris introduced the attorneys to the prospective jurors and explained that this was a libel and slander case. She asked them all some general background questions, then tendered the panel to Jack Harrington for *voir dire*, questioning the prospective jurors. Unlike many federal jurists, Judge Katsoris allowed both sides to conduct their own voir dire and gave them considerable latitude in doing so.

"Good morning," Harrington said. He rose and walked over to the jury box. He was at his charming best, nodding and smiling in particular to two middle-aged women in the front row.

"Have any of you ever suspected that some nasty gossip or rumor concerning you was going around the neighborhood?" Without waiting for an answer, he continued. He knew, as did Tony, that many trials are essentially decided in the *voir dire*, when jurors begin to associate themselves with one side or the other.

"It's a terrible thing when false rumors are spread about an innocent person, and repeated in whispered little comments that are passed from one person to another. I'm talking about the vicious kinds of rumors that can destroy a person's good name in the community forever. That's called slander. And the law provides, as the Judge will instruct you later, that anyone who commits the terrible offense of slander can, and should, have damages assessed against him. Do any of you disagree with the law on that?" No one raised their hand. "And if those lies are put into print and circulated to others, that's called libel. Do any of you disagree that anyone who does that should also be punished?" Again, no one raised a hand.

"Do you all agree that a man or woman's good name is one of their most precious assets?" No one dissented. *He's good*, Tony thought. *Very good.*

"Do you all also agree that if someone libels someone else and ruins their good name, that he or she should be severely punished, and substantial damages assessed against them?" Everyone in the panel seemed to be nodding with Harrington as he finished his question.

"Would any of you have any problem entering a very large verdict against the defendant corporation, if we prove that, through its agents, it committed a terrible libel or slander of the plaintiff in this case, William O'Coogan, a highly-respected member of this community?" No one indicated that he or she would have any problem at all.

Harrington seemed pleased with himself as he turned and began walking back to the plaintiffs' counsel table.

As he reached it, he turned and, as an afterthought, asked one more question.

"By the way, do any of you, or any members of your immediate family, have any connection with the American Dental Society?"

One of the gray-haired women in the front row raised her hand. "Yes," she said quietly.

"And what is that connection?"

"My husband is a dentist, and a member of the ADS."

"Would you say he is an active member?"

"He never misses an annual meeting."

Harrington's embarrassment showed. He'd almost missed that one. He picked up the stack of biographical sheets and thumbed through them, until he found the right one. "Your Honor, the plaintiffs ask that Mrs. Leigh be excused for cause."

Judge Katsoris nodded her agreement. "Mrs. Leigh, you are excused. Thank you for your time. You should return to the jurors' room downstairs." Then, calling the name of the first prospective juror sitting in the rear of the courtroom, the court asked him to take Mrs. Leigh's place in the jury box.

Harrington asked the new man a few questions, particularly including whether he had any dentists in his family, then tendered the panel of four to Tony.

Tony asked a few preliminary questions designed to establish rapport with the panel including whether any of them had any prior dealings with the plaintiffs, the Federal Dental Academy or William O'Coogan. None of them had. Then he moved into one of the defense's most sensitive areas.

"There's one particular aspect of this case that I think you're all going to have trouble with," he began. "That is, how can you give both sides a fair trial? The plaintiff is an individual, William O'Coogan. He claims he's been hurt. The defendant, on the other hand, is a faceless corporation. Oh, it's a not-for-profit corporation, to be sure, and it's comprised of thousands of neighborhood dentists all over the country, probably including your own dentist; but still, it's a corporation. I'm afraid you're all going to have trouble giving the American Dental Society, a large corporation, a fair trial. I think you're all going to have a natural tendency to side with the individual plaintiff and against the corporate defendant. I see that as the biggest problem you're going to have in this trial: how to be fair to both sides." Tony had their attention now. He was speaking not just to the four jurors in the panel, but to all the other potential jurors in the jury box.

"The key question I have for you is this: after all the evidence is in, if it appears that the American Dental Society really should win, will you actually be able to return a verdict for the defendant? Mrs. Hanson," he asked the other gray-haired woman in the front row, "will you be able to enter a verdict for the defendant corporation, if that's what really should be done, after all the evidence is in?"

Mrs. Hanson was flustered when she realized that she was expected to actually answer the question. "Why, yes, of course," she finally said.

"Thank you."

Tony looked at the man seated behind her. "Mr. Czajkowski, how about you?" He was careful to pronounce the name correctly. "At the end of the trial, if the *right* result would be a verdict for the defendant, a corporation, will you actually be able to vote for that?" Tony asked the question forcefully; as a challenge.

"Yes, yes I can."

"Can we count on that?"

"Yes!" He nodded vigorously as he answered.

Thank you, Mr. Czajkowski." *That's the commitment I wanted. All the other prospective jurors heard those questions and answered them in the same way in their minds*. Tony turned to Judge Katsoris. "Your Honor, the defense accepts this panel."

They had their first four jurors at that point: a plumber from the north-west side; a suburban housewife; a South-Side cab driver; and a secretary from Chicago Heights. Tony was a firm believer in the jury system, and these four looked all right.

Judge Katsoris had the second panel of prospective jurors identify themselves, and both sides repeated their questions, with minor variations. Harrington used one of his peremptory challenges to get rid of an accountant from Park Ridge, apparently, he was concerned that the man was too independent to be guided. Tony used one of his premptories to challenge an Italian businessman from Melrose Park. They had their jury of six. The alternate jurors selected were a math teacher at Senn High School and a CTA bus driver.

By then it was a little after noon and the Judge recessed the case until two o'clock. Both sides would present their opening statements after lunch.

Exiting the courtroom, Tony located Dr. Kaminsky and pulled him aside.

"Bob, I owe you a real apology."

"Why's that?"

"I didn't believe you when you first told us that the Dental Academy was an outfit front. To be honest, I thought that you were full of bullshit and that your bullshit was going to get us all in a lot of trouble. But you were right. You were the only one in town who had those guys pegged. I don't know how this trial's going to go, but if you hadn't blown the whistle, probably nobody would have. As far as I'm concerned, you did the right thing."

Kaminsky fumbled for one of the cigars sticking out of his coat pocket.

"Thanks, Tony, you know, I've taken a lot of shit at the ADS for getting us involved in this. So I appreciate it." At that, he turned and walked out into the corridor, lighting up as he did. The pungent aroma of his cigar smoke trailed behind him.

"Tony, do you want to have lunch with us, or would you rather eat alone?" Carol had walked up behind him as he was talking to Kaminsky. She sensed that he might want to lunch by himself to collect his thoughts for his opening statement.

"You go on. Why don't you take Dr. Schofield to Berghoff's next door? I've reserved a table for us. You might want to invite Jake and Dr. Kaminsky, too." He looked to the back of the courtroom to see if Charlie and Chris were still there; if they were, they should be included. But they'd already left. "I've got to restructure my comments to the jury, now that the antitrust counts have all been thrown out. That stuff filled up half my opening statement. I'll just grab a sandwich in the cafeteria downstairs."

Carol left as the crowd in the courtroom thinned out. All that remained, besides Tony, were three reporters talking to each other and two stocky older men with open collars seated in the back bench. Tony assumed they were professional court watchers, the retirees who roam the courthouse corridors looking for good trials to watch.

He was wrong. They were the eyes and ears of a very interested party in Tucson.

Chapter 20

October 18 – 1:00 p.m.

"Thou shalt not bear false witness against thy neighbor!" Jack Harrington's thundering voice filled the courtroom as he began his opening statement.

"That's not only God's law, ladies and gentlemen of the Jury. It also happens to be our law. It's one of the cornerstones upon which civilized conduct is based in our society. And it's the law that you will be asked to enforce in this case."

"Ladies and gentlemen, you have been selected to perform the single most important duty that any citizen in a democracy can perform: to render justice. A terrible thing has happened to my client, William O'Coogan. As the evidence in the trial will clearly show, he has been defamed, libeled and slandered. His good name, the product of a life's work, has been smeared by these defendants. And he has come to this court, and to you, for justice."

He paused, looking at the jurors. He had their undivided attention.

"The evidence that will be presented during the course of this trial will show that William O'Coogan is a successful and highly respected businessman. He has served on, and chaired, many of our most important civic committees. He decided to invest in a new dental school, the Federal Dental Academy, in order to improve the dental health of the people of Chicago. The evidence will also show that the American Dental Society obstructed this new dental school at every turn contending that their so-called standards weren't being met. But the real reason was that its owner William O'Coogan was supposedly connected with organized crime. They didn't say this about Bill O'Coogan or his Academy openly, but quietly; in whispers to the right people, behind closed doors. Confidential notes to the right people. Their conduct was premeditated, malicious. Before long, they had done their job. You know how rumors spread. Everyone in the business and dental communities soon heard that William O'Coogan was somehow involved in organized crime." Raising his voice again, Harrington roared, "No more hideous distortion of truth has ever been uttered in this city!"

"And it wasn't just businessmen in the Loop who heard this terrible defamation. Bill O'Coogan's family, his wife and children, his neighbors and his children's friends, heard the whispered rumors that he was part of the crime syndicate, the so-called Outfit. Can you imagine the humiliation? Well, you won't have to imagine it, because Bill O'Coogan will tell you himself during this trial the terrible agony he experienced when he had to assure his own children that he wasn't a gangster."

"This is the man who was honored just a few months ago by being named the Civic Foundation's Citizen of the Year. This is the man who has served with distinction as chairman of more civic committees than any other living Chicagoan. Chairman of the Better Boys' Foundation; president of the Chicago Athletic Association; president of the Saint George Alumni Association; president of the lake Forest United Way, then the Cook County United Way, raising tens of millions of dollars for the poor; chairman of Cardinal Bernardin's Commission on the Laity; escort to the Pope on his visit to Chicago; and co-recipient, with his lovely wife Mary Francis, of the archdiocese's Catholic Couple of the Year Award in 1981. This is one of our most distinguished and honored citizens."

As he spoke, Harrington walked around behind Bill O'Coogan, putting his hand on his client's shoulder. The white haired lady in the front row of jurors smiled at him. "This is the kind of man we pray that our sons will grow up to be and that our daughters will marry." The white haired juror nodded her agreement.

"What sort of men so hate the truth that they would call someone like William O'Coogan a gangster? Who would tell such grotesque lies? People like the faceless bureaucrats of the American Dental Society, attacking anyone who dare set foot on their self-claimed turf. Hidden away in their marble tower just off Michigan

Avenue, they don't know what truth is! Well, this trial will show them the truth, and it will cast an irrepressible beam of bright light into the dark caverns of the A.D.S.'s bureaucracy. You and I together will cast that beam of truth in there."

"Now, having committed such a terrible libel, dirtying the good name of one of our finest sons, probably forever, regardless of the outcome of this trial, what will be the position of the defendants in this trial that we are starting today? Will they come in and apologize, as any decent person would do? Will they express regret for the unspeakable lies that they have uttered about Bill O'Coogan? I doubt it! My guess is that the weasels who run the American Dental Society, Drs. Schofield, Kaminsky and their ilk, are so arrogant that even now they will refuse to apologize and will, in fact, repeat the same gross lies in this very courtroom."

"Watch and see for yourself what they do. You have a litmus test to judge their integrity. If they have an ounce of decency among them, they'll apologize to Bill O'Coogan right here in this courtroom, with the entire city and its press watching. However, if they are incapable of admitting their sins and insist on repeating those same lies in this trial, then you will know what sort of despicable people the defendants are. You will know then that they should be severely punished. You should send them a message; those who bear false witness against their neighbors will be punished, not only in the next world, but in this world as well."

Jack Harrington sat down and wiped the sweat from his face. The inhabitants of the jury box were on the edge of their seats, then, slowly, one by one, sat back. They understood now, for the first time, what this case was all about.

After a moment of silence the courtroom erupted in a hushed chorus of whispering. Harrington had made a dramatic and powerful opening statement. Perhaps the person who was most impressed was Tony. Harrington, he had to admit, had made a great opening statement.

Judge Katsoris banged her gavel.

"Mr. Jeffries?"

Tony rose slowly, buttoned his suit jacket, and walked around the defense table to stand directly in front of the jury.

"That was an interesting and emotional speech that Mr. Harrington just made to you," he said. "Fortunately, however, what the lawyers say in this trial isn't evidence. It doesn't count. What counts is what the evidence shows. The evidence in this case is going to tell a story dramatically different from the tale that Mr. Harrington just spun for you."

"Let me tell you what the evidence in this case is going to show." Tony stepped over to the defense table, grabbed a thick manila folder, and held it up in front of the jury. "It will show conclusively that William O'Coogan, the plaintiff, has been leading a double life for years. At a superficial, public level he is a successful businessman, socialite and church activist. But at a deeper, darker level he is the financier of one of this country's major Mafia families: the Angelo Bruni family based in Tucson. Using O'Coogan's companies as fronts, Angelo Bruni moves hundreds of millions of dollars around each year; buying a company here, putting financial pressure on somebody there, making campaign contributions to key politicians, buying people's souls, while laundering vast sums of narcotics money. That money is distributed as apparently legitimate income to scores of mob figures and their cronies throughout the country. We will identify for you the men who work in the shadows, receiving Bruni's laundered money through O'Coogan's corporations." Tony laid the thick folder back on the defense table, tapping it with a finger while keeping his eye on the jury.

"We will present expert testimony explaining how each of these payees fits into the organized crime hierarchy. The evidence will show conclusively that William O'Coogan has been deeply involved in mob activities for years, with great success. However, earlier this year he made a serious mistake. He and his mob partners, and you'll know their names well by the time this trial is over, decided to move into an entirely new area, dentistry. What better a front than a dental school? A dental school! What better a beachhead in the growing and important healthcare industry?"

"But someone caught them. Not the FBI, or the attorney general's office, or even the City of Chicago Police Department. No, it was the American Dental Society, which has been given the responsibility for accrediting dental schools in this country through its Commission on Dental Accreditation. They wouldn't approve the school that O'Coogan and his Mafia pals took over, the Federal Dental Academy. They realized that it was nothing more than a mob front, and they refused to accredit it."

Tony paused, stuck his chin out, then continued. "It takes courage, ladies and gentlemen, believe me, to stand up to the mob. But the men and women at the American Dental Society did it. They said, in effect, you're not going to dirty our home. Take your foul game and go somewhere else. And for that they were sued for defamation. For telling the truth, and for keeping the mob out of an area where they had no business going."

"As I'm sure Judge Katsoris will instruct you later, truth is a complete defense in a libel or slander case. During the course of the trial, we will prove to you that William O'Coogan is a working member of the crime syndicate, and has been for years. At the end of this trial, I am confident that you will agree with me that it was heroic, not libelous, for the American Dental Society to say that William O'Coogan and his associates are members of organized crime. I'm confident that you will return a verdict for the defense."

Tony stood in front of the jury and looked at them one by one. He couldn't tell from their reactions whether he had made any impact or not. After a moment, he turned and walked back to the defense table, where he took his seat. The jurors all followed him with their eyes.

"That was terrific, Tony," Carol whispered to him. "I

think you've neutralized Harrington's ranting."

"We'll see." Tony realized then that he was sweating. The moisture of his sweat, coupled with the cool temperature in the courtroom, suddenly made him shiver.

"The Court will stand recessed until nine thirty Monday morning," Judge Katsoris announced. "At that time, Mr. Harrington, you will begin the plaintiff's case. Ladies and gentlemen of the jury, I instruct you not to discuss this case with anyone over the weekend, even family and friends." With that, she banged her gavel once, rose, and stepped down from the bench.

"Not a bad first day," Carol said as they began collecting their papers. "We got the antitrust counts knocked out, got a decent jury, and I think we came out even on the opening statements. That's a pretty good start when you're up against Harrington."

Before Tony could answer, a paralegal from the firm walked briskly up to the table and handed Carol a note.

"We've got a problem, Tony," Carol said quietly after quickly reading the message.

"What is it?"

"We've lost Bill McNulty of the Crime Commission as our expert witness!"

"What?" Tony blurted. A half dozen heads turned.

"His secretary sent a message over about a half hour ago," Carol whispered. "McNulty's just left for an extended vacation to Australia. He'll be gone for at least a month."

"Son of a bitch!" Tony felt that the wind had just been knocked out of him. He began immediately trying to sort out the implication of losing McNulty as Carol continued.

"Back at the office as soon as Judy saw the message she called the office of the Commission, and got a recording that they were closed for the weekend. She then called McNulty's home number in Glenview, but there wasn't an answer. I think he's gone, Tony."

"How could he do this to us?" Tony said, shaking his head. His testimony is critical in identifying the mob figures on O'Coogan's payroll."

"Do you think somebody got to him?" Carol asked.

"Of course; what else? Damn, this screws our case up!"

Carol thought about it for a moment, then spoke up. "What about Jake? Could we use him to testify on that issue?"

"Jake Wysocki?" Tony responded. "We'd never get him qualified as an expert. He might have been on the police force for a long time, but he doesn't have any credentials as an expert witness." He paused, shrugged, then concluded, "But we've got to go with him. We don't have anyone else. We've got to just fight like hell to get the Court to accept him as an expert on the mob."

Across the courtroom, while Harrington and his associate packed their briefcases, Bill O'Coogan watched with some amusement the intense discussion that Tony and Carol were engaged in. He knew exactly what their problem was.

The next morning both major Chicago newspapers had sensational lead articles about the trial. Tony's accusations of O'Coogan's mob involvement were highlighted and quoted. The *Tribune* featured the first of Chris Anderson's syndicated stories linking mob activities in Illinois and Arizona; they announced it would run her entire series of articles on a daily basis, and that Sunday's article would spotlight the cocaine operations of Angelo Bruni, O'Coogan's alleged partner. The *Tribune* stated Chris was in Chicago to cover the closely related American Dental Society trial, and would be supplementing her articles on a daily basis to reflect its developments.

Saturday evening, Jake Wysocki was sitting at his desk in the living room of his brick bungalow on the northwest side of the city. He was paying bills and going over the weekly records of the small security business that he operated providing nighttime security guards, usually off-duty cops, for four plants in the neighborhood. It didn't net him all that much, but it supplemented his police pension. Besides, running his security business made him feel he was still a cop. He really wasn't ready to retire five years ago when they made him give up his badge.

The ashtray to his right was filled with cigarette butts, adding to the stale air that filled the house. Jake added one to it, grinding out a butt while he exhaled a cloud of smoke. He was troubled by a phone call he'd received the night before. Bill Duffy, an old friend, had called about eight from a bar. He was obviously half in the bag. He was the manager of a small assembly plant on Milwaukee Avenue, and had been instrumental a couple of years ago in getting Jake's firm hired for security work. When Duffy called, he told Jake that the company was thinking of hiring a new security firm at the end of the month. He wasn't completely intelligible. It was clear that he was angry, not at Wysocki, but at someone else. Jake figured that he'd get the details later, when Duffy was sober. The business was probably going to somebody's brother-in-law or nephew, and there wasn't much he could do about it. Still, he would hate to lose the income.

Jake thumbed through the day's mail. His wife Clara had passed away two years earlier, he didn't even look at the sale catalogues that he'd received, just tossed them straight into the wastebasket. Then Jake found letters from two of his other clients. That was curious because his clients rarely sent him formal letters. He read one, then the other, and felt anger surging up inside him. They both said the same thing in slightly different language; they were considering replacing Jake's security firm at the end of October.

What the hell is going on here?

He sat there for several minutes staring at the two letters. *We've done a good job for these people*. He also knew his rates were cheaper than the bigger outfits charged, so that couldn't be the problem. There hadn't been any break-ins or security breaches at any of his client's facilities. The more he thought about it, the madder he got. He recalled the old adage: Once is happenstance, twice is coincidence, three times is enemy action. *Some son-of-a-bitch is doing a job on me. And a damn good job at that. My security service is about to go down the tube.*

Then it came to him; O'Coogan, of course. The punks on the street who hated Jake wouldn't do something like this. They couldn't. But William O'Coogan was a businessman; he might be able to pull something like this off, depending on who he knew; and he knew a lot of people at the top. Yes, Jake concluded, O'Coogan, or somebody working for him, is trying to squeeze me. The fact that the contracts hadn't yet been cancelled means that this is a warning. Get out of the case, stop helping Jeffries, and you might be able to save your business. The message was clear.

It also became clear to Jake, the more he thought about it, that if O'Coogan would go to these lengths to put pressure on him, then much heavier and more ominous pressures were likely to be brought to bear against Tony Jeffries.

Jake picked up his Smith & Wesson .38 and began absentmindedly spinning the cylinder. It was something he often did when engrossed in thought.

"Bullshit!" he finally said aloud, slamming the cylinder back into place. *No one's going to push me around like this!* The Dental Academy case had suddenly become very personal. The old cop stood up, loaded his .38 and slipped it into his shoulder holster. Reverting to habit, he pulled a second .38 out of a drawer, checked it, and slipped it into a leg holster he strapped around his right calf. “Jeffries,” he said, “this one’s on the house.”

Chapter 21

October 20

Sunday was a beautiful fall day in Chicago. The trees had begun turning a week earlier and were now in spectacular full color. Temperatures in the low forties lent a crispness to the air.

A Fed Ex truck pulled up in front of 604 Tenth Street in Wilmette a little before eight o'clock that morning. It crunched to a stop in the leaves that had been collected at the curb the day before. The absence of lights indicated that no one in the Jeffries' home was up yet, and the morning *Tribune*, stuffed with all the Sunday extras, was still on the parkway in front of the house.

The uniformed delivery man walked up to the front door and laid down a large, brightly wrapped package. He rang the bell then turned and began walking down the flagstone steps to the sidewalk.

A half-block to the north, Jake Wysocki was parked

in his car, watching with interest. He had been there all night. It's odd, he thought, that the delivery man didn't wait for someone to come to the door. His recollection was that Fed Ex wouldn't deliver anything without getting a signed receipt. And this is a Sunday. *Does Fed Ex deliver on Sunday?*

Then he saw the delivery man begin running as he neared his truck. *Son-of-a-bitch, that guy's not from Fed Ex!* The driver jumped in his truck, gunned the engine, and sped away from the curb, moving north on Tenth toward Jake.

Jake opened the door of this car and stepped out into the street, holding up his left hand. *If there's anything legitimate about this truck it'll stop*, Jake thought. Instead, the driver accelerated as he approached. Keeping his left hand up, Jake reached inside his jacket with his right hand, grabbed his revolver, and raised it.

Jake had time to fire one warning shot into the air; the explosion of the gunshot shattering the early morning silence. The truck continued to accelerate. Standing his ground in the middle of the street, Jake lowered his gun and aimed with both hands at the truck's windshield. He waited as long as he dared.

Behind the onrushing truck, out of the corner of his eye, Jake could see the door to the Jeffries' house open. Young Debbie Jeffries, dressed in her pink bathrobe, stepped outside and was looking at the beautiful big box that someone had left on their porch.

"*Now!* Jake decided. *It has to be now!* Keeping his .38

aimed at the windshield, he fired off three shots in quick succession. They struck the onrushing windshield in a six-inch triangle directly in front of the driver. The vehicle careened to the right, jumped the curb, and smashed into a two-foot thick elm tree on the parkway. An instant later, the door on the left side popped open and the driver rolled out onto the grass. He had a bullet wound in the middle of his forehead and was quite dead.

At the other end of the block, Debbie Jeffries stepped further out onto their porch and looked up the street in the direction of the noise. Then she looked down again at the large present; her birthday was in a week and she knew the box was for her.

"No!" Jake shouted as he ran forward. "Don't touch it!" Debbie didn't hear him as she leaned forward to pick up her surprise gift.

Jake was still carrying his revolver in his right hand as he chugged down the street toward the Jeffries' house. He was breathing hard, he hadn't run this far in a long time. When he saw Debbie reach for the box, he gave another shout and fired his gun into the air again and again until it was empty.

Debbie was startled when she heard the shots and saw a fat old man running down the street toward her waving a gun in the air. She ran back inside the house and slammed the door.

Jake charged across the neighbors' lawn and up to the Jeffries' steps two at a time. Grabbing the box by its cord wrapping, he turned and leaped down the steps to the parkway. The box was bigger and heavier than he'd anticipated. A sharp pain crossed Jake's chest as he carried the box toward the street.

A Dodge van was parked at the curb. Jake ran up to it and flung the box over the vehicle into the street, then dropped to the ground. He felt for the first time the full intensity of the pain in his chest.

There was a sudden thunderous blast. Jake, shielded behind the van, avoided its full impact, but a rush of searing air under the vehicle burned the side of his face. He lay there in the grass trying to catch his breath, while pieces of glass and autumn leaves settled around him.

A little more than a minute later a Wilmette squad car arrived, followed shortly by a fire department ambulance. The scene they found looked more like a war zone than a quiet suburban neighborhood. At the north end of the block a Fed Ex truck, now on fire, was wrapped around a large tree. A bleeding body lay strewn on the grass beside it. At the other end of the block was a second burning vehicle, a van, with another man in the parkway near it. He was struggling to get to his feet. The street in front of the burning van was blocked by a huge crater and was completely impassible. Oily smoke from both fires, and the acrid odor of burnt gunpowder, were spreading over the block. Many of the houses had their doors and windows blown open, especially at the Jeffries' home; little wisps of fire could be seen dancing in the smoke.

One by one, people were emerging from their houses, confused and afraid, many still in their robes. Tony

Jeffries was one of them, pulling on a jacket as he stepped out onto his porch. Karen stood in the doorway behind him in her bathrobe. As soon as Tony saw Jake Wysocki lying beside the burning van, he knew what must have happened.

Tony ran down his steps, then across the lawn to where two Fire Department Paramedics were lifting Jake into the ambulance.

"Jake, are you all right?"

"I don't know, Tony. Got a bad pain." He gestured weakly toward his chest. "Is your family okay?"

"Everyone's fine, Jake. Damn, you're something else."

The paramedics interrupted them by putting an oxygen mask on Jake, then the ambulance pulled away. As it turned the corner, the ambulance's siren began wailing. Tony stood on the parkway and listened to the siren as it tailed off. He could hear it in the distance for a long time. Too long. Evanston Hospital had never seemed so far away.

That evening was the reception to honor the new president of Barat College in Lake Forest. Tony had to attend, he had served on the search committee that recommended the hiring of Sister Mary Kay Beaulieu. Neither Karen nor Tony had recovered yet from the bombing that morning, and Karen refused to leave the kids home alone. Tony understood completely. He assured her that his appearance at Barat would be as brief as possible.

The reception was lavish and well attended. The College's Board of Trustees decided to make the induction of their new president a major public relations event, extending invitations to their best-known and most successful alumni and their spouses. Among them were Caroline Nightingale and her husband Joshua, the senior United States Senator from North Dakota. Senator Nightingale's campaign for the Democratic nomination for the presidency was now in full swing. Some pundits were even calling him the Democratic front runner. The Nightingales were delighted to attend and built a campaign swing through Illinois around the Baret reception. They had attended three fund raising cocktail parties already that evening.

Tony arrived around eight o'clock. He was wearing the dark maroon sport coat and gray slacks that Karen had given him for Christmas last year. The jacket was a little loud for Tony's taste, but very comfortable. He had a mental list of people he should see before leaving, and he set about trying to locate them in the crowd.

As Tony moved through the reception, several people remarked on the explosion that occurred outside his home that morning. It apparently was mentioned on an early evening newscast. Everyone was shocked. Tony was as casual as he could be, and dismissed it as the work of "some crackpot." Someone commented that it was probably a gas explosion. "They happen every day."

The stars of the reception, of course, were the Nightingales. People were hovering around them, shaking their hands and exchanging greetings. Local Democrats in particular were seizing the opportunity to introduce themselves, to have their photos taken with the senator, or offering to work in his campaign. A campaign aide, standing next to Nightingale was busily writing down names, addresses and phone numbers. Another aide, wearing a dark maroon jacket that looked identical to Tony's, was passing out Nightingale buttons; after a while he left the crowd and headed towards the men's room.

Tony was irritated by the political tone of the evening. The new college president, Sister Beaulieu, was not receiving the attention that she deserved. Tony introduced her to several people he knew before deciding he'd had enough and was going to leave.

As he worked his way toward the door, a stocky man in a dark blue suit walked up to him and touched his arm.

"Pardon me, I was told to give this to you," the man said, handing Tony an envelope.

"Are you sure this is for me?"

"Oh yes, Mr. Wexler." At that, he turned and disappeared into the crowd.

Wexler? Of all the nonsense! The guy's mistaken me for someone else!

Tony looked down at the envelope. Across the front was a handwritten: "Conrad Wexler, Nightingale Campaign Committee." Tony realized what must have happened. That aide of Nightingale's in the maroon jacket like Tony's must be Conrad Wexler. The envelope was meant for him.

Well, I can't leave until I get this to Wexler or Nightingale, Tony thought. *Damn, that'll take half an hour in this crowd. I wonder if these papers are that important? If not, I'll just mail the envelope to Nightingale's headquarters.*

Tony opened the unsealed white envelope and pulled out the folded papers inside. He looked at them for a moment, first in confusion, then in horror. Then he stuffed the papers and envelope into his inside coat pocket and pushed through the crowd. He had to get out of there immediately.

At the other side of the room the stocky man was talking to two other men. Their conversation was animated, the other two men were very upset. The man in the maroon jacket saw Tony leaving, and pointed at him. The other two gave him brief, staccato orders, and he hurriedly left through a side door to the parking lot.

Tony was driving south on the Edens Expressway near Glencoe when he first noticed the car following him. It had been speeding until it caught up to Tony, then slowed suddenly and pulled in behind him. Tony was going about sixty in the right lane and the other car was staying on his tail. Tony knew why it was there.

The driver behind Tony flashed his brights on and off. He repeated it several times. Tony ignored him. He wasn't going to pull over. What he had in his coat pocket was too important. He wasn't going to stop for anyone. He pushed his speed up past seventy.

Then he felt a bump. The driver behind him had his brights on, and was hitting the rear of his car. The car careened a bit, but Tony was able to keep it under control. He had to do something. He was hit again. *That bastard's trying to drive me off the road!*

A red van was ahead in the left of the three lanes as they approached the Willow Road overpass. Tony cut to the center lane and took his foot off the gas. The car behind, a light blue Buick, stayed in the right lane and pulled up so that its front was even with Tony's right rear fender. Then Tony cut suddenly to the right. There was a sharp crunch of metal against metal as he forced the Buick off the road and onto the shoulder. The Buick slowed momentarily as it hit the gravel, then quickly accelerated. Tony matched his speed, keeping him on the shoulder; they were now both doing over eighty, with the speeding Buick unable to get off the shoulder and onto the expressway itself. Tony knew that the shoulder was interrupted just ahead by the concrete base of the Willow Road overpass. The driver of the Buick, unfamiliar with the Edens Expressway, slammed on his brakes as he saw what was immediately in front of him at the overpass, but he was going too fast, and crashed into the concrete at the overpass' base with the force of a cannonball. Tony could see the burst of flames in his rearview mirror. He didn't stop.

Within minutes, he was home. He rushed in and showed Karen the document he had been handed by accident.

It was a report from the Land of Liberty Foundation of New York to the Joshua Nightingale Presidential Campaign Committee. "Confidential" was stamped across the top of every page. The report listed all the Nightingale campaign expenses that had been paid by the Land of Liberty Foundation during the month of September. They totaled $4,500,000; and for the year-to-date $52,000,000, along with the use of a private jet and pilot.

"Do you know what this means?" Tony whispered. "The Land of Liberty Foundation is funded with Angelo Bruni's money through Bill O'Coogan's pipeline. The foundation then passes that money to the Nightingale Campaign committee." Karen looked at Tony, shocked.

"The mob has bought itself a god-damn presidential candidate! It's Senator Joshua Nightingale!"

"Oh my God," Karen whispered. She looked at the papers, then quickly back at Tony. "Are we safe here tonight?"

"No, we're not. Even with the squads keeping an eye on the house. Get the kids. We're going to stay at the Orrington tonight. I'll advise Chief Robinson."

Chapter 22

October 21

When the trial resumed Monday morning, everyone was talking about the attempted bombing of the Jeffries' home. The papers ran front page stories that morning, linking the bombing with the trial and with the accusations against William O'Coogan. If the press ever needed confirmation that O'Coogan was connected with organized crime, they had it now. He had gone into the trial as a prominent businessman under questionable attack; suddenly, he was an exposed mob operative. The fact that the bogus Fed Ex deliveryman actually worked for a company that O'Coogan owned added weight to the argument.

There was a lot of talk in the press about Jake Wysocki. At first, his role was unclear. An early edition of the *Sun-Times* even identified him as a suspected member of the assassination team, whose bomb had gone off prematurely. But Tony straightened that out, in interviews both on and off the air. By Monday morning, Jake was a hero. He was still in critical condition in the Evanston Hospital intensive care unit, and it was uncertain whether he'd survive his massive coronary.

By 9:30 Judge Katsoris' courtroom was packed with spectators spilling into the corridor, waiting anxiously for the trial to resume. Jack Harrington and his associate Alice Lattner were unpacking their briefcases and talking quietly. Harrington looked grim. O'Coogan wasn't there yet, he was undoubtedly having trouble navigating the crowd in the hallway. Every reporter in town was there, it seemed, many with a camera man in tow, waiting for O'Coogan to arrive. The hurried fragments of their questions and his answers would later be reported as "exclusive interviews."

On the table in front of Tony was a thick manila envelope bearing the hand-written label "Land of Liberty Foundation of New York." It contained copies of all the checks showing the cash flow from Angelo Bruni's companies through O'Coogan's fronts, including the Federal Dental Academy, to the Land of Liberty Foundation. It also had the report showing how the foundation had donated that money during September, and the preceding months to finance Senator Nightingale's presidential campaign. The Dental Academy was his biggest campaign contributor by far. Tony had been at the office since six o'clock organizing and copying that material. It was going to be the bombshell of the trial.

Tony opened his trial book and flipped through the section on the cross-examination of William O'Coogan. *How do I work in the fact that the man who may be the next president of the United States is on the payroll of organized crime?* He decided that would be divulged in his last series of questions to O'Coogan.

Today the courtroom was too warm. The GSA never got the heating/air-conditioning system to function properly. It was at least eighty degrees in Judge Katsoris' courtroom; somewhere else in the building it was undoubtedly sixty. Mickey, the judge's clerk, unbuttoned his collar and loosened his tie. He was an old-timer from the Bridgeport neighborhood and could never understand why they couldn't get the heat to work the way it was supposed to. Neither could anybody else.

During the lull, Charlie Dickinson walked up to Tony with Chris Anderson at his side. "Tony," he said, "I don't think you and Chris have formally met. As I think you know, she's up here to cover the trial. Chris Anderson.... Tony Jeffries."

"Hi Chris," Tony responded. I kinda figured out who you were the other day from a photo Charlie showed me. Welcome to Chicago."

"Thanks, Tony, Charlie's told me a lot about you. When this trial's over we'd love to get together with you and your wife and Carol. But in the meantime," she added with a smile, "I think we'd all better get back to our seats before someone else takes them."

Charlie nodded, shook Tony's hand and said "Good

luck Tony. Kick their asses for me," then followed Chris back to their seats.

By 9:50, everyone was wondering why the trial hadn't resumed. Patricia Katsoris was a very punctual judge and it was unusual for her to start late. Mickey walked back to the judge's chambers, then returned and just shrugged. If he knew why she was late, he wasn't saying anything.

Lenny Battaglia and two other people from the Dental Academy finally worked their way into the courtroom and stood at the rear looking for seats. There weren't any. A *Tribune* reporter squeezed next to Dr. Kaminsky in the front row quietly peppered him with questions and took notes. Kaminsky loved it.

"This is starting to smell like a locker room," Mickey said as he loosened his collar more.

"I know it," Tony answered. "I hope the judge has the good sense to tell us to take our suit coats off when she gets here. This is going to be a long day."

At 10:10 Judge Patricia Katsoris entered through her private door and rapidly climbed the two steps to her bench. She was not carrying any documents. Mickey intoned the requisite call to order, and everyone scurried for their seats. Moments later the jury was escorted in and took their places in the box.

"Ladies and gentlemen, I apologize for the delay. But we've had an emergency come up this morning, an emergency that deals with this trial," Judge Katsoris announced. "Mr. William O'Coogan, the plaintiff in this case, was found dead this morning in the garage of his

Lake Forest home. He has been murdered."

A wave of shocked whispers swept the courtroom. The reporters took out their note pads and began scribbling furiously. Tony was stunned. He had envisioned many scenarios to end this case, but not this one.

"Since neither a libel, nor a slander cause of action can survive the plaintiff's death, I am compelled to dismiss the remainder of this case," Judge Katsoris continued. "This trial is over. Members of the jury you are dismissed. Thank you for your service." With that, she banged her gavel, and rose to leave the bench.

"Your Honor," the *Sun-Times* reporter called from the first row of spectators, breaking the usual decorum, "how was O'Coogan killed?"

Judge Katsoris, still standing, hesitated a moment before answering. "He was found with an ice pick driven in each of his ears." She turned away and stepped down.

The courtroom exploded in a frenzy as she left. The reporters, who had fought for places in the first row, were now frantically seeking a little privacy for calling in their preliminary reports. The jurors were talking excitedly. Jack Harrington was still seated at the plaintiff's table in stunned silence. The spectators swept around him to fill the front of the courtroom.

Mickey turned to Tony and said loud enough for everyone to hear, "That's a Mafia sign. It means that O'Coogan should have listened to what he was told."

"Unbelievable," Carol whispered to Tony. "It sounds like your message got through to Bruni after all."

"I guess so; but this sure as hell isn't what I had in mind." A sudden chill went through Tony; *he* was the one responsible for O'Coogan's death. He stood and looked around the courtroom. Amid the swirling movement of the crowd, one man stood still and alone. It was an ashen Lenny Battaglia. He slowly turned and left, oblivious to everyone around him.

Tony opened his briefcase and inserted the large manila envelope labeled "Land of Liberty Foundation of New York." He waited a minute for the crowd to thin, asked Carol to collect the rest of their material, then walked out, took the elevator down to the ninth floor, and gave the envelope to John Ellington of the F.B.I.

The dust from the trial's dramatic ending kept settling over the next couple of weeks. Lenny Battaglia vanished; no one could locate him. With his absence, and William O'Coogan's sudden death, Dr. Maria Henriques closed the Federal Dental Academy within a matter of days.

Jake Wysocki made slow progress in his recovery at Evanston Hospital, ultimately surviving with the help of a coronary bypass. His doctors told him to stop playing cop, and retire as a private detective once and for all. He reluctantly agreed on the condition that he could keep his security business as a passive investment. Interestingly, he didn't lose any of his security customers. The three companies that had threatened to cancel his contracts never raised the subject again.

Chris Anderson's series of revelations of mob activity was a sensation, especially coupled with the dramatic end of the trial in Chicago. The *Tribune*, which had run her syndicated articles, reacted eagerly when she inquired about a job. She moved to Chicago in November; before long she and Charlie Dickenson were engaged.

Senator Joshua Nightingale unexpectedly withdrew from the presidential race in late November. He cited "personal reasons." The press was disappointed and urged him to consider a future run.

When the holidays came, Karen and Tony Jeffries decided to take the kids out of town for a family vacation. Tony traded in all his frequent flyer miles (and a few bucks to boot) for a set of six business class tickets to the Caribbean. They opened their presents at home Christmas morning, then flew from O'Hare to Saint Croix for a two-week stay with forays to St. Thomas and Antigua. It was the best vacation the Jeffries family ever had.

It was early one evening in mid-January, shortly after they'd returned from the Caribbean, when Tony received a telephone call at home. It was from the registrar at Glenbrook Hospital. She said that a badly injured patient in their emergency room insisted on speaking to him. His name was Smith and he was in critical condition. Tony had no idea who this Mr. Smith was, but, under the circumstances, said he'd be right over.

He arrived at Glenbrook's ER about thirty minutes later. After identifying himself, he was taken to a room in back where a team of doctors and nurses were working on Mr. Smith. The patient had a large mole on his right cheek, but Tony couldn't recognize him. His face and neck were splattered with blood and an oxygen mask was strapped on. Tubes of various liquids were connected to both arms.

After several minutes the medical team completed its work and left. Only a nurse remained. Tony neared the bed and took a closer look at the patient. It was Lenny Battaglia. His throat had been slit.

Tony looked up at the nurse, then back at Battaglia. A series of temporary stitches held him together.

"Whoever did this missed his carotid arteries," she said in response to his implicit question. "He's lost a lot of blood; but we think he'll make it."

At the sound of the nurse's voice, Battaglia opened his eyes. They opened wider when he saw Tony. In response to his gestures, the nurse removed the oxygen mask. He tried to speak, but the words came slowly, and with great difficulty. "Jeffries. Glad you're here," he whispered.

"What happened to you, Lenny?"

"Bruni. Fuckin' Bruni."

Tony moved closer to the bed. It was hard to hear Battaglia.

"Bruni had this done to you?" Tony asked.

"Yeah."

"Why? Do you know why?"

"Because of the fuckin' trial. He wanted us to drop it. O'Coogan wouldn't do it. Wasn't my fault." Tony could hear the blood gurgling in Battaglia's throat as he strained to get the words out.

"Said I stole money, too. Fuckin' nickels and dimes." Battaglia's voice trailed off.

"Why did you call me? I can't help you."

"I want to deal. The feds. Set it up. I'll talk if I'm protected."

Tony remembered the business card that John Ellington of the FBI had given him last summer. Ellington had written his home phone number on it. Tony checked and found that it was still in his wallet. "I know who to call," he said. "Do you want me to do it tonight?"

"Yeah. I need protection now."

"Okay, I'll make the call."

Within forty minutes Ellington was there together with another FBI agent with a hand-held recorder. Both were dressed casually. The second agent was younger, taller and heavier than Ellington, and looked like he'd been an offensive tackle in his college years. Lenny Battaglia talked to them, with great difficulty, for the next hour. He answered every question they asked, and volunteered information they didn't know enough to ask about. He named Rolf Sorenson's killer and told how he was paid. Tony was disgusted to learn that Sorenson was killed for a lousy five hundred bucks.

Battaglia told them he didn't know anything about

the Land of Liberty Foundation of New York. He was probably telling the truth. O'Coogan wouldn't have let someone like Battaglia in on secrets like that.

Finally, Battaglia was exhausted, and the nurse insisted that they let him rest. Ellington and Tony left at that point. The other agent would stay on until he was relieved. Lenny Battaglia had the protection he had paid for. He would be given a new identity and would vanish yet again.

Months later, Tony read that Lenny Battaglia's mutilated body had been found in the trunk of a car in Naples, Florida. Tony didn't know whether the mob's intelligence sources were that good, or the Bureau simply wanted to wash its hands of him and let some information slip.

Tony never knew exactly how the Bureau used Battaglia's information. Whenever he'd read in the papers about a mob figure being arrested on some federal charge or another, he'd always wonder if that stemmed from Battaglia's revelations.

Angelo Bruni was never arrested; that didn't surprise Tony. The old don had protected himself with many layers of phantom corporations and intermediaries. But Tony knew that he had badly disrupted Bruni's plans, and those of organized crime. Their efforts to establish a foothold in dentistry had failed. Thinking of Senator Nightingale's aborted presidential campaign, Tony knew that much more had failed too.

Tony often thought of the analogy that Jack Roberts had made at The Billy Goat Tavern, that the mob was like a cancer, its spreading couldn't be stopped. But Roberts was wrong. This time, when the smoke and shadows cleared, the cancer was gone, the enemy had vanished. The patient survived.

CPSIA information can be obtained
at www.ICGtesting.com
Printed in the USA
FFHW021859291018
49054351-53338FF

9 781478 799832